William H. Long

Memoirs of Emma, Lady Hamilton

With anecdotes of her friends and contemporaries

William H. Long

Memoirs of Emma, Lady Hamilton
With anecdotes of her friends and contemporaries

ISBN/EAN: 9783337114527

Printed in Europe, USA, Canada, Australia, Japan

Cover: Foto ©Raphael Reischuk / pixelio.de

More available books at **www.hansebooks.com**

MEMOIRS

OF

EMMA LADY HAMILTON

WITH

ANECDOTES OF HER FRIENDS
AND CONTEMPORARIES

NEW EDITION

EDITED AND ANNOTATED

BY

W. H. LONG

EDITOR OF THE " OGLANDER MEMOIRS," &c.

WITH PORTRAITS

W. W. GIBBINGS

18, BURY STREET, LONDON, W.C

1891

EDITOR'S PREFACE.

HE general and increasing interest
shown in the history of Emma,
Lady Hamilton, who, with all her
shortcomings, and in some measure
through them, was one of the most
celebrated women of her age, and
who combined with the acknowledged charms of her
person mental powers of no common range and ver-
satility, is the principal reason for the republication
of her much-maligned " Memoirs," with corrections
and annotations. The story of her wonderfully
chequered career from her cradle to her grave, and
her connection with the greatest naval commander the
world has ever seen, is as attractive and thrilling as a
romance, and will serve for all time—" to point a
moral, or adorn a tale." The first edition of the
" Memoirs of Lady Hamilton," by an anonymous
author, was published by H. Colburn in 1815, and a
second edition, corrected and enlarged, a few weeks
later in the same year. The present edition is a
reprint of the second, with the exception that a long
introduction, written in the most prosy style of

moralizing, and two or three shoit passages in different places, written in a similar general strain, of no
interest, and containing little or nothing bearing on
the story, have been omitted, it is hoped with advantage. The work has been disparaged, but used,
more or less, by almost every author writing on
the story of Lady Hamilton; and the larger proportion of the facts it records have never been contro-
verted, but many of them confirmed, by authorities
appearing since its first publication. The notes have
been drawn from various sources; the chief being—
Clarke and M'Arthur's " Life of Lord Nelson,"
Pettigrew's " Memoirs," and Sir H. Nicolas's well-
known " Dispatches and Letters " of the hero; but
the editor must specially acknowledge his obligations
to the exhaustive work of Mr. J. C. Jeaffreson, on
" Lady Hamilton and Lord Nelson."

March, 1891.   W. H. L.

PREFACE TO SECOND EDITION.

 HE favourable reception which this volume has experienced from the public, manifested by the sale of a large impression in a few weeks, and by the most honourable testimonies in its behalf, expressed in different periodical publications, has enabled the Author to fulfil the promise made in the preface of his first edition, of making such corrections in the narrative as should be called for by the communication of authentic facts and specific information. But while he returns his thanks to several obliging correspondents for some friendly hints and additional circumstances, of which he has not failed to avail himself in the present impression, he feels a honest satisfaction in finding that the integrity of his memoir remains unaffected.

August 1st. 1815.

LIST OF PLATES.

—

CHAPTER I.

Honour and shame from no condition
rise :
Act well your part ; there all the honour
lies. POPE.

NE of our greatest moralists, who owed more to himself than to his relations, has said, in his strong manner, that there is a " scoundrelism about persons of low birth." No man knew better than he did how to appreciate worth in all stations, and no man ever acted with less servility to the great, or with more kindness to the poor. His observation, therefore, must be taken in a qualified sense, as expressing only what he had commonly met with, and proving that the influence of pristine meanness will, more or less, continue through life. Of the truth of this remark, we shall meet with some striking proofs in the following

memoirs, throughout the whole of which, the want of early instruction and example will be seen, and the force of low habits and improper connections will be completely understood.

The person whose adventures we are now to report, as far as they can be traced, and with every allowance for the uncertainty in which the early history of such characters is always involved, owed her origin to a couple that lived together in a menial capacity, in the county Palatine of Chester. The man, whose name was LYON, survived this marriage only a short time, leaving, in 1761, a young widow, and an infant daughter, named EMMA,[1] wholly without support. In consequence of this melancholy change in her circumstances, the poor woman retired to Hawarden, in Flintshire, which was her native place, and where she was now enabled by her industry, and the kindness of friends, to maintain herself and this child, whose education was such as might be expected from the poverty of her mother's circumstances, and the little time that could be allowed from domestic occupa-

---

[1] Her father was Henry Lyon, smith, of Great Neston, Cheshire, and his daughter was baptized there, by the name of *Amy*, May 12, 1765. She was probably born April 26 (the date she always celebrated as her birthday), 1763. Her father died June 21, 1765.

tions. In an account of herself, however, which the subject of this narrative thought proper to dictate at the request of an enterprizing bookseller, for a collection of what he called " Public Characters," it is stated that she received an education superior to damsels of her condition, at the expense of the late Earl of Halifax. This was one of those instances of deception in which she was too apt to indulge, and by which she foolishly hoped to impose upon the credulity of mankind. The truth is, that all the instruction which she ever obtained in childhood consisted in the simple article of reading, and that so very imperfectly, as to be unaccompanied by correctness in spelling,[1] a qualification which she never properly acquired to the end of her days, though she mixed so much with polished society, and had an extensive correspondence.

Yet, in justice to the energies of her mind, it should be observed that she supplied the defects of her original condition by voluntary application and uncommon diligence, at that period when gaiety and business may be supposed to

---

[1] This was a defect she often lamented in later life, but her orthography was fully equal to that of her friend Caroline, Queen of Naples, who could spell neither Italian nor French correctly, and who could not plead the deficiencies of her early education as an excuse.

furnish plausible excuses for neglecting the labour of intellectual improvement.

At the age of twelve or thirteen she was received into the family of Mr. Thomas, a respectable medical practitioner at Hawarden, who was the brother-in-law of the late Alderman Boydell, and father of the eminent surgeon in Leicester Square. Her situation in this place was that of a nursery-maid ; and it is worthy of remark, that in her subsequent changes, she ever preserved a grateful sense of the kindness which she had experienced from the friends of her youth, who were well disposed to give her the instruction that was suited to her condition in life.

Happy certainly would it have been for Emma, had she been suffered to remain in her original state of servitude, but still more so if she had never been transplanted from her native mountains, to breathe the contaminating air, and to witness the licentious manners of an overgrown and luxurious city.

At sixteen she visited London, where she obtained a place with a tradesman [1] in St. James's

---

[1] On first coming to London, probably in the year 1778, she obtained a situation as nursemaid in the family of Dr. Budd, who resided in Chatham Place, Blackfriars, and who was one of the Physicians of St. Bartholomew's

Market : and it is said, that when some years afterwards she moved in a sphere of splendour, she called in her carriage at this shop, and expressed a strong sense of gratitude to her old master and mistress.

In her next situation, which was with a lady of fortune, she had ample opportunities of gratifying her love of reading, by the books obtained from the circulating library for the amusement of her mistress : but the information derived from these volumes was ill adapted to moderate the ebullitions of vanity, to mortify the impetuosity of passion, to chasten the mind, by a consideration of the duties of life, or to point out the dangerous rocks and hidden shoals, which are certain of proving destructive to those who are impelled by emotions, instead of being directed by the sense of religion.

Hospital. Her fellow-servant here, as housemaid, afterwards became Mrs. Powell, the well-known and highly-popular actress at Drury Lane Theatre. Some degree of intimacy was long maintained between these two remarkable women, both destined to rise so far above their original status of domestic service, that their change of fortune reminds one of the favourites in a fairy tale. Years afterwards, when Lady Hamilton was at the height of her celebrity and beauty, she visited Drury Lane with her husband, and the attention and admiration of the audience were divided between the favourite actress and the still more famous wife of the minister.

Novels and romances, in rapid succession, without reflection or discrimination, constituted the chief delight of this young person, who had been sent out into the world unarmed, either by prudent counsel or parental example. Here it would be wrong to omit the very remarkable and feeling censure which was passed on this pernicious waste of time, by the very person of whom we are speaking, and who, as we shall find, suffered so much from the evil. Adverting to what had been her own practice in early life, she used to condemn very pointedly those who, from design or carelessness, threw such allurements in the way of their domestics. So strong, indeed, was her sense of the mischievous tendency of those productions on the minds of the giddy and uninformed, as to declare that if she had the choice, her preference would be given to a servant that could not read at all, to one that was so qualified. This, to be sure, was carrying matters to the utmost extremity; and the reason she was pleased to assign for her opinion, though ingenious enough, cannot be admitted as a sufficient justification of the decision founded upon it. " Wherever," she would observe, " a female servant, especially if she is young, and has a turn for reading, can indulge her inclination by the books which lie in the apartments of her mistress, the business in which she should be employed will surely be neglected, and her mind be raised, by the perusal, above the sphere in which it is her province to move."

An inordinate attachment to books, exhibiting the falsest pictures of human nature, and to the playhouse, where the passions are inflamed rather than corrected, had the most baneful influence on the mind of this giddy adventurer on the perilous ocean of life. That which commenced at the outset in the laxity of discipline, became habitual by the want of monition in the progress ; and this being confirmed by the total absence of example in the heads of the household, had the effect of lessening that delicacy of sentiment, and dread of shame, which will ever prove an adamantine shield to the female heart, and the most powerful guard of its honour.

The next place to which she removed was one that flattered her vanity, and gave a latitude to her inclinations. Her appearance became almost as powerful a recommendation as her character to a lady who figured in the fashionable world, and whose house was the resort of gay persons, among whom were some writers for the stage, and others, who stood high in the public esteem as singers and performers. This was exactly the place that best suited the peculiar inclination of the lively Emma, whose heart was but too susceptible of the allurements which were now most amply spread before her by the folly of the vain, and the designs of the vicious.

The family into which she thought herself happy in being admitted as housemaid, presented to her view a perpetual round of bustling activity, which had no other object than to provide luxury for those who thought only of indulging their love of pleasure, by pampering the senses with new supplies of extravagance. The day was occupied in preparations for the festivities of the evening; and those hours which should have been devoted to rest and reflection, were sacrificed to scenes of dissipation. One part of the week was nearly the same as the other; and there was hardly anything to mark the return of that day which human and Divine authority have combined to render sacred, except in the selection of company, and the change of amusements. The servants were under the necessity of pursuing their ordinary avocations, instead of enjoying that rest which the law enjoined, and their improvement required. In this whirlpool of hurry and pleasure, the domestics had neither time for serious meditation, nor opportunities allowed them to learn their duty. From those who should have established order by their authority, and recommended temperance by their example, no rules of sobriety were received, nor any useful knowledge gained for the regulation of the conduct, and the improvement of the mind. So long as the respective business of each servant was discharged, entire satisfaction was given, and no attention was paid to the manner in which the residue of time was employed, or to the company that they kept.

In such a place, the dangers attending youth and beauty were multiplied by the facilities now offered of indulging that love of theatrical amusement which had already been too strongly excited ; by the incessant flatteries which were addressed to a credulous ear, and the arts that were continually adopted to charm away all apprehension of future misery, in the desire of present gratification. It was impossible that in a house like this, the charms of Emma should pass unobserved by the numerous visitors who were on terms of intimacy with the family. To a figure of uncommon elegance were added features perfectly regular, with a countenance of such indescribable sweetness of expression, as fixed the beholder in admiration. The airiness of her form gave a peculiar grace to her movements, and such was the flexibility of her limbs, that she might have been considered as a mountain nymph. Her agility, however, though light and sportive, had nothing in it of boisterous activity ; nor in the gaiety which she supported did there appear any of that levity which seems to court instead of repelling temptation. Among the many attractions which at this period distinguished the female of whom we are speaking, that of a very musical voice was one which could hardly fail, in the situation where she was placed, to excite attention and inflame vanity. Having the advantage of a good ear, aided by a retentive memory, she was enabled to sing popular airs with considerable effect ; and the opportunities which she enjoyed of frequenting places of public amusement, served to increase the passion for dramatic entertainments. The effect produced by these exhibitions, was that of adding to her love of singing a strong turn for mimicry, which was encouraged by her companions to such a degree, as to become the subject of general conversation.

By the folly of those who should have checked this propensity, instead of giving it countenance, that which was at first a playful act of occasional humour, productive of a little harmless amusement, settled into habit, and drew off the mind from those occupations which, diligently followed, might have rendered this young person a much more useful though a less brilliant member of society. Hereby she acquired a boldness which proved the leading feature of her character through life, to which her ruin was owing in the first instance, and which confirmed her in the habits of intrigue and extravagance, so completely as to render her the deceiver of her own heart, while she was imposing on the credulity of others.

CHAPTER II.

Ah, turn thine eyes
Where the poor houseless shiv'ring female lies.
She once, perhaps, in village plenty blest,
Has wept at tales of innocence distrest;
Her modest looks the cottage might adorn,
Sweet as the primrose peeps beneath the thorn;
Now lost to all, her friends, her virtue fled,
Near her betrayer's door she lays her head,
And, pinch'd with cold, and shrinking from the
    show'r,
With heavy heart deplores that luckless hour,
When, idly first, ambitious of the town,
She left her wheel and robes of country brown.

GOLDSMITH.

HE female who hesitates on the threshold of temptation, by stopping to listen with inquisitive delight to the tale of flattery, is lost. She betrays her virtue, by giving encouragement to the voice of praise, when she should be employed in examining her conduct, to discover what it is that renders her an object of admiration.

Thus it was in the present instance ; and more could not well have been expected, considering the circumstances in which this young person was placed, the gifts with which she was furnished, the graces she possessed, and the companions with whom she daily associated. Her first lapse from the path of virtue was occasioned by an act of good nature ; for in the early part of the American war, a friend or relation having been impressed and sent on board the Tender off the Tower, she had the courage to wait upon the late Admiral John Willet Payne,[1] then a captain, and employed in the regulating service,

---

[1] Captain, afterwards Rear-Admiral, John Willet Payne, was the youngest son of the governor of St. Christopher's, West Indies, and was educated at the Naval Academy at Portsmouth. He served in the West Indies, and in the American War, under Sir Peter Parker, and was aide-de-camp to Admiral Lord Howe at the capture of New York. After much service on the North American Station, he was appointed to the *Phœnix*, Captain Sir Hyde Parker, and was present in the action with Count d'Estaing in the West Indies. He was made a post-captain in 1780, and commanded the *Leander*, 50 guns, and the *Princess Amelia*, of 80 guns. At the conclusion of the war, 1783, he returned to England, where he mixed with the best society, and by his agreeable manners became a special favourite of the Prince of Wales. He was appointed to the post of Keeper of the Prince's Privy Seal, and soon afterwards entered Parliament as member for Huntingdon. On the declaration of war by France in

with a request that he would cause the man to
be liberated. This gallant officer was so much
struck with the appearance of the petitioner,
that he granted her prayer, and became a suitor
in return. These attentions were far from
being unacceptable to one whose principles were
already weakened, and she soon became the
mistress of her new admirer, who spared no
expense in setting off her charms to the best
advantage.

But after some time, the late Sir Harry
Featherston [1] having declared his passion for
Emma in warm terms, her protector consented

1793, he was appointed to the *Russell* (74) and took part
in Lord Howe's victory of June 1, 1794. In 1796 he
commanded the *Impeteux* (80) under Admiral Colpoys,
and Lord Bridport, and in 1797 was made Rear-Admiral
of the *Blue*. His health failing, he was appointed
Treasurer of Greenwich Hospital in 1799, where he
died, November 17, 1802. His brief *liaison* with Emma
Lyon resulted in the birth of a daughter named Emily.

[1] Sir Henry Fetherstonhaugh, Bart., of Up Park,
situated on the border of Sussex and Hampshire, between
Havant and Petersfield. His father, Sir Matthew, the
first baronet, purchased the property in 1746. Sir Henry
died at an advanced age in 1846 without issue, when the
title became extinct. During this connection, which
lasted hardly a year, the fair Emma so gained the esteem
of Sir Henry, that their separation at the end of 1781 did
not extinguish his regard for her; he was her correspondent for years afterwards, and his letters testify by

to yield up the fair one to the opulent baronet, who conducted her to his seat in Sussex. Here for some months she led a life of fictitious grandeur, as the nominal mistress of a noble mansion, though she soon had the mortification of seeing that her real character was known, and despised, even by those who were under the necessity of obeying her commands. The fondness of her lover, the extravagant adulation of his sporting companions, and the continual succession of riotous amusements, could not prevent the intrusion of some bitter recollections, and an inward feeling of resentment at the occasional marks of contempt which were betrayed by the honest rustics, who were as yet far from exchanging their reverence of the institutions of their ancestors, for the frivolous distinctions, and shameful customs, of the fashionable world.

Emma, during her residence at Up Park, displayed her agility in various festive scenes, and she particularly obtained great applause on account of her equestrian powers, sitting her horse with uncommon elegance, and rivalling in

their propriety and tone of respect to the favourable opinion he retained for her. In her declining fortunes, after the death of Nelson, he often wrote to her, and sent her presents of fruit and game.

speed the boldest of her acquaintance. But this course of dissipation was of short continuance; and though roses appeared scattered in every path, the pleasure which they yielded faded quickly away, leaving nothing but thorns behind.

After spending the summer and part of the autumn in the country, the baronet removed with his prize to London, where, for many reasons, he avoided exhibiting her in a public manner, and she was accordingly placed in private lodgings. For some time the condition was easy and agreeable enough to prevent the suspicion of its having any insidious object; but when neglect and indifference became too apparent to escape observation, the keen sense of wrong produced remonstrances, which were received with a coolness that only served to aggravate resentment, and to hasten a separation.

Thus abandoned in her utmost need, without either friend, property, or character, this hapless victim of vanity and deceit was driven to encounter the ruthless storm, dependent upon charms which had already deprived her of peace, and which were now to provide her a guilty support. Of the variety of scenes through which this daughter of vicissitude

passed, after experiencing that treachery which
most commonly follows the sacrifice of virgin
innocence, it is impossible to give an account ;
and even were the particulars most exactly
remembered, or easily collected, still the relation could hardly be attended with any better
effect than that of ministering to an idle spirit
of curiosity, which seeks amusement in tales of
misfortune, and derives a wretched kind of
pleasure even from the follies of mankind.

The gradations from splendid distinction
gained by the loss of virtue, to the extremity
of want and misery, were so rapid, that in a
few months she was nearly an outcast in the
metropolis, when one of those casual occurrences, which sometimes produce a complete
turn in human affairs, may be said to have
restored her again to society.

The encouragement afforded in this land of
credulity to every species of empiricism, never
fails to stimulate the genius of new adventurers,
whose claims to public support have the greater
chance of being successful, in proportion as they
are removed from decency, or are at variance with
probability. At the period of which we are
speaking, one of those impudent pretenders to
superior wisdom, who are continually taking
advantage of the national thirst for wonder and

novelty, contrived to fill his pockets at the expense of the thoughtless and the ignorant, by an exhibition, which, in any other country than England, would have subjected the inventor to exile or imprisonment. This man, who, in point of education and abilities, ranked above the general description of quacks, affected to explain the inmost secrets of nature, and to unfold all her mysterious operations in the continuance of each species of animal being, while to his hearers he ventured to hold out the infallible charm that was to insure the enjoyment of health, pleasure, and longevity. The lectures of Dr. Graham,[1] however, would

[1] Graham was the son of a saddler, and was born in Edinburgh in 1745. He studied medicine, and took his degree of M.D. there, and after practising for a while at Pontefract, went to America, where he posed as a philanthropic physician, whose sole object was the healing and benefit of his suffering fellow-men. He returned to England in 1775, and settled for a time in Pall Mall, London, where he advertised his wonderful cures of diseases of the ear and eye, including many desperate cases which had defied ordinary remedies and physicians. After a visit to Scotland, where he was sought after by patients of the highest rank, attracted by the fame of his marvellous skill, he returned to London, and in May, 1779, opened his "Temple of Health" in the Adelphi. The object of this remarkable institution was, in the doctor's own words, "the propagation of a much more strong, beautiful, active, healthy, wise, and virtuous race of human beings, than the

hardly have answered his purpose, in a lucrative point of view, if he had not enlivened them by descriptions and illustrations, which served to excite sensations, and to provoke desires that

present puny, insignificant, foolish, peevish, vicious, and nonsensical race of Christians, who quarrel, fight, bite, devour, and cut one another's throats about they know not what." It was an original scheme, and by its success the doctor showed he possessed a keen knowledge of human nature. His address was agreeable, his appearance prepossessing, he had a glib tongue, and almost every qualification necessary to make him what he really was—one of the most clever and remarkable quacks that ever existed.

As a crowning attraction to his undertaking, Graham announced the appearance of the "lovely Hebe Vestina, the rosy Goddess of Health," who, according to his advertisements, presided at "the display of the Celestial Meteors, and of that Sacred Vital Fire over which she watches, and whose application in the cure of diseases she daily has the honour of directing." The rosy goddess was the late mistress of Sir H. Fetherstonhaugh, who, to quote the doctor, "on the celestial throne, will exhibit in her own person a proof of the all-blessing effects of virtue, temperance, regularity, simplicity, moderation ; and, in these luxurious, artificial, and effeminate times, to recommend those great virtues." In other advertisements Graham professed to be able to show the whole art of living with "health, honour, and happiness in this world, for at least a hundred years." One of the principal means to attain to this patriarchal age was the frequent use of mud baths, and on stated occasions the doctor exhibited himself, practising his own precepts,

rather stood in need of a restraint than a stimu-
lant. When the popularity of these licentious
discourses began to fail by repetition, the orator
had recourse to a bold device, to awaken the

immersed in mud to the chin, his head covered with a
flowing wig. The beautiful " Hebe Vestina" was also
to be seen in a similar condition, her hair elaborately
dressed in the prevailing fashion, with powder, flowers,
ropes of pearls, and feathers. In 1781 the " Temple of
Health" was removed to Schomberg House, Pall Mall,
and two new attractions, "The Temple of Hymen " and
"The Celestial Bed," were exhibited to the gaze of
throngs of admiring and jeering spectators. The rooms
were most elaborately furnished, with statues, stands of
armour, stained-glass windows with rich curtains, and the
walls covered with mirrors ; strains of soft music filled
the air, heavy with perfumes, till the audience almost
fancied themselves in an enchanted palace ; at least, so
said the doctor. In another advertisement he announces
that "the enchanting glory of these magical scenes will
break forth about seven, and die away about ten o'clock,
during which time Oriental odours and Ætherial essences
will perfume the air, while the hymenæal sopha blazes
forth with the plenitude of the soft lambent celestial fire."
The price of admission to these wonders was only " one
shilling," and the Temple was crowded nightly by people
who eagerly paid half-a-guinea to view the "Celestial
Bed," and other novelties, in " the Holy of Holies," as the
shilling advertised only admitted to the body of the hall.
This "Celestial Bed" was Graham's crowning achievement. It was beautifully carved and gilt, supported by
twenty-eight glass pillars, and surmounted by a richly-gilt
canopy, from which crimson silk curtains were gracefully

public attention, and to draw around his rostrum crowded audiences of the weak and the wicked, consisting of those who, from inexperience, could see no deformity in vice, and of habitual debauchees, who had no higher enjoyment. To gratify a depraved taste, and that from the vilest of all motives, the love of gain, this unprincipled charlatan resolved to introduce a new object of attraction, in the person of some young female, whose figure might render her a perfect model of health and beauty. The difficulty certainly lay in obtaining an object who would submit to be exhibited, in a condition, the very proposal of which could not but

dependent. The bed itself was "magnetico-electric, coverings of purple and curtains of celestial blue surround it, and the bed-clothes are perfumed with the most costly essences of Arabia." The doctor asserted that married couples without children, but desirous of offspring, would surely attain their wishes by sleeping in this wonderful bed—"the only one in the world, or that ever existed." The fee for this privilege was £100 per night, and many persons with more wealth than brains are recorded as having paid it. As the novelty wore off the demand decreased, and the price was reduced to £50, then to £25 per night, and at last whatever sum could be got was taken. In 1784 the farce was played out, the "Temple of Health" was shut up, and all the furniture and apparatus, with the famous bed, disappeared under the auctioneer's hammer.

make the most wretched of the sex shudder at the degradation.[1] Yet the lecturer was not mistaken in his opinion of mankind, when he reckoned upon the complete success of his scheme, not only in gaining auditors, but in finding a subject who would consent, for a reward, to stand in all the simplicity of nature, as the representative of the cheerful goddess of health and inspiring beauty. The event answered his expectations; and thus the unhappy fair one, whose misfortunes were owing in a great measure to her lovely form and mimic powers, now became indebted to the same causes for a deliverance from the lowest state of misery. Disgusting as this incident must be to every one who feels the slightest respect for the honour of human nature, and concern for the interests of virtue, both of which were grossly insulted by an exhibition that would have put a heathen to the blush, still our

---

[1] There is not the slightest evidence that such a scandalous violation of decency ever took place. "Hebe Vestina, the rosy Goddess of Health," was certainly attired and draped in a classical style for exhibition. The connection of Emma Lyon with Dr. Graham, at the furthest could not have been but a very few months in duration, probably in the year 1782; but she may have officiated in the "Temple of Health." prior to being under the *protection* of Sir H. Fetherstonhaugh, a year or so earlier.

indignation ought to be directed against the
lecturer and his hearers, rather than the frail
object of a licentious curiosity and the instrument of gross imposture. But while the fact of
the exhibition stands uncontradicted, the friends
of the female who figured in it have persevered
in denying her connection with the scene. Their
zeal, however, is more gratifying to the feelings
than satisfactory to the judgment; for such a
circumstance could not have been related without
some foundation, and the writer of this had the
whole history from a person of the highest
literary character, twenty-four years ago.

Of this strange folly some distinguished artists,
both painters and sculptors, contrived to profit
in their respective lines, by adopting this elegant form as a model. Many exquisite pieces
were accordingly painted and chiselled after
this finished production of Nature's workmanship ; and the remunerations which she received
placed her in a situation above want.

Still it is not to be disguised, that the declen-
sion from virtue, and the habits which she had
acquired, left too strong a tinge to be wholly
obliterated even by the blow of adversity, and
the change which she had experienced.

Her admirers increased as the representations
of her multiplied ; and the praises which she

continually heard, from those who certainly were
the best judges of symmetry and beauty, tended
effectually to wear away the sense of disgrace,
and to reconcile her mind to the blandishments
of guilt.

Among those who were captivated by the
personal graces of the lively and fascinating
Emma, and who devoted much professional
attention to the delineation of her in various
characters, the eccentric ROMNEY [1] was by far the
most distinguished in his attachment, and the
most favoured by the object of his admiration.

This artist was then at the zenith of his reputation, in Cavendish Square ; but his moral
character may be estimated from the fact, that
he had abandoned a virtuous wife and two children, above twenty years before the period at
which we are now arrived.

The most particular friend and biographer of
the painter, though utterly unable, and no doubt
unwilling, to justify this flagrant instance of
cruelty on moral principles, has yet endeavoured

---

[1] George Romney was born at Dalton-le-Furness,
Lancashire, December 26, 1734. He left Lancashire for
London, 1762, studied from 1773 to 1775 in Italy; and
after a successful career of more than twenty years in
the Metropolis, retired, in 1798, to Hampstead ; but soon
after, his health failing, he returned to his wife and family,
and died at Kendal, November 15, 1802.

to find some motive for the act, which may, as
he thinks, have the effect of lessening its crimi-
nality. This conduct of Romney in leaving a
young family unprotected in a remote part of
the kingdom is ascribed to a romantic spirit of
enterprize, and to the desire of improving his
mind and his circumstances ; but that " beholding in an innocent wife a supposed impediment
to every splendid project, he resolved, instead of
settling as a family man to wander forth alone
into the distant world in quest of professional
adventures."

Such is the sophistry by which the violation
of the first of duties is made instrumentally expedient, if not really necessary, to the attainment of distinguished eminence in an intellectual
and liberal pursuit. But allowing all that the
partiality of friendship can require in behalf of
an esteemed object, we may be permitted to express our concern and indignation at the continuance of this separation, when the only reason
ever offered for it had ceased to operate, and
when that eminence was completely attained, for
which the connubial state and parental endear-
ments had been so long sacrificed. It might
have been expected that a man of such exquisite
sensibility as Romney is described, would, on
entering into the possession of a noble mansion,

and the enjoyment of an ample income, have eagerly called his family to town, to participate in his good fortune. But the case was otherwise ; and while the artist lived in splendour, visited by persons of the highest rank, and earning between three and four thousand pounds a-year, his meek and unoffending partner remained without any attempt to injure him by an exposure of her wrongs ; though such was her condition, that she would gladly have received the scraps which fell from his table.[1]

Yet of this very man, the indiscretion of kindred genius has ventured to record, that " in conversation he was often delightfully eloquent, particularly in describing to a friend pathetic scenes in humble life, which he often explored ; sometimes for the purpose of discovering new subjects for his art ; and frequently for the nobler purpose of relieving distress ; for no man could be more tenderly alive, both to the duty, and the delight of generous compassion, and evangelical charity ! "

---

[1] Romney, after leaving his wife with two children in 1762, visited them only once, in 1767, but he provided for their maintenance, and kept them from poverty. On his return to Kendal in 1799, his youth and health both gone, his wife, to her honour, after thirty-seven years of neglect, received him with forgiveness and kindness, and affectionately nursed him during two years of helpless imbecility.

However tender might have been the feeling, or extensive the bounty of Romney, he certainly paid no attention to the consideration, that "charity begins at home," a maxim, which, though too often perverted to the low purpose of screening a niggardly disposition, under the specious plea of prudence, contains a sound moral truth, equivalent to the declaration of an evangelical writer, who practised what he taught —"if any provide not for his own, and especially for those of his own house, he hath denied the faith, and is worse than an infidel."

The charity of Romney was anything but that which it is said to have been, for it was utterly destitute of religious principle, and had its origin in the school of sentimentalists, where feeling is substituted for duty, and the breach of one obligation finds a covering in excessive sensibility. Severe as these remarks may be deemed, they are called for by the circumstance, that while the painter lived apart from a worthy woman, to whom he was bound by the most sacred ties, he lavished his bounty on one who was above twenty-five years younger than himself, and with whose character he could not fail to be acquainted.

But, like Sterne, whom he admired, Romney had no true feeling; and his propensities to sensual indulgence were well known to all his acquaintance. With Emma he became enamoured while painting her picture, as Apelles fell in love with Campaspe. Certain it is, that the modern artist had no cause to complain of the severity of his mistress; and his fondness for her was carried to such a pitch, that he oftentimes neglected the works which he was employed to execute, from a capricious whim to delineate his idol in some new character or fascinating attitude.

A colour, however, has been given to this connection, for the purpose of making it appear to have been nothing more than pure disinterested generosity on the one side, and filial attachment on the other.

The biographer of Romney has touched this subject with an art, which manifests uncommon anxiety to relate what may be fairly told, without leading the reader to suspect the real nature of this attachment.

" The talents which nature bestowed on the fair Emma," says the historian, " led her to delight in the two kindred arts of music and painting. In the first she acquired great practical ability ; for the second she had exquisite taste, and such expressive powers, as could furnish to an historical painter an

inspiring model for the various characters,
either delicate or sublime, that he might have
occasion to represent. Her features, like the
language of Shakspeare, could exhibit all the
feelings of nature, and all the gradations of
every passion, with a most fascinating truth,
and felicity of expression. Romney delighted
in observing the wonderful command she possessed over her eloquent features ; and through
the surprising vicissitudes of her destiny, she
ever took a generous pride in serving him as a
model : her peculiar force and variation of feeling, countenance, and gesture, inspirited and
ennobled the productions of his art. One of his
earliest fancy pictures, from this animated model,
was a whole length of Circe with her magic
wand. It could not be painted later than the
year 1782, as I recollect a letter from a friend
in that year, describing the very powerful impression made by this picture on a party who
then surveyed it. Some years afterwards, I had
a conversation in Romney's gallery on the same
picture, with an opulent nobleman, now no
more, who discovered a faint inclination to purchase it, but it was reserved for a purchaser of
superior taste. A Calypso, a Magdalen, a
Wood Nymph, a Bacchante, the Pythian
Priestess on her tripod, and a Saint Cecilia,

were all drawn from the same admirable
model.[1]

This statement is intended to impress on the
mind of the reader a persuasion that the painter
was actuated by professional motives only,
which will hardly be admitted as coming within
the limits of probability, by any one who has
made human nature his study ; and by those
who ever had the slightest knowledge of the
parties, it will be treated as a most extravagant
idea, that Romney, who had abandoned his wife,
and lived in luxury, should receive such a
visitor at all seasons, and behold her in every
luscious attitude, from the mere wish of improving his own genius. But in truth, had the
artist been possessed of that charity which is
ascribed to him, he would have seen the gross
impropriety of placing an interesting young
woman in characters which could not be even
represented without a wantonness of counte-·
nance, habiliment, and attitude, wholly repug-
nant to the delicacy of that charm, so beautifully
pourtrayed by the poet, in his description of the
mother of mankind :

> Grace was in all her steps, heav'n in her eye,
> In every gesture, dignity, and love.

[1] Romney also painted her as Miranda, Serena, Joan of
Arc, Magdalen, Bacchante (for the Prince of Wales), &c.

Of the numerous pictures of Emma, painted by Romney, one of the most pleasing represents her as viewing the sensitive plant, with a mixture of surprise and delight. This piece, which is in the possession of Mr. Hayley, has been twice engraved, and that gentleman relates its history in the following manner :—

" During my visit to Romney in November, 1786, I happened to find him one morning contemplating by himself a recently coloured head on a small canvas. I expressed my admiration of his unfinished work in the following terms : —' This is a most happy beginning : you never painted a female head with such exquisite expression ; you have only to enlarge your canvas, introduce the shrub mimosa, growing in a vase, with a hand of this figure approaching its stem, and you may call your picture a personification of sensibility.' ' I like your suggestion,' replied the painter, ' and will enlarge my canvas immediately.' ' Do so,' I answered with exultation, on his kindly adopting my idea ; ' and without loss of time I will hasten to an eminent nurseryman, at Hammersmith, and bring you the most beautiful plant I can find, that may suit your purpose.' " [1]

Granting, as every one must, that this

[1] Life of Romney, p. 121.

portrait indicates an uncommon sweetness of
expression, and great liveliness in the countenance ; still it would be very difficult to show
in what respect it can be considered as peculiarly
marking the characteristic of sensibility, or how
it is at all deserving of that appellation, unless
it be in a punning association of the figure and
the plant. It is a great perversion of taste to
suppose that the feeling, which is moved by the
happiness or the sufferings of others, can be expressed by contemplating an inanimate shrub,
which is wholly destitute of the power of
exciting joy or sorrow.

With this picture of Emma, as the representative of a virtue, to the reality of which,
through life, she was an absolute stranger,
though at any time she could easily assume the
appearance of it, the connection between her and
the painter shall for the present be closed ;
leaving him to the influence of those beauties of
person, and especially to that charming voice,
which lulled in him every serious reflection, by
the dulcet strains of harmony, and the syren
song of pleasure, agreeable to the language of
the amatory poet :

> Music so softens and disarms the mind,
> That not an arrow does resistance find :
> Thus the fair tyrant celebrates the prize,
> And acts herself the triumph of her eyes.
>
> WALLER.

LADY HAMILTON AS SENSIBILITY.

From an engraving by R.ᵈ Earlom after Romney

CHAPTER III.

There is in human nature generally
more of the fool than of the wise;
and therefore those faculties by which
the foolish part of men's minds is
taken, are the most potent of all.

BACON.

T the time when the modern
Phryne was the favourite
model of artists, particularly
of Romney and Tresham, she
lived apparently by her needle,
and with such an appearance
of simplicity, as entirely to disarm the neigh-
bours of all suspicion. Yet under a plain and
almost a rustic garb, with looks of modest
diffidence, and a voice of persuasive mildness,
were concealed the complete knowledge of all
the arts of pleasure, and every propensity to the
indulgence of her passions.

Having once condescended to become the
living representative of the most voluptuous

characters of the Grecian mythology, she made
no scruple of giving to each libidinous figure
all the force and attraction of the naked truth.

In the present instance, it is certain that the
variety of characters sustained, and the capti-
vating attitudes assumed to diffuse a bewitching
allurement into the form and expression, suited
to the personification of a Calypso, a Bacchante,
and a Venus, were attended with pernicious consequences to a female, who, in her attempts to
excel in this particular line, lost the sense of
virtue, and became completely skilled in the arts
of intrigue and duplicity.

Though naturally sensual, extravagant, and
ambitious, she had so effectually obtained the
outward command of her passions at this period,
as to preserve an air of modesty, even while
engaged most eagerly in voluptuous pursuits.
She appeared, indeed, to be the child of nature,
perfectly unconscious of the least design ; and
to her might have been applied in every respect
the very striking and animated description of an
intriguing female drawn by the masterly pencil
of the comic poet :

> Coquet and coy at once her air,
>   Both study'd, though both seem neglected ;
> Careless she is, with artful care,
>   Affecting to seem unaffected.
>
> CONGREVE.

By this address, she contrived to draw into her lure one who was supposed to have been equally skilled in the mystery of deception with herself, and who, though he was enthusiastically devoted to fine forms after the Grecian model, yet was as inconstant to each object of attraction as the flitting insect, which, ranging in every direction where the loveliest odours are exhaled, abides not long on any of the flowers by which they are produced.

Strange, however, it is, that this honourable member of the house of Warwick was for once completely deceived, and caught in his own toils. The birdlime of Emma's charms, heightened by the apparent simplicity of her manner, and certainly not rendered the less attractive by her peculiar neatness in dress, fixed the roving mind of Mr. Charles Greville[1] so effectually, that he left no artifice unessayed to gain possession of what he really imagined to be an uncropt flower, "blushing unseen and wasting its sweetness in the desert air."

Too much practised in the ways of the world, that lead to the female heart, this man of fashion,

[1] Charles Francis Greville, second son of Francis, Earl of Warwick, by Elizabeth, daughter of Lord Archibald Hamilton, was born in 1749, and died unmarried in 1809. His connection with Emma Lyon lasted about four years, from 1782 to 1786.

and but too well acquainted with the avenues
who prided himself as much on account of his
amours as on his collection of pictures and his
exquisite taste in the fine arts, became perfectly
enamoured of the lovely nymph, who happened
to cross his path. The enquiries which he made
about her residence, gave him such complete
satisfaction with respect to the virtue and industry of this young woman, as to convince him
that he had discovered an inestimable treasure,
and consequently to inflame his desires. Chilling indifference, and peremptory repulses, by increasing the difficulties of his pursuit, rendered
him more impatient and determined. Perseverance he knew would make his attentions at
least respected, even though success should not
ultimately attend his efforts. By degrees his
constancy prevailed : confidence yielded to im-
portunity, and with many promises of fidelity, the
lover became rewarded for his assiduity. Quite
overjoyed at his rare fortune, he set about cultivating those talents of Emma, which his acute-
ness could not help discovering, nor his good
taste from admiring. Being himself a connoisseur in music, he spared neither time nor
expense in providing proper instructions for a
person from whose improvement he anticipated
new sources of gratification.

The progress of the pupil gave infinite delight
to her admirer; and such was the force of her
natural genius, that she contrived every day to
evince some fresh excellence, by which means
his affections became perfectly settled; and a
heart naturally volatile, continued to be bound
in the soft enchantment, even when the novelty
of personal charms had no longer any particular
influence. But how successfully art maintained
the dominion which beauty had acquired, will
appear from a trifling incident that occurred not
long after the formation of this connection.
Ambitious of displaying his conquest to the
world of fashion, the lover conducted the lovely
Emma, dressed out in a very elegant style, to
Ranelagh, which was then the favourite theatre
of gaiety and gallantry. Here her form and
agility attracted universal attention, and excited
so much admiration, that for once she gave way
to a natural impulse; and to increase the applause with which she had been flattered, she
gave the company some delightful specimens of
her unrivalled powers, both in musical expression and flexibility of action. The consequence
of all this was, as might be expected, that a
convulsive sensation of astonishment and rap-
ture ran through the whole assembly, the
plaudits of which proved so intoxicating to the

object of them, that she redoubled her exertions, and called forth renewed peals of applause. But all these were so many poisoned arrows to the heart of Mr. Greville, who brought her thither rather to dazzle beholders by her beauty than to gratify idlers by her accomplishments. He now perceived that she was not only fond of adulation, but that she actually courted it, and was quite in her element when surrounded by a host of admirers. This was a distressing thought to one who had in fact placed his affections on Emma, from the persuasion that her mind was not only uncontaminated by the folly of the gay world, but wholly ignorant of the art of gaining its admiration. Being now more than half suspicious of the deception which had in reality been practised upon him, he returned home in a pensive mood ; and so completely overpowered were his feelings, that he could not help expressing them, with strong emotions of concern, at the manifest inclination which she had shown to " please fools rather than to respect his sentiments."

Any other woman than Emma would on such a reproach have thrown herself into hysterics, or recriminated in language of haughty indignation. But with that superiority of duplicity which always distinguished her, instead of having

recourse to such ordinary expedients, she retired
very coolly to her room, and after throwing off
all her elegant attire, she put on the original
cottage dress, in which she had at first made an
impression on the heart of her protector ; then
returning to the place where he sat, she signified
her intention of relieving him from all further
uneasiness, by returning to that station where he
had originally found her, and where, as she said,
it would always afford her pleasure to receive
him still as a friend. The effect of this declaration was electrical : the clouds of jealousy were
dispelled in a moment, and the connection, which
seemed to have been on the very point of dis-
ruption, became more closely cemented than ever.

Mr. Greville, who was at that time in an
office of considerable distinction at court, maintained his mistress in a style of elegance corresponding to his rank ; and after making every
allowance for her situation, and natural turn for
expense, it must be admitted that at this period
she deported herself in a manner which gave
him and his friends much satisfaction. One
of her first acts, when placed in this state of
splendour, was to send for her mother, who now
assumed, though by what legal claim cannot be
clearly ascertained, the name of Cadogan.[1]

---

[1] Her mother's maiden name was Mary Kidd, and
Mary Lyon by marriage. After the death of her hus-

Pleasing as it is to record this instance of dutiful respect to her parent, from whom she was never afterwards separated during a space of above twenty years, it would be still more satisfactory if the writer could detail correspondent particulars of tenderness towards the fruits of this union. There were three[1] of these children, two girls and a boy : the names of the former

hand she was known as Mrs. Doggen, or Dogan ; but, on coming to reside with her daughter and Mr. Greville in Paddington Green, London, her surname was lengthened to Cadogan, by which she was always afterwards known. The good woman, though mixing much with high society through her daughter, still retained some of the plebeian tastes of her early condition. At an entertainment given in honour of the English fleet at Naples, at the drinking of a toast, Mrs. C. exclaimed, "They may talk of their Lachrymæ Christi and stuff, but give me a glass of London gin before a whole bottle of it!" As there happened to be a few bottles of gin on board one of the ships, her wish was speedily gratified. But she certainly possessed some sterling qualities, for Lord Nelson wrote of her with respect and sent her presents, and Sir W. Hamilton, who must have known her intimately during her residence under his roof, left her an annuity of £100 for life.

[1] This is improbable, and there is no evidence to support such an assertion. If she was the mother of *three* children by Mr. Greville, it is remarkable that, in their correspondence for years afterwards, there is not the slightest mention of anything of the kind, nor allusion to any issue as the result of their intimacy.

were Eliza and Anne : the latter was called
Charles, after his father, but the surname of
each was wholly fictitious ; and even the mother,
who always passed for their aunt, for reasons
which it would be in vain to enquire, and useless to conjecture, thought proper at this time
to take upon herself the name of Harte.

Nothing perhaps can more strongly pourtray
the moral and political evil of concubinage than
the insulated condition into which it commonly
throws the innocent offspring of such illicit
connections. These unfortunate children rarely
enjoy the benefit of parental affection ; and to
that social friendship which is cemented by the
ties of legal consanguinity they must for ever
remain utter strangers. Even when they experience proper kindness, enjoy the advantages
of education, and are raised by an adequate provision or a suitable occupation above the fear of
want, and the reproaches of the world, still the
recollection of their origin cannot but produce
momentary uneasiness, and expose them to occasional marks of contempt. Cut off by the immorality of their parents from the privilege of
bearing a name which may gain them the respect
of their contemporaries, persons of this description are deprived of that powerful incitement to
great actions which arises from hereditary virtue.

Instead of this, they have every reason to conceal the particulars of their descent, and for the most part they have but too much cause to bury in oblivion the names of those from whom they derive their being. In general, the pathetic complaint of one who was himself of this wretched class, may be adopted by them all :

> No mother's care
> Shielded my infant innocence with prayer :
> No father's guardian hand my youth maintain'd,
> Call'd forth my virtues, and from vice restrain'd.
>
> SAVAGE.

The truth of this was felt by the children of whom we are speaking ; for in England they never knew what parental care was ; and when at last they were taken under the protection of the mother, it was by the pretext of an alliance which never had an existence; while on neither side did they obtain the instruction and means of support for which they had a fair claim on those who gave them birth.

In the year 1789 a revolution took place in the affairs of Emma, which was of the utmost importance to her whole destiny, and ultimately to that of others. Mr. Greville being under the necessity of retrenching his establishment, by a temporary embarrassment in his concerns, endeavoured to convince his mistress of the necessity of a separation, on such terms as could be most accommodating. While this plan was in agitation, Sir William Hamilton,[1] ambassador at the court of Naples, came to London on some private business ; and being introduced by Mr. Greville, who was his sister's son, to this accomplished woman, he expressed his admiration of her person and manners with such warmth, as suggested a thought to the nephew of adopting a measure by which he could both benefit the lady and rid himself of an expensive burthen. The enchanting vocal powers of Emma, added to the excellent character which was given of her by Mr. Greville, quite enraptured Sir William, who made an offer, which was readily accepted, of taking her with him to Italy, for the purpose of rendering her still more accomplished. Matters being thus amicably adjusted to the satisfaction of all parties, the lady and her mother soon after quitted England for Naples, to which city they travelled overland by the way of Germany.

[1] The date of this affair is entirely wrong. The assured income of Mr. Greville was £500 per annum, and, by "keeping up appearances," he had gone beyond his means, and was considerably in debt. Consequently, the arrival of his uncle, Sir W. Hamilton, in London, in the summer of 1784, on a long leave of absence, was very gratifying to his favourite nephew and prospective heir to his property. For the real facts of the matter, see note page 55.

CHAPTER IV.

There is no reason why we should
not sometimes blame, and sometimes
commend the same person; for as
none are always right, so neither is
it probable that they should be invariably wrong.

POLYBIUS.

IR WILLIAM HAMILTON,[1]
who discharged the office of
envoy at the Neapolitan court
for the long period of thirty-
six years, was in some respects
a very estimable man.   He
was the foster-brother of our venerable monarch

[1] Sir William Hamilton, was a younger son of Lord
Archibald Hamilton, Governor of Greenwich Hospital,
who was a younger son of William, third Duke of
Hamilton. Sir William was born in 1730, and began life,
according to his own account, "with an ancient name
and £1,000." He improved his fortunes by marrying, in
1755, a Welsh heiress, the daughter of Hugh Barlow, Esq.,
of Lawrenny Hall, Pembroke. As he informed his nephew

(George III.), to whom, at an early age, he was appointed equerry, and in whose first parliament he sat as one of the members for the Borough of Midhurst. His talents were respectable, and his manners rendered him a proper person to act as the representative of his sovereign in a place which was at that time the resort of families of the first distinction. When Sir William (then Mr. Hamilton) succeeded Sir James Grey, as the envoy at the court of Naples, that city was the centre of attraction to inquisitive travellers, not only on account of its natural beauties, and the salubrity of the climate, but in consequence of the remarkable discoveries which were daily brought to light in the excavations, where Herculaneum and Pompeii had been overwhelmed by the eruptions of Vesuvius. Among the vast influx of strangers drawn every year to Naples, by the desire of beholding these interesting curiosities,

years afterwards, he married not from choice, but rather against his own inclination, but the lady had an estate worth nearly £5,000 a-year, and a watchful regard to his own interest was the chief motive in this *mariage de convenance*. The only issue of this union was a daughter who died in 1775, and the mother left Sir William a widower in 1782. From 1764 to 1800 he filled the post of English ambassador at Naples. He married his second wife, Emma Lyon, or Harte, September 6, 1791, and died April 6, 1803.

were many learned men from all parts of Europe,
of whose observations the British ambassador
could not fail to profit ; while they, on their
part, were grateful for his attentions, and soli-
citious of his correspondence.   Thus he became
a virtuoso, a naturalist, and an antiquary, by
the peculiar nature of his situation, and the
conversation which perpetually occurred at his
table.   His judgment, however, was such as
enabled him to make a proper use of the opportunities he enjoyed, and being of an active mind,
he was not to be intimidated by ordinary difficulties.   He explored the beautiful country
where he resided with uncommon diligence,
and repeated his observations on Vesuvius, and
other volcanic mountains, with all the patience
and industry becoming the man of science, who
is neither content with a superficial inquiry,
nor satisfied while any objects remain which
he has not completely investigated, or about
which the smallest uncertainty may be supposed
to exist.   The value of such a resident in that
part of the world was duly appreciated in his
native country, where he was elected a fellow
of the Royal Society, to which learned body he
made many valuable communications that were
inserted in their transactions from the year 1766
to 1794.   Most of these papers are descriptive

of the eruptions which the author witnessed, or of districts over which he passed soon after they had been devastated by earthquakes. Besides these productions, Sir William Hamilton favoured the world with a very splendid work, entitled "Antiquités Etrusques, Grecques et Romaines,"[1] illustrated with plates, in two volumes folio. His motive in publishing this collection in a foreign language might, perhaps, admit of an apology, though it would be difficult to satisfy any Englishman of the propriety of adopting the French tongue, on a subject which by no means required the assistance of such a mode for the purpose of elucidation, or the advantage of general circulation. Considered as a classical work, the Latin would have been the most proper vehicle ; but when the official situation of the author is taken into the account, it will be hardly possible to advance a single reason why he should have given the preference to the French language on this occasion, when his own was equally copious, expressive, and adapted to the subject. Charles III., King of

---

[1] This work was in 4 vols.; the first two were published at Naples in 1766, the others a few years later. The profit of the publication was given to the editor D'Hancarville.

Naples, certainly evinced more discrimination and sound sense in the disposal of the great work which he caused to be published, relating to Herculaneum, Stabiæ, and Pompeii, in two folio volumes. When the editor, Monsignor Bajardi, who was a learned prelate of the Roman Church, waited on the king to receive his directions for the distribution of the copies, which had been printed at the royal charge, in order to be presented to the learned, and deposited in public libraries, the king said to the bishop, without deigning to notice the French, Spaniards, or Italians, "Give five hundred to the English." Bajardi, who was a man of liberal sentiments, and far from being unfavourable to our nation, replied with a bow, " In that case, I fear, the rest of Europe must go without their share." To which the king answered, " Why, then, let the press be set over again."

This monarch, it must be confessed, paid more respect to the character of the English nation than the ambassador, who chose to publish a magnificent work on a general topic in that very language, which, perhaps, of all others, was the one that he ought to have rejected.

In 1772, our author printed an octavo

volume of "Observations on Mount Vesuvius, and Other Volcanoes." ,This subject he discussed at great length, four years afterwards, in two folio volumes, bearing the title of "Campi Phelegræi, or Observations on the Volcanoes of the Two Sicilies," to which he afterwards added a supplemental volume.

The interests of truth, however, require it to be told, that, great as the diligence of our ambassador was in promoting the knowledge of this branch of natural history, his acquaintance with preceding writers on the subject was but scanty, and he had besides so very slender an acquaintance with philosophical language, as to be under the necessity of calling in the assistance of others in the arrangement of his observations. The person to whom he was under the greatest obligations for the composition of these works was a monk of Mount Etna. The great merit of Sir William Hamilton consisted in his exertions to bring a valuable accession of discoveries to the store of science, and in giving a liberal patronage to the fine arts. Even before he left his native land, and when he was but a young captain in the Guards, he had evinced his judgment in the formation of a valuable cabinet of pictures, some of which were purchased at the sale of Sir Luke

Schaub's gallery, and to which he afterwards
made such additions as opportunities offered,
and a limited income afforded. It was, in
fact, this particular bias of his mind for
works of elegance that led him to seek the
appointment which he obtained, and for which
unquestionably he was, on various accounts,
eminently qualified. This situation also
offered some advantages in another point of
view, by enabling him to make such purchases
as would be profitable to himself, and acceptable to his country. Many commissions of
this kind were imparted to the ambassador by
personages of the highest distinction; and so
well were they executed, as to increase the
number of applications from all parts of Europe.

Among the various objects which engaged
the particular attention of Sir William, the
favourite one was that of collecting the most
beautiful vases, especially those of Grecian
workmanship. When he had made himself
master of a considerable number of these
remains, he caused drawings to be taken of
the finest specimens, from whence engravings
were executed under his own eye, and for the
most part in his own house. Of these a fas-
ciculus was published in the year 1791; and
another of equal, if not superior beauty,

four years afterwards. Besides the prospect
of lucrative advantage from the sale of the
work itself, the author was actuated by another
consideration, in which he completely succeeded.
The plates were sent to England, that from
them some idea might be formed of the
collection which they represented. A negotiation was accordingly entered into for the
purchase of the cabinet at the national expense ;
and the royal approbation having been obtained,
parliament voted the sum of seven thousand
pounds for this purpose, after which the vases,
bronzes, and medals, were presented to the
British Museum. There were not wanting,
however, some persons of literary and scientific
reputation, who considered the price set upon
this collection as far above the real value.
The late ingenious Mr. Wedgewood, indeed,
took occasion to observe, in an examination
before a committee of the House of Commons,
that in his manufactory he had produced
imitations of the vases, to such a degree of
beauty, as, by exportation alone, brought
three times the money into England which
the originals had cost the nation. But this
testimony can hardly weigh anything in favour
of the extravagance of the grant, since it was
the consequence of what could neither have

been foreseen, nor even contemplated, at the
time when the negotiation for the purchase
took place. It is not a little extraordinary
that the ambassador should, very shortly after
the disposal of this collection, have formed
another, exceeding the former in number and
value. Antiquities of this description must
have been very common in that country, to
have enabled the collector to quadruple the
number of vases in four or five years ; yet such
was the case ; for early in 1796 we find him
endeavouring to transfer this fresh stock to
Prussia, through the mediation of the Countess
of Lichtenau, mistress of Frederick William,
which lady was then travelling for her health
in Italy.

In the manner of conducting this business
there certainly was nothing of the dignity of
an ambassador, but much of the finesse of a
trader in curiosities ; for the dealer, in praising
his wares, took care to say that the Grand
Duke of Russia would be glad of them, but that
he did not wish to see them carried so far to
the north. Adverting to the sale of his first
collection, Sir William magnified the beauty
and number of the present, which, though so
vastly superior in all respects, he declared his
willingness to part with to his Prussian majesty,

for the same sum as that which he had received
from the British parliament for the articles
deposited in the Museum. The proposition,
however, came to nothing, and most, if not all,
of these vases, afterwards found their way to
England. That the public minister of a great
nation should be impelled by any cause to truck
his cabinet for sale in a foreign market, and that
too by the brokership of a courtezan, must
certainly be considered as a proceeding little
in itself, and totally unworthy of the official
character of the person who was driven to
such shifts. But, in truth, whatever were the
motives by which his Excellency was actuated
in these trafficking concerns, he could hardly
have said with strict justice, when parting with
his treasures, " poverty, not my will, consents,"
since his establishment was liberal, and his
fortune more ample than he chose to acknowledge. His purchases at Naples were, indeed,
large, but his profits upon them were so very
considerable, that he could not fail to realize a
handsome income, during the number of years
in which he may be said to have almost enjoyed
a monopoly in this peculiar line of commercial
speculation. Every picture of value, and every
antique gem, were offered to the English ambassador, in the first instance ; and as there

were not always persons at Naples who would purchase such articles upon anything like liberal terms, he, of course, was sure of obtaining many bargains, which, by long experience, and a most extensive connection, he well knew how to dispose of to the best advantage.

Flattered as our ambassador was by the marked attentions which he received from the most illustrious persons in all parts of Europe, he had not the smallest reason to complain of any neglect on the part of his own country. His situation was not only highly honourable, but lucrative; and besides the Order of the Bath,[1] he received from his sovereign many testimonies of personal esteem under His Majesty's own hand.

[1] He was created Knight of the Bath in 1771, and was made a Privy Councillor in 1791.

CHAPTER V.

O you! whom Vanity's light bark
    conveys
On Fame's mad voyage, by the wind
    of praise,
With what a shifting gale your course
    you ply,
For ever sunk too low, or borne too
    high!   POPE.

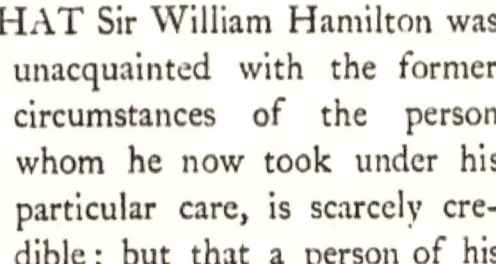

HAT Sir William Hamilton was unacquainted with the former circumstances of the person whom he now took under his particular care, is scarcely credible; but that a person of his talents and experience should voluntarily condescend to take the cast-off mistress of his own nephew is too revolting to the feelings of human nature to be supposed.[1]   The age of

---

[1] Sir W. Hamilton was certainly quite aware of the nature of the connection between his nephew and Miss Lyon, but the real causes of the subsequent curious

this gentleman, his long absence from England, and his confidence in the honour of a near relation, can alone account for an act, which in any other view would be equally a disgrace to

arrangement that took place between them was for a long time a mystery. According to reports at the time current, all equally veracious, the ambassador, after an absence of twenty years from England, returned to find his nephew on the brink of marriage with his mistress ; and to prevent such a misalliance married her himself. Another account was, that the uncle agreed to pay the debts of the nephew, on condition of the latter surrendering his mistress to him. The real motives are not far to seek. Mr. Greville, regarding himself as the heir of his uncle, had the strongest objection possible to his relative contracting a second marriage with the possibility of children, and much preferred his forming another union without the sanction of the Church. He saw also that Sir William was fascinated by the voluptuous beauty and accomplishments of the *quondam* "Goddess of Health," and having in contemplation himself a matrimonial alliance with a lady of rank and fortune, which would be greatly to his advantage, and to which his connection with Emma was an obstacle, there was a double advantage to be gained in getting her off his hands, and by so doing obliging his uncle and himself. An agreement was presently arrived at between the uncle and nephew, by which the former provided securities for the payment of the debts of the latter, and besides made some testamentary arrangements in his favour ; and also stipulated that Emma Lyon should follow Sir W. Hamilton to Naples, with the ostensible object of completing there her education in music and singing under the care of the ambassador, but in reality to become his mistress. As

his heart and his understanding. But in suggesting the single apology that can be possibly devised for the extraordinary conduct of the ambassador, no excuse will be thereby afforded

she was much attached to Mr. Greville, it was represented to her that the embarrassed state of his affairs made their separation for a time absolutely necessary, but that after a few months he would rejoin her in Italy. She certainly had no suspicion of the real motive for sending her out of England till some time after her arrival at Naples, but believed the arrangement to be made solely for the benefit of Mr. Greville and herself. Early in the year 1786 Emma and her mother, under the escort of Mr. Gavin Hamilton the painter, who was returning to prosecute his studies in Rome, left England for Naples, where they arrived on April 26 of the same year. The youthful beauty soon discovered that she had not been consigned to the care of Sir W. Hamilton solely for her educational improvement, and sent letter after letter of passionate entreaty to Greville, to which he returned no answer. As an example, showing the depth of her affection, and her constancy towards him in her embarrassing position, she wrote in one of her earlier appeals to him, and it is but a sample of the others : "My dear Greville, I live but in the hope of seeing you ; . . . remember you will never be loved by anybody like your affectionate and sincere Emma. Pray, for God's sake, wright to me and come to me, for Sir William shall not be anything to me but your friend." When at last Greville replied, it was to inform her that their connection was at an end, and advised her to consider her own interest by yielding to the wishes of his uncle. Her reply to this suggestion can be best given in her own words : " As to what you

to those who took an advantage of his weakness.

There was a great want of decency in the transaction, if the parties had a knowledge of each other's previous habits and connections ; but if, as is most probable, his Excellency was imposed upon by the artifice of the female, and the disingenuity of her paramour, no language can be too strong to reprobate proceedings, which, besides the gross immorality that marked them throughout, carried the strongest appearance of being a confederacy to entrap a credulous old man into an imprudent alliance.

Emma improved greatly [1] by the instructions

write to me to oblidge Sir William I will not answer you. . . . If I was with you, I would murder you and myself both. . . . It is not to your interest to disoblige me, for you don't know the power I have hear. Onely I will never be his mistress. If you affront me I will make him marry me." But after several months she consented to the proposals of Sir William, and carried out her threat of marrying him five years later, in 1791.

[1] Her operatic and histrionic improvement under the guidance and tutelage of Sir William, are pronounced by her contemporaries to have been extraordinary. Her singing and acting, we are told, rivalled the performances of the most celebrated professionals : "With a common piece of stuff, she could so arrange it, and clothe herself, as to offer the most appropriate representations of a Jewess, a Roman Matron, a Helen, Penelope, or Aspasia. No character seemed foreign to her, and the grace she

which were provided for her at the charge of the ambassador, who at length became so thoroughly enamoured, as to make her his wife in a private manner. It being, however, necessary, according to the etiquette of the court of Naples, that she should be acknowledged by the English sovereign, previous to presentation and admission there, Sir William hastened with her to London, early in the summer of 1791, as well to celebrate the marriage, according to the rites of the Established Church, as to give his lady that honorary distinction which his public situation rendered indispensable. This circumstance serves as an additional proof that the ambassador was in a great degree ignorant

was in the habit of displaying under such representations, excited the admiration of all who were fortunate enough to have been present on such occasions. The celebrated Shawl Dance owes its origin to her invention ; but it is admitted to have been executed by her with a grace and elegance far surpassing that with which it has ever been rendered on the stage of any of our theatres." She was offered two thousand guineas to sing for the season at the Opera House, London. A witness of her representations some years later wrote : "I saw her represent in succession the best statues and paintings extant. She assumes their attitude, expression and drapery with great facility, swiftness, and accuracy. Several Indian shawls, a chair, some antique vases, a wreath of roses, a tambourine, and a few children are her whole apparatus."

of the footing on which his nephew and Emma had lived, otherwise it is hardly to be imagined that any man of common sense and delicacy of feeling would venture to bring a woman of such a description to the very place where all her former history could not fail to be remembered. The manner, therefore, in which Sir William Hamilton brought forward the object of his choice, however much it might reflect on his judgment, considering the disparity of their years and condition in life, did at least free him from the suspicion of being privy to his own dishonour. It is not to be credited that such a man would take a pride in proclaiming himself a dupe on the subject which of all others renders the mind most tender to the idea of wrong. Yet on the supposition that the ambassador was fully apprised of the precise nature of the connection that had subsisted between Emma and his nephew, he must have been not only this very dupe, but, what is worse, wholly unconcerned at the scandalous degradation into which he had suffered himself to be inveigled.

A good-natured husband may sometimes be induced by the remains of affection to throw a veil over some slight levities, and even to pardon errors of greater magnitude ; but there are few even of the most vulgar and depraved description who will take a pleasure in blazoning their own disgrace.

While, however, justice forbids us to believe that in the present instance the respect due to personal honour was compromised, on the part of him who was most affected by the folly, no condemnation can be severe enough for those who took a pleasure in countenancing it by their applause.

An authority, on which we may rely with full confidence, has given us a curious account of the arrival of this remarkable couple in London, and of the bustle which their intended nuptials occasioned in the circles of fashion. The biographer of Romney, having noticed the hypochondriacism under which his friend laboured at this time, tells us how very fortunately he was relieved from his complaint.

" An incident most seasonably occurred, which raised to joyous elevation the sinking spirits of the artist, for nature had given him a heart that could most sincerely exult in the good fortune of those he regarded. The fair Emma, whom he had so often painted with admiration and delight, surprised him by an early visit one morning, in a Turkish habit, and attended by · Sir William Hamilton.

" Romney had ever treated her with the

tenderness of a father, which she acknowledged on this occasion with tears of lively gratitude, in announcing to him her splendid prospect of being soon married to Sir William, and of attending him to the court of Naples.

" Romney had conceived such very high ideas of the beauty, the talents, and the heart, of this lady, that I believe the joy of a father, in the brilliant marriage of a favourite daughter, could hardly exceed that of my friend on this occasion. In his letter dated the 19th of June, 1791, he says :—

" ' At present, and the greatest part of the summer, I shall be engaged in painting pictures from the divine lady. I cannot give her any other epithet, for I think her superior to all womankind. I have two pictures to paint of her for the Prince of Wales. She says she must see you before she leaves England, which will be in the beginning of September. She asked me if you would not write my Life :—I told her you had begun it :—then, she said, she hoped you would have much to say of her in the Life, as she prided herself in being my model. So you see I must be in London till the time when she leaves town.'

" In another letter, dated July 7th, he says :—

" ' I dedicate my time to this charming lady :
there is a prospect of her leaving town with Sir
William, for two or three weeks. They are
very much hurried at present, as everything is
going on for their speedy marriage, and all the
world following her, and talking of her, so that
if she had not more good sense than vanity,
her brain must be turned. The pictures I have
begun are Joan of Arc, a Magdalen, and a
Bacchante, for the Prince of Wales ; and
another I am to begin as a companion to the
Bacchante. I am also to paint a picture of
Constance for the Shakspeare Gallery.'

"His intended picture of Constance," says
the biographer, "was, I believe, never begun ;
but his Joan of Arc had a countenance of most
powerful expression. The head was thought
one of the finest that he ever painted from the
features of his favourite model."[1]

So much has been already said of Romney,
that any farther remark on the character and
conduct of the painter might appear invidious ;
yet the studied partiality with which these
anecdotes are related, and the rapturous language in which the artist speaks of his living
model, whom he compliments as " a divinity,"
ought by no means to pass without censure.

[1] Life of Romney, p. 157.

Neither Romney nor his friend could be ignorant of the scenes through which this female had passed : what an insult, therefore, must it be to the dignity of the sex to place a person of this description above all womankind ! If anything can be supposed to exceed the indiscretion of Romney, it must be that of the biographer, who, without any inducement or reflection, suffered such prurient effusions of his friend's folly to meet the public eye, instead of consigning them to the flames.

The expected marriage took place soon after by license,[1] and what is observable enough, the bride on that occasion took the name of Harte, though that by which she had always been known in the country was Lyon ; and this she owned herself to be the true one, on meeting with an old fellow-servant sometime after the death of her husband.

To account for this conduct, we must suppose, that having, according to the custom of persons in her condition, changed her name, and becoming known to Sir William by that only, she was under the necessity of adhering to it, lest by disclosing the truth, some suspicion

[1] The marriage took place at Marylebone Church, September 6, 1791.

might have risen in his mind of the duplicity that had been practised upon him.

It reflects little credit on the leaders of what is called the fashionable world, that they should at this period have been so lost to the sense of decorum, and the respect due to the established forms and orders of society, as to vie with the greatest eagerness for the honour of receiving one whose sole pretension to the distinction lay in a relation that rather served to aggravate than to obliterate the errors by which it was preceded, and out of which it actually arose. The acquirements in singing and acting which Emma brought from Italy, and the conquest which she had made of a man in high station, now hoary in years, rendered her so very popular among the gay and trifling, that her former situation, as the mistress of a person then living, and the mother of children by him, was either willingly forgotten, or remembered only to produce a laugh at the capriciousness of fortune. Into one quarter, however, the folly could not penetrate, and a public reception at court was peremptorily forbidden, certainly not from any fastidious adherence to antiquated rules, nor from an unreasonable prejudice against obscurity of birth and poverty of condition, but wholly through that inflexibility of moral principle

which scorns to smile at the folly which it dis-
approves, and avoids giving encouragement to
vice, out of courtesy to those who have been
infatuated by its delusive arts. The following
anecdote, which may be relied on as coming
from a quarter that gives it authority, will show
in a very striking manner the contrast between
the sentiments of the sovereign and those of the
admirers of Emma. On the day that Sir William Hamilton was married, he had a private
interview with His Majesty, by appointment,
when the king, in course of conversation, mentioned the report that was circulated respecting
the intended nuptials of the ambassador, adding
with a good-natured smile, " But I hope it is not
true." To this his Excellency immediately
rejoined, " May it please your Majesty, the ceremony took place this morning."

The qualifications which obtained this woman
the extravagant admiration of the polite circles
where she found admittance, were far from
being such as did any honour to their judgment, or furnished an apology for the conduct
of Sir William Hamilton in making choice of
her for a wife. The nature of these accomplishments is well described in a letter from one
of those who enjoyed most delight in contemplating them, and who had abundant opportunities of witnessing their effect.

" In my last letter," says Romney, " I think I informed you that I was going to dine with Sir William and his lady. In the evening of that day there were collected several people of fashion to hear her sing. She performed both in the serious and comic to admiration, both in singing and acting : but her Nina surpasses anything I ever saw ; and I believe, as a piece of acting, nothing ever surpassed it. The whole company were in an agony of sorrow. Her acting is simple, grand, terrible, and pathetic. My mind was so much heated, that I was for running down to Eartham to fetch you up to see her." [1] In another letter, the artist gives the following curious anecdote :—

" She performed in my house last week, singing and acting before some of the nobility, with most astonishing powers : she is the talk of the whole town, and really surpasses everything both in singing and acting that ever appeared. Gallini offered her two thousand pounds a year, and two benefits, if she would engage with him, on which Sir William said pleasantly that he had engaged her for life."

Romney was anxious to paint as many portraits of this favourite model as he could, during her stay in England, and she frequently sat to

[1] Life of Romney, p. 181.

him for that purpose. On one occasion, however, the artist being apprehensive that he had lost somewhat of her esteem, was weak enough to whine at her capriciousness of behaviour with the puerility of a lover, instead of treating the person who behaved in such a way with proper contempt. The friend to whom he poured out his silly complaint, and who should have laughed or scolded him out of his whimsies, encouraged him in the folly by which he was infatuated, and sent him a copy of verses, to be presented as a propitiatory offering to the offended " divinity."

These stanzas were addressed to Cassandra, which was one of the characters represented in a picture of her painted by the disconsolate artist, whose vapours, however, were dissipated before the verses reached him, and who thus expressed the state of his mind to the author:—

" Cassandra came to town on the sixteenth, and I did not see her till the twentieth ; so you may suppose how my feelings must have suffered : she appointed to sit on the twenty-third, and has been sitting almost every day since ; and means to sit once or twice a day till she leaves London, which will be about Wednesday or Thursday in the next week. When she arrived to sit, she seemed more friendly than she had been, and I began a picture of her as a present for her mother. I was very successful with it, for it is thought the most beautiful head I have painted of her yet. Now, indeed, I think she is as cordial with me as ever, and she laments very much that she is to leave England without seeing you.

" I take it excessively kind in you to enter so deeply into my distresses. Really my mind had suffered so very much, that my health was much affected ; and I was afraid I should not have had power to have painted any more from her : but since she has resumed her former kindness, my health and spirits are quite recovered."

That Romney should have lamented as a distress the apparent coolness of another man's wife, while he was totally unconcerned about the condition and feelings of his own, ought to have excited indignation rather than pity in the mind of his friend. Instead of this, the whole correspondence that passed on the subject has been printed, with some pathetic remarks on the acute sensibility of the painter, and no moderate encomium on the amiable qualities of the lady.

Neither of the parties merited the praises which have been so profusely bestowed upon them ; for at this very time they were both in circumstances which demanded a different course of action as some atonement for their past errors. Romney would have been more properly employed in healing the wounds which he had inflicted on the heart of an unoffending woman, than in running after a Syren, and crying like a foolish boy when she behaved towards him with a little levity. With respect to the object of his admiration, it may be sufficient to say, that the extraordinary elevation to which she had been raised was not owing to any mental grace, but to attractions, which, however powerful they might be in exciting pleasure, were far from having any tendency to promote virtue. When this woman became so unaccountably the wife of a man of rank, her proper line of conduct would have been the study of humility, and of the means of acquiring a meek and quiet spirit befitting her new state, and indicating some concern for the irregularities of her youth. The reverse of all this marked her character at the most interesting period of her life, when many causes concurred to recommend a lowly disposition and a serious deportment, instead of that hilarity and mimicry which procured her the applause of the thoughtless, and confirmed her in the love of vanity and the practice of deception.

CHAPTER VI.

For that fair female troop thou saw'st,
    that seem'd
Of goddesses so blithe, so smooth, so
    gay,
Yet empty of all good, wherein consists
Woman's domestic honour and chief
    praise,
Bred only and completed to the taste
Of lustful appetence, to sing, to dance,
To dress, and troule the tongue, and
    roll the eyes :
To these that sober race of men, whose
    lives,
Religious, titled them the sons of God,
Shall yield up all their virtue, all their
    fame,
Ignobly——   MILTON.

T the beginning of September, Sir William Hamilton and his lady left England for Naples, where, on their arrival, some little difficulty is said to have been experienced with respect to the introduction of the wife of the ambassador at court, owing to the strict regulations

and ceremony observed by the queen : but if this report be true, the obstacle did not long remain, for in a few months her ladyship was admitted on terms of cordial intimacy at the palace, and at length she succeeded in gaining an entire influence over both their majesties, who frequently visited the English minister in a friendly way, and received his lady at all times with the greatest familiarity.

No situation on earth perhaps could have so well suited the mind of this extraordinary woman as Naples, which for dissipation stood unequalled by any city in Europe. Ferdinand IV. [1] gave himself up to the sports of the field,

---

[1] Ferdinand was the third son of Charles of Bourbon, King of the Two Sicilies. He was born in 1751, and on the accession of his father to the throne of Spain in 1759, according to treaty, he became King of the Sicilies. In April, 1768, he married Maria Caroline of Austria. During his youth his physical welfare was promoted to the neglect of his intellectual development, and at the age of sixteen he was considered to be the best shot, the cleverest fisherman, and the most daring horseman to be found in his dominions. He was good-tempered on the whole, and fond of practical jokes. His minister, Sir John Acton, as his opinion of him, said : " Ferdinand is a good sort of man, because nature has not supplied him with the faculties necessary to make a bad one." On his restoration to the throne of Naples in 1815 he abolished the Sicilian Constitution, and after a reign of 66 years, died in January, 1825.

and to excursions in his pleasure-boats. His great ambition was to be the boldest huntsman in his kingdom, and the most expert mariner in the bay of Naples. On most of his enterprizing expeditions against the boars and the foxes in the woods and mountains, he was accompanied by the English ambassador, who, at the age of sixty, prided himself on his agility in running, his dexterity in fishing, and his skill in shooting. The hunting diversions sometimes continued for several weeks; and Sir William says, in an account of one of them, written to his wife:—" The king has killed eighty-one animals of one sort or other to-day: and amongst them a wolf and some stags. He fell asleep in the coach, and awaking, told me he had been dreaming of shooting. One would have thought he had shed blood enough."

While Ferdinand and his courtiers were enjoying themselves abroad, the queen and her ladies devoted all their time to scenes of pleasure at home. In these festivities, of which the wife of the English minister had often the management, and in which she was generally a principal performer, the utmost latitude was given to every kind of licentiousness. Hardly a day passed without some new amusement; and it seemed as if in this modern Cytherea, the cares of government, and the duties of every station, were made subservient to the study of pleasure. The house of the ambassador exhibited, under the plea of hospitality, a similar round of extravagance ; and, at a time when the revolutionary spirit, excited by the commotions in France, was spreading over the continent, the senses of all orders in Naples, as well foreigners as natives, appeared steeped in the lethargy of folly, and to have no feeling for anything but the grossest objects of voluptuary indulgence. Corruption pervaded all the departments of the state : and the manners of the people partook of the principles and example of their superiors. There was no gradation of honest industry and virtuous independence between pride and beggary ; no class of active citizens, that, from a spirit of patriotism, endeavoured to uphold the credit of their country amidst the dissipation of the rulers and the idle habits of poor. At this eventful period, the greatest economy was necessary in the management of the revenue, and the most vigilant measures were required to place the kingdom in a state of defence ; but, instead of being moved by the misfortunes which had fallen upon the other branches of the Bourbon family, their Sicilian majesties continued in the same improvi-

dent course which they had pursued many years,
neither instituting any reform in the administration, nor laying the slightest restraint upon their
own vitiated appetite for frivolous amusements
and sensual indulgence. It is painful to reflect,
that the character of the English nation was
considerably injured by the share which our
ambassador and his wife took in these follies,
being more anxious to cultivate the royal
favour, than to support their own dignity, and
the honour of their country. Sir William
Hamilton did not want talents suited to his
office, but he had lived so long at Naples, and
was so much accustomed to the trifling manners
of the court, and the wretched condition of the
people, that while the one perverted his judgment, the other blunted his feeling. It is no
wonder, then, that a man of this easy temper
should have suffered his young partner to exercise all her art in consulting the inclinations of
the queen, when he, at the age of sixty-three,
did the same in following the sports of the king.
It is difficult to say which of the two gained the
completest ascendency, but there can be no doubt
that the influence of the lady was attended with
the greatest consequences ; and it may be safely
affirmed, that the hold which she had over the
mind of the Queen of Naples amounted in effect

to a complete sway over the sovereign. Yet, like most friendships of this sort, where the knowledge of dangerous secrets gives an advantage to the inferior, which often provokes resentment on the one side, and insolence on the other, the two personages of whom we are speaking had occasional bickerings, some of which were attended with strange and indecorous circumstances. The freedom of access to the royal apartment, which had been given to the wife of his Excellency, proved at last very irksome, by her frequent intrusions when the queen wished to be alone, or when she was engaged in a private conversation with some who did not choose to have their opinions witnessed by a third party. One day, her Ladyship, going as usual to the palace, was stopped in her progress through the rooms by a servant, who respectfully informed her that her Majesty was engaged, and desirous of being undisturbed by any visitors. The indignant Emma, who knew that the person thus favoured was a countrywoman of her own, and one for whom she felt a great dislike, made light of the prohibition, and forced her way into the presence without the least ceremony. Such a breach of decorum could not well pass without resentment; but unfortunately, in the present instance, the rudeness on the one side

excited a storm of fury on the other, and a blow
from the queen, applied not very gently in the
face of the intruder, produced another in return,
to the great astonishment of the attendants,
who rushed in to separate the combatants. This
strange conflict, which in any other court would
have been followed by a sentence of perpetual
exclusion, was productive of no other consequence than a little idle discourse among the
people of Naples, and some merriment on the
part of the king, and his confidential companions. The temporary gloom occasioned by
this affair was soon dispelled, and her Ladyship
returned to court, apparently in as much favour
as ever. It is not to be supposed, however, that
the queen was so totally regardless of what was
due to her dignity, as to forget the outrage that
had been committed, and the insult which she
had received; but an imprudent familiarity
having brought the parties on a kind of level,
which became more fixed by their mutual
acquaintance with each other's conduct, an act
of oblivion took place, and a reconciliation was
effected.

Among other persons of distinction, who
made Naples their principal residence, a little
after the marriage of the ambassador, the late
Earl of Bristol was one of the most conspicuous.

This nobleman, who was both a spiritual and a temporal peer, being for many years Bishop of Derry, spent all his time in foreign countries, to the entire neglect of his diocese, though it is one of the richest in Ireland. The prelate, who was somewhat advanced in years when Sir William Hamilton returned from England with his lady, presently became enamoured with her person and accomplishments. This perhaps may be considered by some of her admirers as an evidence of her merits; but when the character of his Lordship is known, the attachment will be found to reflect no more credit on his understanding, than it did honour to the object of his esteem. Though an ecclesiastic of the highest station, the bishop was an avowed sceptic in religion, the doctrines and institutions of which he would not scruple to ridicule in the company of women, treating even the immortality of the soul as an article of doubt and indifference. He affected a peculiar singularity in his dress, generally wearing a white hat, and a coat of coloured silk, so as to have very rarely the smallest external sign of the episcopal function, and never showing in his conversation any of that gravity which became his age, rank, and profession. Besides giving his sanction to every kind of fashionable amusement, he kept a box at the

Opera ; and even the diversions which in Italy are freely practised on Sunday evenings never drew from him any discouragement.

He commonly went by the title of the count bishop, and his company was greatly courted on account of his lively conversation, blunt freedom, and the fund of anecdote which he possessed. Being on a visit to a friend in 1782, he related the following pleasant story of himself : that going to the Grande Chartreuse, whilst the society were at dinner, he found the convent door shut, and, on knocking, the porter told him that no one was permitted to enter while the monks were at their meals : upon this, he gave the porter a letter to the abbot from a neighbouring prelate, in which the bishop called him his brother, the Bishop of Derry. Immediately after the letter was delivered, the doors flew open, and the whole convent, on their knees, met his Lordship, craving his blessing ; which he, without any ceremony, delivered to them as he passed along. The good brotherhood were wholly ignorant where Derry was situated ; and relying upon the testimonial which he brought, they of course took him for a catholic bishop. Without attempting to undeceive them, his Lordship blessed them all, throwing out his

benedictions very gravely with his hands.
When the monks became better informed of
his character, they had no doubt a very different
opinion of the efficacy of his blessings.

At the time when Lord Bristol was at
Naples, living on the most familiar footing
with the ambassador, an illustrious personage [1]
of this kingdom visited that city, where he
was entertained with all the respect due to
his family. One evening, there was a splendid
party at his Excellency's house, and among the
rest Mrs. Billington, with several other persons
of eminence in musical science, both singers
and performers. The treat afforded by such
a combination of taste and talent was of course
very great ; but in some of the finest airs, the
young prince marred the music, by interposing
his own powers, with the design of helping
those who would have been better pleased by
his silence. The Bishop of Derry, who was
naturally impatient, endured all this for some
time, with only muttering now and then a
peevish pish or two; but at length the inter-
ruptions became so annoying, that he could
contain himself no longer, and turning to the
royal singer, he said, " Pray cease : you have
the ears of an ass." This coarse censure,

[1] William Henry, Duke of Gloucester, brother of
George III.

however, produced no other effect than to stimulate the performer to fresh exertions; and he also ventured to sing one or two songs for the entertainment of the company, all of whom, with the exception of the bishop, affected to be uncommonly delighted. His Lordship, instead of joining in the praises that were bestowed, and scorning to pay a compliment at the expense of his veracity, said to a lady who sat next to him, loud enough to be heard by every one in the circle, "This may be very fine braying, but it is intolerable singing."

Of his uncommon freedom of speech, indeed, we may form a judgment from his behaviour at a public dinner given in Germany, by the late King of Prussia, to the Duke of Brunswick, and several of the princes of the empire, after the peace concluded by that sovereign with the French Republic. The Bishop of Derry, being offered some capon, declined it, on which the King of Prussia asked him whether he disliked that dish: "Yes, Sire," replied he: "I have an aversion to all neutral animals."

This pointed attack on the truckling politics of the Prussian monarch brings under our observation the history of his mistress, the unfortunate Countess of Lichtenau, whose origin was nearly as low as that of the heroine

7

of these Memoirs. The countess, in the year 1795, visited Italy for her health, and while at Naples, she contracted a great intimacy with Sir William Hamilton and his lady, through Lord Bristol, with whom she had been acquainted in Germany, and who kept up with her a very extraordinary correspondence. It was during the residence of the countess at Naples, that the English ambassador endeavoured, by her interest, to dispose of his second collection of vases to the King of Prussia, representing them as not only valuable in the light of antiquities, but as being particularly serviceable to the improvement of the porcelain manufactory in that monarch's dominions. Though this negotiation was unsuccessful, the friendship of the ladies continued to be very warm, at least, so long as the countess remained in that country. The following curious billet will serve to elucidate pretty clearly the group of friends therein mentioned, and particularly the principles of the Bishop of Derry, of whom the writer speaks in language very near approaching to blasphemy.

" *Naples*, 29*th March*, 1796.

" My very dear friend,

" I desire most anxiously to hear from you,

how your health is, and when you will return
among us. The good and beneficent Lord
Bristol, who is in despair at not seeing you,
waits your arrival with the same solicitude as
the Jews looked for the coming of our Lord
among them. My husband salutes you with
all his heart. The good and sincere Denis
speaks of no one but you, and we all join
in wishing that you may not see *** at Rome,
who has been very wicked and dishonourable
here ; but the particulars are too long to be
detailed. I think she will never be permitted to
visit here again. She has betrayed the noble
family at whose house she was cherished, and
has caused therein so much confusion, that it
will be very difficult to restore order. Your
good heart would suffer to see it. Adieu, dear
countess ; continue to love your sincere and
constant friend,

" Emma Hamilton."

The irreligious comparison contained in this
epistle, though it shows the levity of the person
who wrote it, carries at the same time clear
evidence of having been dictated by the old
nobleman himself, who took a delight in such
profane allusions, and in playing most irreverently
with sacred things. His own letters to the wife

of the English ambassador exhibit melancholy
instances of this voluntary degradation of
character, and scandalous abuse of that trust
which demanded at least some outward respect
from one, who, while he ridiculed religion in
his heart, spent the revenues which he derived
from it in foreign lands upon players, buffoons,
and women of light reputation.

One of the letters of his Lordship concludes
with these delicate lines :

> " O ! Emma, who'd ever be wise,
> If madness be loving of thee?"

At another time he says :—

" Yesterday we dined on Mount Vesuvius ;
to-day we were to have dined on its victim,
Pompeii : but ' by the grace of God, which
passeth all understanding,' since Bartolomeo
himself, that weather soothsayer, did not foresee
this British weather, we are prevented.   In
the meantime, all this week and the next is
replete with projects to Istria, Procite, &c. &c.,
so God only knows when I can worship again
my Diana of Ephesus."

This last allusion, so indecently coupled with
an apostolic benediction, has a reference to the
part of Diana, which was personated by her

Ladyship with great effect, and of which there
is an engraving executed at Naples, after a
picture painted by the order of her husband.

Yet the bishop was not altogether blind
to the improprieties of his dearest connections
at this very period ; for being one day at Sir
William Hamilton's, and engaged in a conversation with Emma, a lady was announced of
a character so notorious that, his Lordship
instantly took up his hat and prepared to
depart. " Why, my Lord, you are not going,
are you ?" said Lady Hamilton. " Our company is not I hope disagreeable." To this he
replied, " It is permitted to a bishop to visit
one sinner ; but quite unfitting that he should
be seen in a brothel."

How justly the Bishop of Derry has obtained
the character of great liberality, will appear
from the following remarks on two unfortunate
princes, who, without the slightest offence of
their own, were driven from their respective
countries, by the overwhelming violence of the
revolutionary tempest. In July, 1795, his
Lordship informs his " dearest Emma," among
other articles of intelligence, " that in Amster-
dam, and other towns of Holland, there are the
greatest insurrections in favour of that fool the
Stadtholder. All this, however, can only tend

to facilitate peace, but not at all to restore that despicable, odious family of the Bourbons,—the head of which is now at Verona, where we left him eating two capons a-day ('tis a pity the whole family are not capons !) ; and, what is more, dressing them himself in a superb kitchen —the true chapel of a Bourbon prince."

After this cruel reflection on the present amiable sovereign of France, who would have expected to see in the same letter such fulsome compliments as these?

"Emma ! if that dear Queen of Naples does not write herself to the Prince D'Oria for me, I won't look at your beautiful face these six months, ' coute qui coute.' " At another time, he says of the modern Messalina, "Send me word, dearest Emma, how the invaluable, adorable queen finds herself. The weather changed so unmercifully yesterday, that Lovel and I both grew ill ; and this makes me the more anxious to hear of our too sensible and ines- timable queen. My warmest wishes—physical, political, and moral—ever attend her."

Disgusting as these extracts must be to every mind, where the sense of honour and the love of virtue continue to predominate, they are yet not without their uses, particularly as they serve to show the pernicious consequences that always

result to those who abandon the station in which
they are placed for a life of greater freedom. It
has been urged as an excuse for this nobleman,
that he devoted the whole of his ecclesiastical
revenue to the encouragement of the fine arts ;
and the author has been informed by one who
was intimate with his Lordship, that being at
table, where many ingenious persons were assembled, the prelate said: " Ah, I assure you,
the Bishopric of Derry is a fine thing ; worth
twenty thousand a-year, and all for you gentlemen ! "

This it must be confessed was a strange mode
of appropriating the revenues of the church,
and an extraordinary atonement for the neglect
of his Lordship's episcopal duties. While he
abandoned his station as a lord of parliament,
and as the bishop of a see, which required constant inspection, worthless parasites revelled on
his bounty in foreign countries, and a set of
hungry harpies continually hovered around him,
to gather from his prodigal hand that super-
fluity of wealth which was neither the product
of his own industry, nor inherited from his
ancestors, but came to him as a trust to be
employed for the glory of God, the benefit of
his country, and the relief of the poor. The
consequence of all this irregularity was such as

might have been expected. The unsettled life
which he led impoverished his mind, corrupted
his manners, and destroyed his religious principles. But he suffered for his folly in another
respect, by falling into the hands of the French,
when they ran over Italy, in 1799 ; and these
marauders, without paying the least respect to
his rank or age, threw him into the castle of
Milan, where he endured a close and rigorous
confinement about eighteen months. On re-
gaining his liberty at the interposition of the
Austrian court, his Lordship hastened to Rome ;
and after travelling through various parts of
Italy, his constitution, which had been very
active and good, began to manifest signs of
decay. In his last illness he experienced the
usual sincerity of such attachments as are formed
from caprice on one side and interest on the
other ; for all his domestics plundered his
property, neglected him when he wanted their
assistance, and quarrelled with one another about
the division of the spoil. In this wretched
state, remote from his family, surrounded by a
host of mercenary ingrates, and unsupported
by the consolations of religion, Lord Bristol
breathed his last, in the seventy-third year of
his age, at Albino, near Rome, August the 8th,
1803. Of this event Lord Nelson gave an

account to his fair friend and correspondent, with a manifest reflection on the bishop, for not having remembered Lady Hamilton by a testamentary bequest. His Lordship concludes his letter with this account of the deceased prelate :—

" There will be no Lord Bristol's table. He tore his last will a few hours before his death. It is said that it was giving everything to those devils of Italians about him."

Such was the character and the end of Frederick Hervey, Earl of Bristol,[1] and Bishop of Derry, who dissipated a long life, a princely fortune, and respectable talents, in the pursuit of pleasure, from the same motives which actuated the Epicureans of old, whose creed and practice were comprehended in the resolution, " Let us eat and drink, for to-morrow we die."

[1] Frederick Augustus Hervey was born 1730, made D.D. and Bishop of Derry in 1768, and succeeded his brother as fourth Earl of Bristol in 1779. He married Elizabeth, daughter of Sir Jermyn Davers, Bt. Any addition to the traits of his character as given in the text would be superfluous. After his decease at Naples, July 8, 1803, his remains were sent to England for interment, on board the *Monmouth*. Mr. Elliot, the British Minister at Naples, wrote to Lord Nelson, that, knowing the superstitious dread which sailors have of the presence of a corpse on board ship, he had caused the body to be packed and shipped as an *antique statue*.

CHAPTER VII.

No levell'd malice
Infects one comma in the course I
hold :
But flies an eagle flight, bold, and
forth on,
Nor leaves a tract behind.

SHAKSPEARE.

IR WILLIAM HAMILTON soon found that an imprudent marriage at his time of life brought with it as many cares as pleasures ; and he had the mortification of knowing, that the new relation into which he had entered, instead of giving satisfaction at home, was likely to prove the justifiable pretext for his recall.

This may be gathered from a letter, written by the ambassador, while he was on a hunting excursion with the King of Naples, in which he says, " You see what devils there are in England ! They wanted to stir up something against me ;

but our conduct shall be such as to be unattack-
able : and I fear not an injustice from England.
Twenty-seven years' service—having spent all
the king's money, and all my own, besides
running in debt, deserves something better
than dismission."

Of this complaint, an explanation may be
requisite, and it is not difficult to find one that
would be ample enough to have warranted the
measure, which his Excellency so feelingly deprecated.

The continent of Europe at that period stood
in the most critical circumstances, for the progress of the revolutionary principles, which had
already succeeded in overturning the constitution
of France, could not be supposed by any rational
understanding to have a favourable aspect on the
peace and happiness of other nations. If ever,
therefore, any time demanded statesmen of
pre-eminent talents and virtue at the head of
their respective courts, and in the office of
ministers from one to another, it was that very
era to which our attention is now directed. In
former days, perhaps, it mattered not much
whether an envoy at Naples was a man of extraordinary intelligence or not, as little more was
requisite for the adequate discharge of the duties
imposed upon him than great courtesy of

behaviour, and a dignified support of the character and honour of his country.

But the tremendous explosion which had now burst forth in the moral world, rendered many changes necessary in the administration of the several governments, particularly in their diplomatic intercourse with each other. Among the rest, Naples was one which stood in great need of an alteration in this respect, and that for the very reason assigned by our ambassador as the ground of his pretensions to his continuance in that situation.

His pursuits and amusements could interfere but little with his public avocations while that part of the world remained tranquil ; but the French revolution gave a shock to every establishment, and portended plainly enough to every man, that did not wilfully shut his eyes, a long and sanguinary war throughout Europe. Sound policy, therefore, pointed out the necessity of endeavouring, by virtuous and able agents, to rouse the sluggish courts to a sense of their danger, and by making them sensible of their proper interests, prevail upon them to adopt such measures as were best calculated to enable them to maintain their independence against a ruthless enemy.

Sir William Hamilton might be an excellent

connoisseur in bronzes, medals, and pictures ;
but he ought at this time to have given way
to some person of a more comprehensive genius,
and one whose mind entered deeply into the
circumstances of the times. Instead of that
piercing judgment, which, being always on the
wing, explores every passing occurrence, to trace
the effects which it is likely to produce, the
mind of our ambassador exhibited nothing but
phlegm, except when in the course of his enquiries
some object of great curiosity was offered for his
purchase, or he happened to be engaged in the
hunting parties of the monarch, with whom he
chanced to be a favourite. Of the puerile
character of Ferdinand, a singular anecdote is
related by Sir William, in one of his letters
written during an excursion with his Majesty.

" Yesterday, the courier brought the order of
St. Stephano, from the Emperor, for the Prince
Ausberg, and the king was desired to invest
him with it. As soon as the king received it,
he ran into the prince's room, whom he found
in his shirt, and without his breeches ; and, in
that condition, was he decorated with the star
and ribbon by his Majesty, who has wrote the
whole circumstance to the emperor.

" Leopold may, perhaps, not like the joking
with his first order. Such nonsense should, cer-

tainly, be done with solemnity ; or it becomes, what it really is, a little tinsel, and a few yards of broad ribbon."

This was, no doubt, an imprudent act of levity at a time when so many attempts were making to level all distinctions in society, and to represent crowns and mitres, sceptres and croziers, as nothing better than the baubles of childish superstition, or the ensigns of an arbitrary usurpation of the common rights of mankind. But if the King of Naples acted on this occasion in a manner unbecoming the respect due from one sovereign to the institutions of another, the conduct of our ambassador cannot be altogether excused, in writing as he did on the subject. Slight incidents will sometimes illustrate the real character of men, much more than a long train of public actions. Sir William, in bestowing this contemptuous appellation on one of the imperial orders, paid no flattering compliment to the red ribband with which he himself was decorated ; and though a man of sense will despise the folly of those who court such honours for the mere sake of shining above others, he will not on that account cast an odium on distinctions, which, however unworthily they may have been bestowed, were originally intended as the rewards of merit, and still continue to be the

badges of public approbation. The freedom
with which the ambassador imparted state
secrets, and his opinions on public men and
affairs, to his wife, within a few months after
his marriage, cannot be justified by the high
opinion which he entertained of her fidelity and
understanding. This very woman he knew had
been already honoured with the particular notice
of Ferdinand, who endeavoured to gain her
private favours by the offer of a *carte blanche*
for the statement of her own demands.

The paper containing the royal proposals, and
the several letters which the king had written to
her, were, most respectfully, and with much
feeling expression, put by her into the hands of
the queen, who either was, or pretended to be,
very much affected by so extraordinary an
instance of virtue and liberality.[1] It is, how-

---

[1] The king may have been attracted by the charms of
Lady Hamilton while living under the protection of the
English Ambassador before her marriage to him ; but that
his written proposals to her were submitted to the inspection of the queen by the person to whom they had been
addressed, is exceedingly doubtful. Lady Hamilton was
not on close terms of intimacy with the Queen of Naples
till long after her marriage, nor was she presented to
the queen till some weeks after her second arrival at
Naples, from England, as the acknowledged wife of the
ambassador. But it may be noticed that a similar story is
related in Solari's " Venice under the yoke of France and

ever, to be feared, that there was more art
than sincerity on both sides, for the one well
knew that her safest course lay in making a
friend of the queen, rather than in shining as
the favourite of a monarch, who could hardly be
said to be his own master ; while her Majesty,
who cared as little about the amours of her
husband, as she did about the propriety of her
own conduct, thought that by attaching such a
person to her interest she should be able to
gratify her love of pleasure, in a variety of ways,
without any observation. Nor was this all ; for
though these two females, both equally voluptuous, vain and ambitious, had not the slightest
esteem for each other, they were sensible that

Austria"; with the additional circumstance, that the
whole affair was but a clever design of Emma Lyon, or
Harte, to enlist the feelings and interest of the queen in her
favour, and so to bring about her long cherished scheme
of marriage with Sir W. Hamilton. Both stories are probably equally authentic ; but that such was the secret
object of Emma for some years before the wished-for event
came off, is evident from a letter she wrote to Romney,
December 20, 1791. "Tell Hayley," she says, "I
am always reading his 'Triumphs of Temper.' It was
that that made me Lady H——, for God knows I had for
five years enough to try my temper, and I am afraid if it
had not been for the good example Serena taught me, my
girdle would have burst; and if it had, I had been undone,
for Sir William minds temper more than beauty."

the appearance of an ardent affection would be for their respective advantage, and the security of that power which they had but too much reason to apprehend was in a perilous state.

The queen, who was really a woman of sharp intellect, could not be altogether unconcerned about the dreadful scenes which were passing in France ; and she knew that in the event of the flames of war spreading into Italy, the chief if not the only security her dominions could hope for lay in an alliance with Great Britain. Our ambassador was already under some apprehension of being recalled, and of this the queen was not ignorant. She, therefore, had reason to dread such a change, because whoever might be appointed the successor, it was impossible that he could remain any time there without witnessing the corruptions of the court, the depravity of the people, and the absolute necessity of procuring a renovation of the Neapolitan state.

Her Majesty had been now acquainted with Sir William Hamilton much above twenty years, and from him she had nothing to dread, for which reason she felt it necessary to exert herself to the utmost in rendering his situation agreeable at this crisis, and to secure his residence at Naples, by all her influence at the courts of Vienna and Madrid.   Sir William was in consequence not only distinguished by numerous marks of favour, but his lady became the confidential friend of the queen, who occasionally imparted to her information of such importance, as when communicated to the government at home, removed from ministers all idea of placing an agent who had thus given them new proofs of his penetration and intelligence.

Thus, the intimacy which subsisted between these celebrated women, was cemented by duplicity, and arose solely from selfish motives, without having any real principle of regard to the public weal of either country.

Had the Queen [1] of Naples, who at that time

---

[1] The Queen of Naples was Maria Caroline, daughter of Maria Theresa of Austria and Francis Duke of Lorraine, afterwards Emperor of Germany. Her husband, Ferdinand, on attaining his majority at the age of sixteen, made proposals for the hand of her sister, Maria Josephine, who, just as the marriage had been arranged, died suddenly. Maria Caroline then took the place of her sister, and at the age of fifteen married Ferdinand, April 7, 1768, and became Queen of Naples. She inherited the beauty of her mother, with a good deal of her pride and masculine understanding. General Pépé, in his Memoirs, says of her, " Her mind was of the most powerful stamp—by nature she was both proud and haughty, and she nourished in her bosom the most

stood at the head of affairs, been actuated by the smallest degree of parental love for her subjects, she would have turned her thoughts to the correction of abuses in the administration, and to the organization of those means by which the

inordinate love of power." She soon discovered the character of her husband, weak both by nature and education ; and having given birth to a prince, by right of her marriage treaty and the laws of Naples, claimed the right of sitting in the State Council, and of having a voice in its deliberations. She gave great attention to state affairs, and though Ferdinand reigned, the queen really governed Naples. On the advance of the French in 1798, she, with the rest of the royal family, retired to Sicily ; but was reinstated at Naples by the English fleet under Lord Nelson. On the appearance of the proclamation of Napoleon in 1806, that the Bourbons had ceased to reign, she sought refuge in that island a second time, while Joseph Bonaparte occupied the throne of Naples. From Sicily a guerilla warfare was kept up on the mainland, attended by acts of the greatest atrocity ; and expeditions were dispatched against different parts of the south of Italy, to no purpose but to impoverish the Sicilians, though the queen pawned her jewels toward the payment of the expenses. From England the Sicilian Court received £300,000 as a yearly subsidy, but the money was squandered among the Neapolitans and Calabrians, and no commensurate benefit resulted from this lavish expenditure. By her high-handed proceedings Maria Caroline became very unpopular in Sicily, the English ministers were disgusted with their ally, and came to the conclusion that the best remedy for such a state of things was to deprive the queen of her influence. All negotiations and

kingdom might most effectually have been defended by its own resources. But nothing was farther from her thoughts; for though she hated the republican principles of the French, as tending to subvert every throne in Europe, she regarded with abhorrence the only proper means that could be devised for the security of that where she was placed. Having been long accustomed to the exercise of power, and habitually practised in the ways of sensual pleasure, she had a numerous train of nobles to gratify with

remonstrances with the Sicilian Court proving to be useless, in 1811 Lord William Cavendish Bentinck was appointed British minister, and Commander-in-chief of the British troops in Sicily. The obstinacy of the queen defied all attempts at conciliation, and the minister told her at their last interview, that there must be "either a Constitution or a Revolution." Maria Caroline resolved on an armed resistance, but was compelled by the council to submit and to withdraw from Palermo. The executive power was vested in the king, and Sicily received a constitution, which lasted till abolished by Ferdinand on his return to Naples in 1815. The queen, continually intriguing to disturb the peace and to subvert established authority, was confined to one of her country seats, and at length sent from Sicily in an English ship of war to Sardinia, *en route* for Austria. She eventually reached Vienna, and died there, September 7, 1814, about four months before the death of Lady Hamilton at Calais, and less than a year before the final restoration of her husband and family to Naples.

great places of trust, and particular dependents
of all sorts to support by pensions. Instead,
therefore, of making any sacrifices for the public
good, or laying a restraint upon her vicious
inclination, at an awful crisis, when the fate of
her nearest relations was in a state of dreadful
suspense, she listened only to those who, like
herself, considered the nation in no other light
than as a vast reservoir purposely created for the
supply of luxuries to pamper their appetites.

To uphold the authority of the court, and to
prevent the introduction of those doctrines,
which were calculated to make the people acquainted with the reciprocal duties of sovereigns
and subjects, a most enormous and expensive
system of espionage was carried on, by which
the government became terrible without adding
to its security.

Such was the country where Sir William
Hamilton, after a residence of near thirty years,
was most anxious still to remain in his official
capacity, though he was sensible of the disorders
which pervaded the kingdom, and aware of the
dangers by which it was surrounded. It was
natural perhaps for the ambassador to feel a
strong partiality for a place where he had so
long enjoyed ease, honours, and pleasure ; nor
can he be blamed for the feeling which he

expressed at the bare report of his being super-
seded. Old age contracted in one office does
not commonly bring with it a conviction of its
own infirmities, nor do the changes that take
place in the sphere where a man has long
moved induce a suspicion that he who has lived
to behold them may have had correspondent
ravages in his own mind and person. So long as
he enjoys health and spirits, he considers these
things as matters of ordinary occurrence; and
instead of taking a hint from the revolutions
which he beholds, to retire in time, he adheres
more closely to his situation, assigning as his
reason for this determination the years he has
spent in the office, and the experience which
he has thereby acquired. Thus it was in the
present instance, though nothing was more easy
than to have shown that the grounds alleged for
the residence of Sir William at Naples were such
as proved the necessity of his recall. During
his long abode in that place, the character of
the court, and the state of the nation, had been
greatly degraded; and of late years this deteriora-
tion had proceeded with a velocity that ought
to have made an intelligent and virtuous observer
more disgusted at such a sink of debauchery,
than desirous of continuing to witness its folly
and its downfall. But, like the patriarch of old,

the ambassador had been so long accustomed to
the scenery and manners of Naples, that he
could not bear the idea of withdrawing from it,
though the political hemisphere began to give
alarming symptoms of pouring down an overwhelming torrent on that and all the neighbouring states.

Wrong as it was in Sir William to cling thus
closely to his appointment, at a juncture which
was pregnant with events, against which he
could be ill provided by his studies and habits,
still greater blame attaches to the councils of
those who complied with his wishes in continuing him, when they ought to have been sensible
that an energetic administration at home must
be crippled in its exertions, if it does not
employ legislations of a similar character
abroad. Unfortunately, however, while the
greatest zeal was manifested by the English
government for the preservation of social order
throughout the family of Europe, the good
intentions of our ministry were frustrated by
the superior talents of the agents who were
employed in foreign courts by the other powers.
It may seem strange that political discussions
should have a place in such a memoir as the
present, but as great events often spring from
little causes, there will be no difficulty in show-

ing that the marriage of Sir William Hamilton, and his consequent reluctance to quit Naples for England, brought after it a train of momentous circumstances, which ended in a separation of the once united kingdom of the Two Sicilies. Our design here is somewhat above that of affording a little momentary entertainment to the lovers of anecdote, and those who take a delight in reading the details of human folly and depravity. Even the intrigues of Cleopatra, her vice and extravagance, might have been buried in oblivion, had it not been for their political effects, the history of which could not well be understood without a minute account of her character, and a narrative of her conduct and connections. Differing in degree, but corresponding in disposition and adventures, the wife of the English ambassador at Naples has obtained, and will continue to occupy, a place in history, which therefore gives the particulars of her life more importance than such a subject could otherwise possess.

Sir William Hamilton and his lady both choosing, for many substantial reasons, to remain in Italy rather than to return to their native country, employed themselves with the greatest assiduity in cultivating the favour of the king and queen, who on their part were, for reasons

just as liberal, equally desirous of retaining his
Excellency at their court. The ambassador
accordingly did all that lay in his power to
gain the goodwill of the monarch, by presenting
him with double-barrelled guns, procuring brass
carronades for his yacht, and, what was worse,
by spending that time in field sports which
ought to have been employed in counteracting
the influence of the French, German, and other
agents, by endeavouring to infuse an energy
into the Neapolitan government, and laying
before every member of it a full exposition of
the evils which threatened the existence of the
state. The apathy of Sir William at this period
was rendered still more culpable by the part
which he suffered his lady to take in the private
pleasures of the queen, to whose propensities and
connections he was far from being a stranger.
The palace of Naples might indeed have rivalled
that of Agrippina, in the nature and variety of
wanton amusement, and the arts made use of to
gratify the vilest passions. Nor did that government in tyranny and cruelty fall short of the
Roman empire in its worst state ; as the following instance will sufficiently prove. There was
an English banker at Naples of considerable
reputation, on whom the English ambassador
was accustomed to draw his bills, and Lady

Hamilton did the same, by her husband's permission. But her demands in this way became at length so quick and exorbitant, that Mr. Mackinnon, the banker, though he had authority to advance money on a public account to his Excellency, thought it prudent to refuse compliance with her Ladyship's order, till he should receive further instructions.

Whether this act of resistance to her will produced what followed, must be left to the judgment of the reader; but so it was, that the next day a file of musketeers surrounded the banker's dwelling, and having taken Mr. Mackinnon into custody, they carried him to the castle Del Ovo, where he was closely confined, and exposed to every nuisance. After remaining in this durance some time, without knowing the cause of his imprisonment, or having the means of bringing his case before a legal tribunal, a basket of iced fruits was brought him one day as a present. This article of luxury, which is always a choice treat at Naples, could not fail to prove very acceptable to one who had been compelled to live on the coarse fare of a prison. Mr. Mackinnon, however, having experienced some civilities from the officer of the guard, fortunately gave him an invitation to partake of

this agreeable entertainment. The officer, looking at the fruit, and then at the prisoner, asked
him how it was possible that a man who had
lived at Naples so long as he had done, should
think of receiving conserves, or anything of this
kind, from unknown persons ; on saying which,
he gave some of the contents of the basket to
a dog, which died in convulsions in a few
minutes.

The gentleman, whose life was thus attacked
by the most infamous means, contrived to make
his escape by the assistance of some friends, who
sent into the castle a large basket, or hamper,
filled with clothes. Soon after, one of the
strongest porters in Naples was employed to
bring out this basket, in which the banker was
deposited, covered with linen so effectually as
to be completely concealed. The porter without knowing what he was employed to carry,
staggered under his load till he came outside the
castle, and on reaching a low and narrow bridge,
he placed the basket on the parapet, where it
actually rocked to and fro by the violence of the
wind, which blew very hard from the sea.
Luckily, however, the labourer, after resting a
little while, and execrating his heavy burthen,
took it again upon his shoulders and arrived
safely at the place appointed, without meeting

with any molestation. It may naturally be
supposed that Naples was no longer a safe
residence for one who had thus eluded the
vengeance of his enemies ; and Mr. Mackinnon
accordingly made the best of his way out of a
country which was overrun with spies, and
wholly destitute of justice. On his arrival in
England, in very distressing circumstances,
which were aggravated by the loss of his
wife, he laid his case before government, and
printed a statement of his sufferings, but without meeting with any recompense.

CHAPTER VIII.

A rebellion or an invasion alarms
and puts the public upon its defence;
but a corruption of principles works its
ruin more slowly perhaps, but more
surely.   BERKELEY.

HE murder of the virtuous but too gentle Louis XVI. and of his accomplished queen, by the wretches who profaned the name of liberty in France, seems at last to have roused the Neapolitan court to some apprehension of their danger; and when the war broke out that year, this state made a common cause with the other powers against the new republic, which threatened to annihilate every monarchy in Europe.

In August following, the inhabitants of Toulon, and the neighbouring parts, being wearied out by the sanguinary oppressions of the revolutionary government, determined to throw off the yoke, and to put themselves under the protection of the English. For this purpose a deputation waited upon Admiral Lord Hood, then commanding on that station ; and his Lordship perceiving the importance of the proposition, readily acceded to it, at the same time taking every step that he could to preserve the Toulonese from their inveterate enemies. Knowing the necessity of a military force under such circumstances, Lord Hood dispatched Captain[1] Nelson of the *Agamemnon* to Sir William Hamilton at Naples, requesting his good offices with the government there, to send such a supply of troops as could be spared. On the arrival of the English ship in the bay, the captain waited on the ambassador, who introduced him to their Sicilian majesties. In a

---

[1] Nelson at this time—September, 1793—was thirty-four years of age, and had not lost his eye nor right arm. He was caressed by the nobles, feasted at Court, and he and his crew styled by the king "the Saviours of Italy and of his dominions." In a letter to his brother William, Nelson says : " The king received me in the handsomest manner ; I was three times with him out of the four days, and once to dinner, when I was placed at his right hand before our ambassador and all the nobles present." This was the first time Nelson and Lady Hamilton met, and it is clear from his letters to his wife, that he regarded her only as any honoured guest would an agreeable hostess.

letter which the brave commander wrote to his wife, giving an account of his mission, he says : " Lady Hamilton has been wonderfully kind and good to Josiah" (the son of Mrs. Nelson by her former husband). " She is a young woman," he adds, " of amiable manners, and who does honour to the station to which she is raised."

Of this first aquaintance, which afterwards proved so extremely important in its consequences, a strange account has been related in a book purporting to be the authentic Memoirs of the Life of Lord Nelson, compiled by one Harrison.[1] The statement in that work of the introduction of Nelson to her Ladyship is so palpably contradictory to truth and common sense, that it is a wonder how any person could ever have invented it. Having noticed the surrender of Toulon to Lord Hood, and the arrival of the *Agamemnon* at Naples, this biographer says :—

" In the meantime, Captain Nelson had been introduced to the king and queen of Naples, from whom he met with a most cordial and gracious reception : nor must his singular previous introduction by Sir William to Lady Hamilton be passed over without particular

[1] Published in 2 vols. 8vo, 1806.

notice ; on the result of which so much of the felicity of this exalted hero's future life seems evidently to have in a superlative degree depended. On Sir William's returning home, after having first beheld Captain Nelson, he told his lady that he was about to introduce a little man to her acquaintance, who could not boast of being very handsome ; ' but,' added Sir William, ' this man, who is an English naval officer, Captain Nelson, will become the greatest man that England ever produced. I know it, from the few words of conversation I have already had with him. I pronounce that he will one day astonish the world. I have never entertained any officer at my house, but I am determined to bring him here. Let him be put in the room prepared for Prince Augustus.' Captain Nelson was accordingly introduced to her Ladyship, and resided with Sir William Hamilton during his short stay at Naples ; and thus commenced that fervid friendship between the parties, which continued to glow, with apparently increasing ardour, to the last moment of their respective existences, whom it has been Lady Hamilton's severe lot to survive.

"The introductory compliment which has been paid by Sir William Hamilton to Captain Nelson's transcendent abilities, was not ill

SIR WILLIAM HAMILTON, K.B.

from an engraving by W.T. Fry after C. Grignon

requited by one of the latter's first salutations
of the worthy envoy : 'Sir William,' said he,
in consequence of the dispatch made use of in
obtaining the Neapolitan troops, 'you are a
man after my own heart : you do business in my
own way. I am now only a captain, but I will,
if I live, be at the top of the tree.'

" These reciprocal good opinions of each
other," continues the pretended historian, "which
form the basis of all substantial friendships,
could not fail to unite such excellent and
enlightened minds in a sincere amity. It
can never appear wonderful, then, that Lady
Hamilton, herself a person of very considerable
talents, and possessing a warm and affectionate
heart, naturally attached to splendid abilities,
should be forcibly struck with the pleasing
manners, extreme goodness and generosity of
mind, and evident proofs of comprehensive
intellect, which she continually witnessed in
the new friend of her intelligent husband,
during the few days of his continuance at
Naples.

" The frank and friendly attentions of her
Ladyship, at the same time, it must necessarily
be supposed, made no slight impression on the
susceptible bosom of Captain Nelson, who was
charmed with the characteristic sweetness of

disposition which she so fascinatingly displayed for the promotion of his ease and comforts."[1]

Some excuse might seem to be justly due to the reader for so long and fulsome an extract, filled with falsehood from beginning to end ; but when he knows that the volumes from whence it is taken were put together under the eye and by the dictation of the very woman who is flattered in the tale, he will see in the whole romantic representation a complete reflection of her mind.

The simple truth is, that Captain Nelson, bearing his Majesty's commission, and charged with particular dispatches to the English resident, went to his house immediately on his arrival, and was there, as a matter of course, received and entertained with the respect due to his rank. According to the fable, Sir William Hamilton picked the hero up by chance, or fell into conversation with him accidentally ; and being pleased with his behaviour, gave him an invitation to his house ; a circumstance altogether as probable as the prediction which the one is said to have delivered, and the boast which the other is reported to have made. Nothing of the kind took place ; nor had the ridiculous story any

[1] Life of Horatio Lord Nelson, by James Harrison, vol. i. pp. 10-79.

other authority than the fertile coinage of her
Ladyship's brain, and the blazoning illustration
which it received from the amanuensis who was
employed in her house at Merton to put together those memoirs. Every one who knew
Sir William Hamilton, was too well acquainted
with his phlegmatic character, to believe that he
ever caught such a fit of prophetic enthusiasm ;
and with respect to the naval commander, though
it cannot be denied that ambition was his ruling
principle, his understanding was at this time too
good to suffer him to play the gasconading part
which is here described. Certain it is, that the
visit was productive of momentous effects ; but
whether these conduced anything to the felicity
or the fame of the hero, remains to be developed
in another place. The whole fictitious narrative, however, affords another evidence of this
woman's extraordinary duplicity, and of the folly
with which it was invariably blended, since it
cannot but occur to every person of common
discernment, that the manner in which Sir
William is said to have spoken of his new acquaintance could not be true ; and they who are
conversant with the etiquette of the service,
must know that the entertainment of an officer
so employed was a regular act of duty, which
could not have been omitted without a breach

of good manners. If Sir William Hamilton
never received a naval officer as an inmate into
his house before Captain Nelson, he must have
conducted himself in a very uncourteous manner
to the various gentlemen of that profession, who,
during his embassy, anchored in the bay of
Naples. But many instances might be adduced
to free the English ambassador from this wrong;
and there are persons high in the service, now
living, who have experienced at his house the
most hospitable entertainment.

Such a tale, therefore, destroys itself by
some glaring inconsistencies, which cannot be
cleared without a manifest injury to the parties
who are the objects of its praise. Notwithstanding this, Mr. Southey, the last biographer
of Nelson, in a compendium abstracted from
other collections, purposely to render it a
manual for seamen, has been imprudent enough
to select this anecdote among others, because it
would, if true, serve to show what an idea was
formed by discerning minds of the peculiar
grasp of Nelson's powers, even before he had
distinguished himself by any exploits, and of
the presentiment which he had of his future
elevation at a time when he could have little
expectation of the kind. The inclination to
invent predictions, and other portents, indicative

of the fate of great men, is of very ancient
date, and has been carried to an extravagant
length in many instances ; but if they were all
examined with accuracy, and compared with
the circumstances to which they relate, most, if
not all of them, would sink into the ordinary
conjectures of human speculation, or be resolved
into the partiality of friendship, seeking for
signs and prodigies after the fact.

Nelson sailed from Naples well pleased with
the success of his mission, and six thousand
soldiers were sent in the fleet belonging to that
nation, to co-operate with the English and the
royalists at Toulon. But though their Sicilian
majesties had a radical hatred to the new state of
things in France, and were very glad to lend what
assistance they could towards the suppression of
the anarchy which prevailed there, neither they
nor their ministers adopted any course for the
reformation of their own states. It is remarkable enough, that at this period an Englishman
should have had the direction of public affairs
at Naples, while two of the same nation possessed the particular confidence of the king and
queen. Sir John Acton, a baronet of an ancient
catholic family in Shropshire, having entered
into the imperial service in 1763, was raised for
his services to the rank of major-general : and

on being sent to Naples, in 1778, he was there made secretary of state, with the department of the navy and commerce, and the rank of lieu-tenant-general. In 1780 the administration of the army was placed under his direction, and in 1785 he was appointed counsellor of state, and knight of the royal order of St. Janiver, and of St. Stephen of Tuscany. Four years afterwards he was made minister for foreign affairs. Sir John Acton was a man of ability, and much attached to his countrymen, but he had little English feeling, and very imperfect notions of the science of government ; for having been so many years in the service of an arbitrary state, and accustomed to nothing but absolute authority on the one hand, and implicit obedi-ence on the other, he scarcely felt a wish to raise the people above their degraded condition. Under the administration of this chevalier, Naples might, at least, have been prepared for a great moral and political change, if he had possessed as much public spirit as private virtue ; but unfortunately Sir John Acton,[1] like the

---

[1] In a letter from Lord Nelson to Admiral Goodall, March, 1801, it is stated, " Acton is married to his niece, not fourteen years of age, so you hear it is never too late to do well. He is only sixty-seven." The issue of this marriage was three children. Sir John died at Palermo, 1811.

English ambassador, had lived too long out of his
native land, and been too much habituated to
foreign institutions, to be desirous of promoting
the cause of liberty. One of the most effectual
means of regenerating a weak and disordered
community is by giving encouragement to
industry ; but nothing of this kind took place
at Naples, where a nuisance was not only
tolerated, but even countenanced, which in any
other state would have been considered as an
evil equally injurious to the people, and dishonourable to the government. The Lazzaroni
of Naples, consisting of many thousands of
vagabonds, without any settled residence or
regular occupation, formed a distinct community in that city, not only under the eye of
the sovereign, but distinguished by particular
expressions of his approbation. A conscientious
and intelligent minister, who considers himself
in the light of a public steward, will see the
obligation which lies upon him to purge out by
every means in his power such disorders as tend
to injure the public morals, and to disgrace the
state. Sir John Acton, on the contrary, even
at the time when the French revolution glared
as a beacon to all the nations around, never
once adopted any measure for the removal of
this scandalous abuse, though the want of a

disciplined army, and an appointed navy, both of which might have been easily supplied, was perceived and felt every day. But the truth is, the Neapolitan court relied more for their defence on the fleet and supplies of Great Britain, than on their own energies and resources.

A country so completely lost to its own character and interest, was, therefore, little deserving of our confidence and support; yet with the generosity which has invariably distinguished this nation, when called upon by the weaker powers, who have been in danger of coming into collision with the more formidable, Naples was favoured as an ally of importance, and by her arts and promises she obtained more notice and greater contributions than she was entitled to, either by her circumstances or fidelity.

At this crisis, when so much depended upon the inherent morality and loyalty of those states, who hoped to escape the misery into which the people of France had fallen through the corruption of their principles, it was evident that none had any just claim to assistance while they remained unconcerned about the symptoms of their own decay. This, however, was the case with the kingdom of the Two Sicilies at the

commencement of the revolutionary war : and it
was equally discreditable to the prime minister
there, and to our ambassador, that amidst all
the horrors of the republican tyranny, and the
apprehensions of invasion, nothing was done to
rouse the Neapolitan court or the people to a
sense of their respective duties. The former
still continued immersed in luxurious habits,
following despicable amusements ; and the
latter, though attached to their king and
country, were without that impulse to great
exertions which springs from patriotism, and a
grateful sense of national blessings.

While the English were contending for the
liberty and independence of Europe, the King
of Naples and Sir William Hamilton appear to
have been almost indifferent to the struggle,
and unmoved by the perils which were gather-
ing in every quarter. The beginning of
1794 presented an awful prospect, and yet in
January of that very year, the ambassador,
being on a hunting excursion, wrote thus to
his wife :—

" By having grumbled a little, I got a better
post to-day (*i.e.*, for shooting) ; and have killed
two boars and a sow, all enormous. I have
missed but two shots since I came here : and,
to be sure, when the post is good, it is noble

shooting !—the rocks and mountains are wild as the boars. The news you sent me of poor Lord Pembroke gave me a little twist; but I have for some time perceived, that my friends, with whom I spent my younger days, have been dropping around me.

" Lord Pembroke's neck was very short, and his father died of an apoplexy.

" My study of antiquities has kept me in constant thought of the perpetual fluctuation of everything. The whole art is really to live all the days of our life ; and not with anxious care disturb the sweetest hour that life affords— which is the present ! Admire the Creator and all His works, to us incomprehensible ; and do all the good we can upon earth ; and take the chance of eternity without dismay."

Though private letters, which were never intended for the public eye, are not objects of criticism as compositions, the facts which they mention, and the sentiments they convey, afford matter for discussion, as throwing light upon the events of the time, and illustrating the characters of the persons to whom they relate. When we follow the King of Naples among the woods and mountains, we ought to feel no surprise at hearing that his troops behaved like poltroons at Toulon, where their presence did

more harm than good to the wretched inhabitants ; nor have we much cause perhaps to
censure the backwardness of the Neapolitan
Commodore Fortiguerra in that business, especially when it is known, that during the
king's absence, a set of foreign agents did all
that lay in their power to divide the counsels
of this miserable government.

The reflections of Sir William Hamilton on
the sudden death of an old acquaintance were
certainly not those of a man whose hopes are
full of immortality. They have all the air of
Pyrrhonism, and breathe nothing superior to the
refined theism of Rousseau, who in his last
moments desired to have a look at the sky,
that he might feast his expiring vision with
objects which he should behold no more for
ever.

The following year our ambassador was busied
in arranging a second collection of his vases, of
which he published in folio an elegant set of
engravings, executed with great spirit and accuracy. About this period, also, he caused a collection of plates to be engraved by Rehberg
from paintings representing Lady Hamilton in
a variety of characters and attitudes; but
neither of these speculations, for such they were,
answered the expectations of the artist who em-

barked in the concern, or of his Excellency, who
shared with him in the adventure.

Such were the pleasures and the pursuits of
the English envoy, at a time when his country
was embarked in a tremendous conflict with the
foes of order abroad, and struggling hard to
prevent anarchy at home.

In the summer of the next year the French
republicans succeeded in frightening the timid
cabinet of Madrid into a separate peace ; but
the negotiations were so secretly carried on,
that the other powers had no apprehension of
such an alienation. Lady Hamilton, however,
had the merit of discovering the design before
it actually became public, and she lost no time
in communicating the intelligence to the nearest
commander, who happened to be Captain
Nelson.

The manner in which this extraordinary
woman obtained possession of this important
state secret indicated uncommon quickness of
penetration, and great readiness in the choice of
means for the accomplishment of her object.
Being one day with the king when a packet of
letters was brought to him from Spain, she perceived that while he carelessly threw down all
as he glanced over them, there was one, which
after fixing his attention for some moments he

carefully put into his pocket. Rightly thinking that this epistle contained some intelligence of peculiar importance, her Ladyship the same day bribed the page to take it from his master's pocket during his afternoon's sleep. Having read and hastily copied this letter, which apprized Ferdinand of the intended peace with France, and consequent rupture with England, she gave it again to the page, and sent off a dispatch to Captain Nelson.[1]

---

[1] The whole of this story is sheer romance. An important letter from the King of Spain to his brother, the King of Naples, informing the latter of the intention of Spain to join France against England, was received in 1796, and secured by Lady Hamilton, according to the account given by Lord Nelson in the well-known codicil to his will, written on the morning of the battle of Trafalgar. But it is more likely that the letter, being opened by the Queen of Naples, was by her sent to Lady Hamilton for the information of her husband, as, under the cover of familiar correspondence with her, all political intelligence that the queen considered of importance to the English government was transmitted to the ambassador. A letter from the queen to Lady Hamilton, dated April 29, 1795 (?) (published in Pettigrew's "Life of Nelson," vol. 2), clearly established this. It commences : " My very dear Lady,—My head is so confused, and my spirits so agitated, that I know not what to do. I hope to see you to-morrow morning about ten o'clock. I send you a letter in cypher, come from Spain—which must be returned before twelve o'clock, so that the king may have it. There are some

After this defection of one of our allies, and a general treachery or imbecility in the rest, it was found that we had little chance of preserving the Italian states, when they were so entirely dead to their own honour and interest. Naples, indeed, was one of the last powers that concluded an armistice with the French, which was followed by a treaty, in consequence of the departure of the British fleet from the Mediterranean ; and the king on this occasion wrote a letter to Admiral Sir John Jervis, in which he lamented this proceeding very bitterly, and beheld the ruin of his kingdom in the retreat of the British fleet. But as an ingenious writer, in his account of these events, observes, " The court of Naples, owing to the spirit of the queen, who at that time was convulsed at the name of a Frenchman, appeared ready for making exertions for the support of the good

facts very interesting to the English government, which I wish to communicate to them, to show my attachment to them, and the confidence I feel in the worthy chevalier. I only beg of him not to compromise me." This is probably the identical letter that Lady Hamilton " bribed the page to take from his master's pocket during his afternoon sleep—read and hastily copied," as stated in the text. It is not at all likely that she had to give herself so much trouble ; and the date of the letter should possibly be 1796, instead of the preceding year.

cause : but a variety of reasons prevented this court from acting with a corresponding degree of energy. The nation was loyal, but its government had grown feeble : and its statesmen had no fixed principle of integrity." [1]

[1] Life of Lord Nelson, by the Rev. J. S. Clarke, &c., vol. i. p. 251.

CHAPTER IX.

Nothing is more easy than to find
fault with others, but it is vain and
useless, unless it tend to the correction
or prevention of similar errors.

PLUTARCH.

HE peace which the Neapolitan
cabinet concluded with the
French republic, at the close
of the year 1796, was far from
ameliorating the condition of
the nation, or correcting the
evils of the government. The king was chagrined, indeed, by a measure into which his
necessities had driven him, and the queen was
disgusted at the appearance in her capital of
those revolutionary leaders, who in their own
country had brought some of her nearest relations to the scaffold. But these feelings were
nothing more than the agitation of impassioned

minds, mortified at sustaining a disgrace which they wanted fortitude to prevent, and virtue to improve. Their Sicilian majesties were indignant at the insolencies of the French generals, and alarmed at the intrigues which were carried on in their territories by the emissaries of that nation. They had also but too much reason to apprehend that the plan of republicanizing all Italy was completely determined upon, though, according to the wonted perfidy of the Directory, it was evident, that previous to the accomplishment of this object, each of the states would be exhausted of its wealth, and then cast aside like a squeezed orange.

Yet with these existing evils, by which they were surrounded, and the gulf of ruin yawning before them, the court of Naples, and those who were in the administration of affairs, still continued to pursue their accustomed circle of dissipation, neither changing their own manners, nor instituting any regulations for the good of the people. Much as the violence and rapacity of the French must be detested by every liberal mind, and despicable as their pretences to liberty truly were, still it cannot be denied that their progress in many countries had a tendency to open the eyes of the inhabitants to those abuses which facilitated the success of there publicans, and gave them so many advantages over ancient establishments. The lower orders of the people could not help repining at their own degraded condition, nor avoid observing the corruptions of their rulers, who were without energy to prevent danger, and, when it came, had no sentiment of feeling for any but themselves.

No nation can sink so completely into ignorance and imbecility, as to render the mass of the population wholly indifferent to oppression, or contented with their own abject poverty, while they see their lords rioting at ease, and indulging in every luxury.

So long as Naples enjoyed the advantages, political and commercial, of an alliance with Great Britain, the inhabitants had many sources of profit, the benefit of which made the greater part less sensible of the radical evils of their government, and careless about the scandalous immoralities of the court. But when the march of the French produced a stagnation of trade, and frightened away from their shores the gay and the wealthy, the invalids who courted health, and the young who came for pleasure, it was impossible that the Neapolitans, who had been accustomed for so many years to derive from these migrations the most substantial advantages, should not be sensibly affected by the loss which they had sustained.

In this state of things, by which industry was paralyzed, and mendicity increased, the higher ranks remained unmoved at the distresses which prevailed around them, nor once stopped to consult upon the means of averting the destruction which was advancing with rapid strides upon the nation. The retrenchment of useless expenditure, combined with a vigorous system of legislation, and an attention to the wants of the poor, might have done much at this crisis in conciliating the people, and stimulating them to the defence of their country Instead of all this, matters were suffered to become worse every day, and an army of spies was kept up to observe the conduct of families, and the discourse of individuals. Amidst all this public distress and private suffering, the palace of Caserta exhibited the same festivities and revelries, to call them by no worse a name, that had defiled this royal residence in former times. Many persons were taken up, and cast into the various prisons of the kingdom, under the general charge of being republicans or jacobins : but though it is probable that some of these characters might have been poisoned by the doctrine of equality, which then prevailed, their errors will not excuse the oppressions of the government by whom these deluded beings were incarcerated in gloomy dungeons, for no other offence than their opinions. Such was the mode by which the weak rulers of this state vainly thought to suppress the murmurs of the people, and to prevent a revolution. Being destitute of public and private virtue, they were mistrustful of all around them, and naturally concluded, from the cast of their own minds, that the rest of mankind were as vicious as themselves.

Severity, perhaps, might in some instances have been necessary for the general safety, but nothing could be more unjust, than to drag poor men from the bosom of their families, load them with irons, and imprison them without a hearing, while thousands of thieves were living under the protection of the government, and midnight assassins were let off with a comparatively trifling punishment. Such was the actual state of Naples at the period of which we are speaking ; and yet, though the queen was active in these efforts to keep down the progress of free inquiry, she has found admirers and apologists even in this country. To her courteous manners and uncommon ingenuity alone can this partiality be ascribed ; for as sovereign princes seldom descend to a familiar intercourse with persons of inferior station, the reception which strangers experienced at the court of

Naples, where they were entertained with remarkable hospitality, made them blind to the
deformities of the state, the depravity of the
great, and the miseries of the people. In the
oppressions which were exercised, as well as in
the follies that were practised, the wife of the
English ambassador had a leading concern, and
she frequently urged on the mind of the queen
the necessity of vigorous measures against those
who propagated calumnies to the disadvantage
of the royal character, and doctrines calculated
to awaken in the people a sense of their degradation. That her Sicilian majesty should be
deeply impressed by these representations was
natural, considering the deplorable fate of her
own sister, the unfortunate Maria Antoinette of
France; nor was she to be blamed for pursuing
such a course as appeared to be most likely to
prevent a similar calamity in her own kingdom.
But she should have considered that the only
effectual method of securing the loyalty of the
people, was by rendering herself deserving of it,
and studying to improve their condition and
morals. Both the queen and her adviser were
bitter enemies to the revolutionary principles,
and inflexibly bent on the destruction of those
who had the effrontery to assert the right of
subjects to investigate and censure the conduct

of their rulers. Lady Hamilton and her husband never failed in their interviews with the
King and Queen of Naples to dwell on the
advantages which England had experienced in
the prompt and vigorous steps that had been
taken to repress sedition, and to check the projects of those who aimed to subvert the constitution. All this had a very powerful effect
upon minds already alarmed for their safety,
and conscious that their subjects had but too
much reason to complain. But there was a wide
difference between the two nations ; and the
proceedings adopted in England for the preservation of the public tranquillity were the result
of legislative inquiry, and strictly within the
letter and spirit of the constitution, while in
Naples private resentment and personal animosity might easily be gratified under the
pretence of guarding against the dangerous
designs of the disaffected. Besides, in that
country, the objects of suspicion or dislike were
separated from their friends, and without legal
advice, which indeed could be of no service in
a state where it depended on the will of the
government whether these unfortunate persons
should have the advantage of a trial or not.

Lady Hamilton has been immoderately praised
for her fidelity to the Queen of Naples, and for

her zeal in opposition to the revolutionary designs of those who were inimical to monarchy. It would, however, have been a far more honourable testimony, to have recorded her exertions in the cause of humanity, and her interference on the behalf of those sufferers who were experiencing the vengeance of a corrupt and arbitrary ministry. At all events, it was little to the credit either of her Ladyship or her husband, that the British character should be so injured, as to be charged with countenancing measures that would have disgraced Constantinople or Morocco.

When the ascendency of the French could no longer be prevented, nor their demands refused, the state prisoners at Naples, who had been confined on suspicion of having sinister designs against the public peace, were brought to a hearing, and discharged. It is not improbable that the republicans carried themselves at this time with a consummate degree of arrogance, nor is it unlikely but that some of those who on this occasion experienced their fraternal kindness were dangerous characters, and actuated by the worst of motives. Nothing, however, in the conduct of the one or the other could justify the unfeeling language of Lady Hamilton to Admiral Nelson, in a letter dated from Naples,

the 30th of June, 1798. " The jacobins have
all been lately declared innocent, after suffering
four years' imprisonment ; and I know they all
deserved to be hanged long ago : and since
Garrat [1] has been here, and through his insolent
letters to Gallo, these pretty gentlemen, that
had planned the death of their majesties, are to
be let out on society again.   In short, I am
afraid all is lost here ; and I am grieved to the
heart for our dear charming queen, who deserves
a better fate ! "

This passage furnishes a complete evidence of
the share which our countrywoman had in the
internal concerns of that kingdom, and, what is
worse, of the bad manner in which her influence
was exercised.   An abhorrence of jacobinism,
when properly understood, was laudable; and a
tenderness for the interests of the queen did
credit to one who had experienced so much of
her kindness.   But it is shocking to see with
what levity this woman could speak of an imprisonment of four years, without a trial, in a
country like Naples, where the murderer had
more chance of meeting with lenity than a man
of principle, whose only crime was that of

---

[1] The French Minister at Naples, and " a most impudent, insolent dog," according to another letter of Lady
Hamilton.

having so much stern virtue as to reprehend boldly the errors of government.

In this letter to the English admiral, her Ladyship speaks most indignantly of the French encroachments, and her conviction that "the court of Naples would be obliged to declare war, if they meant to save their country."

Sir William Hamilton was also convinced of the great danger which menaced that kingdom about the same time, and of the only hope which remained to its ministers ; for in a letter to Earl St. Vincent,[1] then commanding our fleet in

---

[1] Lady Hamilton also, doubtless with the approval and knowledge of the queen, wrote to Lord St. Vincent, giving him a piteous account of the daily troubles and vexations of her Majesty, and urging and imploring him to take speedy measures for the protection and safety of her friend and the royal family. The high-flown reply of the Admiral to this appeal was more in the style of Don Adriano de Armado, than in that of the stern and unbending disciplinarian who commanded the British fleet. On May 22, 1798, he wrote: "My dear Madam,—I feel myself highly honoured and flattered by your ladyship's charming letter. The picture you have drawn of the lovely Queen of Naples and the Royal Family, would rouse the indignation of the most unfeeling of the creation at the infernal designs of those devils, who, for the scourge of the human race, govern France. I am bound by my oath of chivalry to protect all those who are persecuted and distressed, and I would fly to the succour of their Sicilian Majesties, was I not positively forbid to quit my

the Mediterranean, his Excellency says, " Notwithstanding its apparent peace with the French
republic, this monarchy is threatened with immediate destruction. The last message from
the French Directory at Paris was exactly the
language of a highwayman—' Deliver your
money, or I will blow your brains out.' As it
is natural for a person in danger of drowning to
catch at every twig, your Lordship will see that
the greatest hope this government entertains of
being saved from impending danger, is in the
protection of the king's fleet under your Lordship's command."

But the court of Naples had no right to look
for such a support, after having acted with so
much indifference to the great cause in which it
had embarked with the other allies, at a time
when the encroachments of the French might
have been stopped by a cordial co-operation on
the part of the confederated powers, and by the
full exertion of all their means for the restoration of order to distracted Europe. A rein-
forcement, however, was sent to the British

---

post before Cadiz. I am happy, however, to have a knight
of supreme prowess in my train, who is charged with this
enterprise, at the head of as gallant a band as ever drew
sword or trailed pike.—Your true knight, and devoted
humble servant, St. Vincent."

commander, and a separate squadron, under
Nelson, was detached to watch the motions of
an armament then preparing for sea at Toulon.
That officer lost no time in apprizing Sir William
Hamilton of his appointment : and it is but
justice to the latter to say that he manifested
great activity in furthering the views of his
friend, and the good of the service. The
expedition at Toulon naturally excited much
alarm at Naples ; and when it appeared off that
coast, conjecture was very busy about its des-
tination : but Buonaparte relieved the king, by
a message stating that his fleet had another
object than Sicily. Nelson, in his pursuit,
touched also at the bay of Naples, merely to
gain intelligence, and to request the assistance
of some light vessels, of which he was in want.
On this business he employed Captain Troubridge : and here we are under the disagreeable
necessity of copying a tale from the Life of
Nelson, which was manufactured under the
direction of Lady Hamilton shortly after the
death of the hero. According to this account,
Troubridge was sent to obtain permission for
the British fleet to victual and water in any
of the Sicilian ports. "With this view," says
the author of the narrative, "the captain
reached Naples at five in the morning, when

Sir William Hamilton immediately arose, and communicated on the business with the king of the Two Sicilies and General Acton ; who, after much deliberation, agreed that nothing could possibly be done which might endanger their peace with the French republic. Lady Hamilton, in the meantime, aware what would be the decision, and convinced, by all she heard from Captain Troubridge, of the importance to the British fleet, as well as to the real security of the Neapolitan and Sicilian territories, that the ports of these countries should by no means be closed against those who were alone able to protect them from the force or perfidy of General Buonaparte ; without consulting anything but her own correct judgment, and well-intentioned heart, she contrived to procure from some being of a superior order, sylph, fairy, magician, or other person skilled in the occult sciences, as many in Naples, as well as elsewhere, positively profess themselves to be, a small association of talismanic characters, fraught with such magical and potential influence in favour of the possessor, that the slightest glance of the mystic charm no sooner saluted the eye of the Sicilian or Neapolitan governor, than he was incapable of regarding any other object except what the bearer presented to his dazzled view,

or of hearing any other injunction but that
which the same person addressed to his astonished ear ; while his tongue was, at the same
time, impelled to secrecy, by the dread of an
assured death. Possessed of this treasure, Sir
Horatio had immediately sailed ; but, as his
possession of this talisman was to remain a pro-
found secret, till those periods should arrive
when it must necessarily be produced, the same
sort of correspondence continued to be kept up
between the parties, as if no such favour had
been conferred on the hero by any friendly enchantress whatever."

The language in which this story is told
perfectly corresponds with the credit that is due
to it ; for in none of the Arabian romances is a
wilder fiction to be found. But it is necessary
to complete the fable, from the only authority
on which it rests. After relating the unsuccessful search of Nelson in his first visit to the
coast of Egypt, and his return to Sicily, as well
for refreshment as in quest of the enemy, the
writer gives this extraordinary relation :—

" Such instructions had been sent to the
Governor of Syracuse, through the preponder-
ancy of French interest at this period, that he
would have found it difficult even to enter, and
probably have obtained little or no refreshment of

any kind, though much was absolutely necessary, had he not, very fortunately, experienced the beneficial effects of Lady Hamilton's powerful influence, secretly exerted, in the only quarter which was not rendered impenetrable, by the menacing insinuations of the then Gallic resident at Naples. It was the assistance he now procured, by virtue of the talismanic gift received from Lady Hamilton, and without which he could not, in any reasonable time, have pursued the French fleet, and possibly might never have come up with them, that he so solemnly recognized, a short time before his death, as to make it the subject of a codicil annexed to his will, in which he expressly *bequeaths that lady to the remuneration of his country.*"[1]

True it is, that this great man did so recommend her Ladyship to the gratitude of the nation, and equally true it is that she continued through life to abuse the government for not conferring on her a pension adequate to the extraordinary services which she affected to have rendered on this as well as on other occasions. In her own memorial to the minister, she observes, "The fleet itself, I can truly say, could not have got into Sicily, but for what I was happily able to do with the Queen of Naples,

[1] Harrison's Life of Nelson, Vol. i. pp. 244, 252.

and through her secret instructions, so obtained ; on which depended the refitting of the fleet in Sicily, and, with that, all which followed so gloriously at the Nile." [1]

According to this story, the claims of Lady Hamilton were of a very strong nature ; and many persons have, in consequence, been disposed to censure the successive administrations of the country for a supposed injustice to her Ladyship, and disrespect to the memory of the

---

[1] Though empowered by his instructions to take by force any supplies he needed from the Sicilian ports, Nelson was thoroughly convinced that by the instigation of Lady Hamilton, a secret letter was written by the Queen of Naples "to all governors of the Two Sicilies," ordering them to receive the British fleet with hospitality, and that in consequence of this he was willingly furnished with all that he required at Syracuse. On the last day of his life he wrote in the noted codicil to his will. " The British fleet under my command could never have returned the second time to Egypt had not Lady Hamilton's influence with the Queen of Naples caused letters to be wrote to the Governor of Syracuse, that he was to encourage the fleet being supplied with everything, should they put into any port in Sicily." That the queen, in opposition to the king and council, who through fear of the French had decided that but three or four English ships should be admitted into any Sicilian port, privately sent a letter or letters in favour of Nelson, is generally granted, but the part really taken by Lady Hamilton in the matter has been the subject of much discussion, and remains doubtful.

illustrious friend who took so lively a concern
in her interests.   But if Nelson himself was
deceived by female artifice, of which, unhappily,
too many proofs are blended with his brilliant
exploits, the dispassionate reader will not be
disposed to charge the British government with
ingratitude, for having rejected those pretensions, though they came supported by the
powerful weight of his authority.   On this
account, therefore, a few words will be necessary,
that an opprobium so injurious to the national
character may be removed, and that future
historians may avoid staining their pages by
quotations from fabulous narratives.

When Nelson sailed in quest of the enemy,
he received considerable assistance from Sir
William Hamilton ; who was in the confidence
of the King of Naples, and the intimate friend
of the Minister Acton.   Ample means were at
the disposal of our ambassador for the good
of the service, and he employed them well on
the present occasion ; by keeping small vessels
on the lookout along the coasts, and active
agents employed in various parts of Sicily.
The Neapolitan cabinet, or at least that part
of it which had the conduct of affairs under the
queen's influence, had, many months before this
period, made an urgent application to the Court

of London for assistance, and the presence of
a British fleet. When the squadron, therefore,
arrived, and in such force as to relieve, in
a great degree, those states from their fears,
who were most apprehensive of falling beneath
the republican dominion, the government of
Naples must have been wholly regardless of its
fate, if it had withheld such assistance from
its deliverers as could be supplied without any
hazard. So far indeed were their Sicilian Majesties from wanting the inclination to grant
what was required in the first instance, that an
immediate consultation was held on the subject,
and various instructions were sent to different
parts of the kingdom, enjoining the respective
authorities to afford all the relief in their power
to the English fleet. Policy, indeed, was used
in this business; and while public orders were
sent for the purpose of satisfying the French
ministers, private injunctions were dispatched,
not only to the municipal officers in the several
districts, but likewise to many noblemen, and
others, whose loyalty could be relied on, and
who were known to be ardently affected to the
English. There was, however, no need to " spur
a free courser ; " for the Sicilians, both high
and low, had such a rooted animosity to the
French, that it would have been impossible to

have restrained them from contributing the most prompt and efficient aid to our ships, on their arrival in any of their ports. Such indeed was the fact ; for no sooner did Nelson appear off Syracuse, than his fleet was surrounded with boats and vessels of all descriptions, laden with articles of provision. The stores of private houses were opened to supply his necessities, and every peasant in the mountains was happy to bring down the produce of his garden and his vineyard, for the comfort of the English. But had it been otherwise, and had French influence so far prevailed over common humanity in this instance, every one who knows the naval power of this country will be convinced, that neither water nor other articles of life would be wanting, where guns could command respect, and money procure a supply.[1] It is not meant to deny that the British envoy acted with a be- coming energy on this occasion ; or that his wife failed to use her influence, both at Naples

[1] By the secret orders of the Admiralty to Nelson, he was instructed—"to treat as hostile any ports within the Mediterranean (Sardinia excepted) when provisions or other articles you may be in want of, and which they may be enabled to furnish, shall be refused ;" and by the "Additional Instructions" of Lord St. Vincent he was advised that—"their Lordships expect a favour- able neutrality from Tuscany and the Two Sicilies ; in

and in Sicily, for the advancement of her friend's wishes, and the good of the cause in which he was engaged. The part which Sir William Hamilton took was consistent with the duties of his station, and his lady assisted him in the business with her wonted activity and address. But when this is granted, no more remains to be claimed ; for an accredited minister could not well have done less, without subjecting both himself and his employers to censure. That the fleet of Nelson was more quickly victualled than it otherwise would have been, through the exertions of the ambassador, and the friendship that subsisted between Lady Hamilton and the queen, may be true ; but that without their interference no supplies could have been obtained in Sicily, or an admission into its ports permitted, is too gross for belief. The English admiral, with an inferior force, had, not long before, entered Sardinia in distress; and yet he paid no respect to the prohibition that was issued by that monarch against the admission of our ships into his harbours. It

any event you are to extract supplies of whatever you may be in want of, from the territories of the Grand Duke of Tuscany, the King of the Two Sicilies, the Ottoman territory, Malta, and the *ci-devant* Venetian dominions, now belonging to the Emperor of Germany."

is not, therefore, to be credited, that this intrepid officer would have hesitated for a moment in acting with the same promptitude at Sicily, if a churlish spirit and vacillating policy had presumed to thwart him in his great purpose, by withholding from his squadron that supply which he could have obtained on the instant, without asking leave of the governor, or availing himself of any other influence than that which he commanded.

The gallant admiral was indeed persuaded that her Ladyship had rendered him great service in his search after the French fleet, and he had perhaps a commendable wish to procure for her a substantial benefit from the British government; but it is to be lamented, that, for the attainment of this object, anything like art or exaggeration should have been practised.

Lady Hamilton did not want friends in power to bring forward her case in the strongest manner, which would in all probability have been successful, had she been contented with resting her plea for a pension on the simple ground of her husband's long services, without setting up pretensions of her own, and such as could not stand a strict investigation : but when this assumption was made, she lost that interest which otherwise might have been exerted in her behalf. Ministers could not, even with their utmost inclination to do honour to the sentiments of Nelson, sanction what was manifestly a perversion of facts, and which, if true to any extent, would have been a reflection on the character of an envoy, whose years and experience rendered him too respectable to suffer such a stain on his memory, as must have been the case if a grant had been made to his wife, for a public service which it belonged to him to discharge. They who demand more than is their due, are always in danger of losing what they might have gained by candour and moderation ; since it is in the nature of things that we should examine narrowly into the conduct of those who endeavour to take an advantage of our credulity.

There was something in the nature of this claim so important, as connected with the national glory, that an explicit statement, and an accurate detail of circumstances, became necessary for the purpose of showing its truth and its value. Instead of this, the writer of the Life of Nelson, who was hired to set off the subject to the best advantage, found himself so embarrassed, that he could not venture to tell his story in an unvarnished manner ;

but he clothed it in a fantastical drapery, suited
to the pantomimic trick in which he was conscious of being an agent.

The victory of Aboukir diffused a general
joy over the countries which had been trem-
bling at the gigantic progress of the new republic. Naples felt as if she had been released
from the grasp of the destroyer ; and the
honourable Captain Capel, who touched there
in his way home with the dispatches, gave this
account of his reception to the admiral : " I
am totally unable, Sir, to express the joy that
appeared in every countenance, and the bursts
of applause and acclamations we received.
The queen and Lady Hamilton fainted : in
short, Sir, they all hail you as the saviour of
Europe."

The conqueror himself, in a letter to Lady
Nelson, thus described the feelings of the
Queen of Naples, and the exultation that
prevailed in consequence of his achievement :
" The kingdom of the Two Sicilies is mad with
joy : from the throne to the peasant, all are
alike. According to Lady Hamilton's letter,
the situation of the queen was truly pitiable :
I only hope I shall have not to be witness to
a renewal of it. I give you Lady Hamilton's
own words : 'How shall I describe the trans-

ports of the queen? 'Tis not possible : she
cried, kissed her husband, her children ; walked
frantic about the room ; cried, kissed, and embraced every person near her ; exclaiming,
O brave Nelson ! O God bless and protect
our brave deliverer ! O Nelson, Nelson ! what
do we not owe you ! O victor, saviour of Italy !
O that my swoln heart could now tell him
personally what we owe to him ! ' "

It is observable, however, that at this time
Nelson had a repugnance to visit Naples for
the purpose of refitting his ships ; and, in a
letter to Lord St. Vincent, he says of his voyage
thither, " I detest it ; and nothing but absolute
necessity could force me to the measure. Syracuse
in future, whilst my operations lie on the eastern
side of Sicily, is my port, where every refreshment may be had for a fleet."

Naturally fond as the hero was of pleasure,
and vain of honours, he seems, at this period,
to have dreaded that seat of dissipation to which
he was now approaching, and where the syren,
by whom his life became afterwards ruled, was
then preparing her softest allurements and most
powerful enchantments. The reception which
the admiral experienced at Naples is thus described in a letter to his lady, for whom he still
continued to cherish the fondest affection, and

to whom he delighted to impart the sentiments by which he was actuated, and the occurrences which distinguished his eventful life :

" The poor, wretched *Vanguard* arrived here on the 22nd of September. I must endeavour to convey to you something of what passed : but if it were so affecting to those only who were united to me by bonds of friendship, what must it be to my dearest wife, my friend, my everything which is most dear to me in this world? Sir William and Lady Hamilton came out to sea, attended by numerous boats, with emblems, &c. They, my most respectable friends, had really been laid up and seriously ill ; first from anxiety, and then from joy. It was imprudently told Lady Hamilton in a moment, and the effect was like a shot ; she fell apparently dead, and is not yet perfectly recovered from severe bruises. Alongside came my honoured friends : the scene in the boat was terribly affecting : up flew her Ladyship ; and, exclaiming, ' O God, is it possible ! ' she fell into my arms, more dead than alive. Tears, however, soon set matters to rights ; when alongside came the king. The scene was, in its way, as interesting : he took me by the hand, calling me his deliverer and preserver, with every other expression of kindness. In short,

all Naples calls me *Nostro Liberatore*. My
greeting from the lower classes was truly affecting. I hope some day to have the pleasure of
introducing you to Lady Hamilton : she is one
of the very best women in the world : she is
an honour to her sex. Her kindness, with Sir
William's, to me, is more than I can express.
I am in their house ; and I may now tell you,
it required all the kindness of my friends to
set me up. Lady Hamilton intends writing to
you. May God Almighty bless you, and give
us, in due time, a happy meeting ! "

The scene mentioned in this letter as having
been so terribly affecting, was no more than one
of those fine pieces of acting which fired the
brain of Romney, the painter, and made him
desirous of running into Sussex to bring up his
friend, the poet, to witness a performance which
he wanted words to describe. The truth is, that,
as the boat drew near to the *Vanguard*, Lady
Hamilton began to rehearse some of her theatrical airs, and to put on all the appearance of a
tragic queen. There was a great swell, at this
time, in the bay ; and, just as the barge reached
the ship, the officer, who saw through her
affectation, exclaimed, with an oath, that, if she
did not immediately get up the side, the consequences might be dangerous ; for that he could

not be answerable for the safety of the boat.
On this, our heroine laid aside her part, till she
reached the gangway, where, instead of fainting
on the arm of Nelson, she clasped him in her
own, and carried him into the cabin, followed
by Sir William Hamilton, and the rest of the
company.

Here the author of the historical romance,
which we have already been compelled to notice
more largely than could have been wished, relates a strange incident, which, as he says, would
have afforded abundant matter for observation in
the days of superstition ; but which, without previously ascertaining the fact, is gravely attempted
to be accounted for on natural principles.

" While the company were partaking of some
refreshment in the cabin of the *Vanguard*, a
small bird familiarly perched on the admiral's
shoulder. On the circumstance being remarked
—' It is,' said he, ' a very singular thing : this
bird came on board the day before the battle
of the Nile : and I have had other instances of
a bird's coming into my cabin previously to
former engagements.' This," adds the writer,
" is the more remarkable, as the same thing is
said to have afterwards happened prior to the
battle of Copenhagen." [1]

[1] Harrison, vol. i. p. 320.

The narrator of this prodigy dismisses it by supposing that these were merely birds of passage, which mode of reasoning might be satisfactory enough for a solitary instance ; but philosophy itself will be confounded by the frequency of the recurrence on the eve of different battles, in remote parts of the world. But the story stands on too slender a basis to require either moral argument, or the aid of science ; and it would have been creditable in the writer of Nelson's life, had he suppressed an anecdote for which he could adduce no legitimate authority. Supposing such a circumstance to have occurred at Naples, it is accounted for more rationally by what is told, in this very memoir, of the practice of the Lazzaroni, who kept small birds in wicker cages, which on the approach of the hero of the Nile they opened, and gave the little prisoners their liberty. One of these birds most probably entered the cabin windows of the *Vanguard*, and attracted the notice of the admiral ; but the rest of the story carries too much the air of invention to merit farther attention.

However commendable it might have been in any individuals to show their gratitude by some signal acts of liberality and splendour, for the decided turn given to the affairs of Europe, in the defeat of the French fleet on the coast of Egypt, little can be said in praise of the extravagant shows, which, on this occasion, were displayed by our ambassador at Naples. The pageantry of these entertainments, and the profusion of expense that was incurred, to gratify an idle vanity, were wholly unworthy the character of that nation which this waste was intended to honour. But the mummery exhibited by the British envoy in that capital was equally impolitic and frivolous ; since, while it was conceived in the spirit of the French, it tended to irritate them and their friends more bitterly against the Court of Naples.

The birthday of Nelson happening a little after his arrival, furnished an occasion for a fête which was given by Lady Hamilton : and such was the attention of the court, that though it was a time of state mourning, the sables were, by order, laid aside in honour of the day. In a letter to Lady Nelson, dated September 28, 1798, the admiral says :—

" The preparations of Lady Hamilton for celebrating my birthday to-morrow are enough to fill me with vanity ; every ribbon, every button has Nelson, &c. The whole service is marked H. N. glorious first of August. Songs and sonnetti are numerous beyond what I ever could deserve. I send the additional verse to 'God save the King,'¹ as I know you will sing it with pleasure. I cannot move on foot, or in a carriage, for the kindness of the populace : but good Lady Hamilton preserves all the papers as the highest treat for you."

At this festive scene, which consisted of a ball and supper, eighteen hundred persons are said to have been entertained ; but the harmony was somewhat interrupted by an altercation between the admiral and his son-in-law, which might have been attended with serious consequences, if Captain Troubridge and another officer had not conveyed the young man out of the room.² The occasion of this disturbance

---

¹ This additional verse, from the pen of Miss Knight, ran thus :—

> "Join we great Nelson's name,
> First on the rolls of Fame,
> Him let us sing.
> Spread we his fame around,
> Honour of British ground,
> Who made Nile's shores resound,
> God save the King."

² This was Nelson's fortieth birthday, and the grand *fête* cost Sir W. Hamilton over 2,000 ducats. In the saloon, underneath a magnificent canopy, was erected a rostral column, bearing the words, "Veni, Vidi, Vici," and the names of the heroes of the Nile. The feelings of Captain Nisbet were excited by wine and anger, but a

was some intemperate language which Mr.
Nisbet incautiously applied to Lady Hamilton,
whom he accused in plain terms of having supplanted his mother in the affections of the
admiral.

The terms in which this accusation was conveyed, and the time chosen for making it, cannot
certainly be justified ; but on the other hand it
ill became the lady who was the object of it to
relate the adventure at all, much less in a manner
that served to throw the whole odium upon the
indiscreet relative of her admirer, without the
slightest explication of the cause of that rude
behaviour which she was so careful to set forth
in the blackest colours in the life of the hero.

Whatever might be the conduct of the
young man who has been so severely censured,
and however much it is to be lamented that
he should not have deported himself with more
decorum ; still, if he had not perceived some
very unbecoming circumstances in the intercourse which excited his resentment, it is not
to be supposed that he would at a public
entertainment have provoked the vengeance of

reconciliation between him and his stepfather was effected
by the mediation of Sir W. and Lady Hamilton. Nisbet's
temper was probably quick, and his manners the reverse
of polished. *See note at end of Chapter.*

his powerful friend by insulting the wife of the English ambassador. Had not the consciences of the parties been a little affected by the coarse and unseasonable sarcasms which were then thrown out, it is most reasonable to believe that some degree of punishment would have been inflicted, and a proper apology required as an atonement for the outrage. On the contrary, though Nelson was for the moment highly exasperated, and the lady ever after felt a rancorous hatred against Mr. Nisbet, they both suppressed their emotions, and endeavoured to soothe one whose observation they dreaded. This was invariably the practice of the modern Calypso, who no sooner discovered any symptoms of jealousy or disgust in the friends of the hero, than she immediately began to exert her diligence in flattering them by her assiduities and attentions. Many instances might be adduced of this consummate art ; and thus it was at the period of which we are speaking, for instead of acting with the becoming dignity of insulted virtue, she employed all her allurements to deceive the young man who had branded her with the foulest invective, and she succeeded so well in her schemes, that Nelson, writing to his wife shortly after the · disagreeable scene which took place on his

birthday fête, expressed himself in this language :
" The improvement made in Josiah by Lady
Hamilton is wonderful : your obligations and
mine are infinite on that score : not but Josiah's
heart is as good and as humane as ever was
covered with a human breast. God bless him,
I love him dearly, with all his roughness." [1]
That this great commander acted with duplicity,
may perhaps to some appear too harsh a conclusion, and yet it can hardly be denied that
his language and his conduct were somewhat
at variance at this time, for which the most
plausible account seems to be, that he was
now so completely under the influence of an

---

[1] Lady Hamilton in a letter to Lady Nelson, dated
the same month, December, 1798, says : " Lord Nelson is
adored here, and looked on as the deliverer of this
country. I need not tell your Ladyship how happy Sir
William and myself are at having an opportunity of
seeing our dear, respectable, brave friend return here,
with so much honour to himself and glory for his country.
We only wanted you to be completely happy. Josiah
is so much improved in every respect, we are all delighted with him. He is an excellent officer and very
steady, and one of the best hearts in the world. I love
him much, and although we quarrel sometimes, he loves
me, and does as I would have him. He is in the way
of being rich, for he has taken many prizes. He is
indefatigable in his line, never sleeps out of his ship,
and I am sure will make a very great officer".

artful woman, as to have forgotten the respect that was due to the dignity of his character. Of this influence a striking proof appears in a letter written by him to Earl St. Vincent, in which he says, "I believe Lady Hamilton has written so fully, and, I will answer, so ably on all subjects, that but little remains for me to say. Your commands respecting the queen were executed with so much propriety, that if I had never before had cause for admiration it must then have commenced. Her Lady-ship's and Sir William's inexpressible goodness to me is not to be told by words, and it ought to stimulate me to the noblest actions ; and I feel it will."

The weakness manifested in this letter shows how much the heart of the writer had been affected by the wiles that were practised upon him, and how strangely he was attached to the interest of the queen, whose court he had not long before characterized as completely infamous.

The day after the entertainment which has been just described, his Lordship, in a dispatch to his commander-in-chief, thus expressed his honest feelings : "I am very unwell, and the miserable conduct of this court is not likely to cool my irritable temper. It is a country of fiddlers and poets, whores and scoundrels."

That Nelson should with such sentiments
continue to be fascinated by those who formed
a part of this wretched community, is greatly
to be lamented, but this instance serves to
prove that human nature is sure to be overcome
where a man has not fortitude enough to run
away from temptation. The valour which
" seeks reputation in the cannon's mouth " is
of a different quality from that calm and stedfast
virtue which resolutely opposes the blandishments of vice. Our brave commander, who
suffered himself, contrary to his better judgment,
to be lured into the circle of folly, saw plainly
enough that he was in a perilous condition,
and while he continued to be infatuated by
an attachment to the seat of pleasure, he had
the good sense to condemn the frivolous
manners, and corrupt principles, of those persons
with whom he had a daily intercourse.

It may however be wondered, that, with this
impression on his mind, he should still remain
so strangely prepossessed in favour of those,
who, if they did not exactly correspond with
the description which he drew, did at least
give their countenance to those characters, by
admitting them to their private parties and
public entertainments. Nelson could not have
known the Neapolitans so exactly as to have

painted them in the way he did, but through the information which he obtained from his English friends ; and therefore, if he had not been as blind to their failings, as he was quick-sighted to the deformities of others, he would have despised them for their meanness and hypocrisy, in associating with persons, who, in any other place, must have been expelled from society. At an entertainment which was given by the admiral on board of his own ship to a large party of the Neapolitan nobility, Lady Hamilton, in the midst of the feast, said in a low voice to an officer now high in the service, " In all that company before you, there is not a woman that is virtuous, nor a man that does not deserve the gallows." Yet these very persons were the chosen friends of the ambassador and his wife. These made up the assembly who celebrated the admiral's birthday ; and these, in short, constituted that precious set for whom he made the most dreadful sacrifices.

But if such was the court of Naples, their conduct cannot be justified, who for many years gave a particular sanction to the depravity which prevailed there ; nor can any apology be found for the attempts which were made to uphold that system of corruption and oppression, by the power of the British navy, and by the influence of our national character.

* * *

NOTE.

Captain Josiah Nisbet was the only son of Dr. Nisbet, of the island of Nevis, West Indies, who died insane about eighteen months after his marriage. His widow, Frances, became the wife of Captain Nelson, March 12, 1787, when her son Josiah was three years old. He served as midshipman on board the *Agamemnon* (64), and as lieutenant in the *Theseus* (74), with his step-father, whose life he saved by binding his shattered arm when wounded in the disastrous attack upon Santa Cruz, July 24, 1797. By the interest of Nelson he was promoted, and appointed to the command of the *Dolphin*, attached to the Mediterranean fleet. In December, 1798, he was made post-captain, and commanded the *Thalia* (36), on the Mediterranean station. His conduct was not considered satisfactory by Lord St. Vincent, who made a complaint against him to his stepfather. Early in January, 1799, Nelson, in a letter to St. Vincent, said: "Let me thank you for your goodness to Captain Nisbet, I wish he may deserve it ; the thought half kills me;" and in another letter to Captain Ball, a few months after : " I hope Captain Nisbet behaves properly ; he is now on his own bottom, and by his conduct must stand or fall." The desired improvement evidently did not take place, as in October of the same year, Nelson wrote to Admiral Duckworth, concerning the *Thalia* : " I wish I could say anything in her praise. Perhaps you may be able to make something of Captain Nisbet, he has by his conduct almost broke my heart." Shortly afterwards Captain Nisbet ceased to command the *Thalia*, and was never more actively employed.

CHAPTER X.

Never did base and rotten policy
Colour her working with such deadly
wounds.

SHAKSPEARE.

HE naval victory gained on the coast of Egypt, and the consequent disasters to which it exposed the flower of the French army, commanded by the most fortunate of the revolutionary generals, stimulated Austria to embark in a new war, with the hope of crushing the insolent republic. In this design it found a willing ally in the court of Naples, which engaged to raise eighty thousand men for the common cause. Ferdinand, indeed, showed more energy on this occasion than he had ever displayed before, but unluckily his soldiers wanted courage, and General Mack, their commander, seems to have been deficient both

in talents and honesty. The king marched
with thirty-two thousand men to Rome, but the
cowardice of his troops gave the enemy an
easy victory, and he was glad to hasten back
to his capital, for the purpose of saving himself
and his family.

Nothing now remained for the court but to
remove to Sicily, which was effected by the
prompt assistance of Lord Nelson, whose
squadron was then fortunately lying in the bay.
Great address was requisite in the management
of this business ; but it is no more than justice
to Lady Hamilton to state that she displayed
throughout the whole of the concern an equal
degree of heroism and judgment. Having discovered a subterraneous passage, which led from
the royal apartments to the seashore, she accompanied Lord Nelson one evening by this
way, and thus arranged secretly the proper steps
for conveying on board his ship the most valuable of the property.

An accident, however, occurred, which had
very nearly proved fatal to the whole design,
for a bell having been touched, gave an alarm
to a sentry at a little distance, who would have
gone to the place, had not her Ladyship, with
great presence of mind, hastened to the man
with an apology for unintentionally making the

noise, and requesting him to avoid disturbing the family. By this quickness, she succeeded in preventing any discovery, and the conveyance of the treasures through the passage to the boats continued till the royal fugitives were ready for their departure. Of these transactions, which were obliged to be conducted with great privacy to prevent giving any cause for suspicion to the Neapolitans, an account was drawn up by Lord Nelson himself, and transmitted to Earl St. Vincent, from which it will be proper to extract some particulars :—

" On the 14th of December," says his Lordship, "the Marquis de Niza, with three of the Portuguese squadron, arrived from Leghorn, as did Captain Hope, in the *Alcmene*, from Egypt. From that time the danger for the personal safety of their Sicilian majesties was daily increasing ; and new treasons were found out, even to the minister of war. The whole correspondence relative to this important business was carried on with the greatest address, by Lady Hamilton and the queen, who, having been in constant habits of correspondence, no one could suspect them. Lady Hamilton, from that time to the 21st, every night received the jewels of the royal family, &c., &c., and such clothes as might be necessary for the very

large party about to embark, to the amount, I
am confident, of full two millions five hundred
thousand pounds sterling. On the 18th,
General Mack wrote that he had no prospect of
stopping the progress of the French, and en-
treated their majesties to think of retiring from
Naples, with their august family, as expeditiously
as possible. From that day, various plans were
formed for the removal of the royal family from
the palace to the water-side. On the 19th
I received a note from General Acton, saying
that the king approved of my plan for their
embarkation. During that day, the 20th
and 21st of December, very large assemblies
of people were in commotion, and several
were killed. On the 21st, at half-past eight,
P.M., three barges, with myself and Captain
Hope, landed at a corner of the arsenal.
I went into the palace, and brought out the
whole royal family, put them in the boats, and
at half-past nine they were all safely on board
the *Vanguard, Samnite*, and *Archimedes*, with
about twenty sail of vessels, left the bay of
Naples. The next day it blew much harder
than I ever experienced since I have been at sea.
Your Lordship will believe my anxiety was not
lessened by the great charge that was with me ;
but not a word of uneasiness escaped the

lips of any of the royal family. On the 25th, at nine, A.M., Prince Albert, their majesties' youngest child, having ate a hearty breakfast, was taken ill, and at seven, P.M., died in the arms of Lady Hamilton. And here it is my duty to tell your Lordship of the obligations which the whole royal family, as well as myself, were under, on this trying occasion, to her Ladyship. They necessarily came on board without a bed, nor could the least preparation be made for their reception. Lady Hamilton provided her own bed, linen, &c., and became their slave ; for, except one man, no person belonging to the court assisted the royal family. At three, P.M., being in sight of Palermo, his Sicilian majesty's royal standard was hoisted at the main-top-gallant mast-head of the *Vanguard*. At two, A.M., December 26th, we anchored, and at five I attended her Majesty and all the princesses on shore ; the queen being so much affected by the death of Prince Albert, that she could not bear to go on shore in a public manner. At nine, his Majesty went on shore, and was received with the loudest acclamations, and apparent joy."

These, indeed, were the genuine effusions of loyal attachment on the part of the Sicilians, who, having for many years groaned under a wretched government, now entertained a confidence that the presence of the king among them, and the establishment of his court at Palermo, would ameliorate their condition, and correct the abuses of which they had but too much reason to complain. The event proved, however, that the minds of the weak and vicious are not changed by the difference of situation, or improved commonly by the visitation of calamity. Their Sicilian majesties, and the parasites around them, no sooner recovered a little from the fears which depressed their spirits on leaving the ancient capital of their dominions, than they began to indulge in those habits to which that very loss was to be attributed. Ferdinand found on this island an abundant employment in shooting; and his queen, with Lady Hamilton, and other favourites, sought relief in balls and card parties. While the inhabitants of Sicily were astonished at the splendour and gaiety which prevailed, they were mortified to perceive that nothing like a reformation of public abuses took place, but that, on the contrary, all posts of honour and profit, as they became vacant, were conferred on the Neapolitans. This scandalous policy corresponded with the shameful extravagance which marked the conduct of the court, though

at the same time, every ducat was wanted for
the service of the state. To the miseries of the
lower orders, this profligate government was
wholly insensible, and, as is usual with depraved
minds, instead of reflecting on their errors, and
endeavouring to seek for some mode by which
to regain the goodwill of mankind, and to
obtain internal tranquillity, they had recourse to
amusements of the most frivolous kind, thinking
perhaps that such a course was an indication of
fortitude. But if they so deceived themselves,
it was impossible that such proceedings could
succeed in imposing either upon the inhabitants,
or the English who were compelled to witness
this round of licentiousness.

While these follies were acting in Sicily, the
city of Naples was in a state of such confusion,
that any man of patriotic sentiments might have
been of essential service. When the army
failed in its duty, the populace rose against the
French, drove in their advanced posts, and would
have succeeded in exterminating the whole, if a
man of enterprise had been at their head ; for
such was their energy and determination, that
when the invaders planted artillery in the streets,
the Lazzaroni rushed upon the guns, and stabbed
the soldiers. Still there was no virtue in this
zeal, though by judicious management it might

have been rendered beneficial to the cause of
general order, in destroying a horde of
marauders, who came into that country, as
they did everywhere else, for plunder and
ambition, under the pretence of liberty and
equality.

The loyalty of the Neapolitans was not the
result of principle, but passion, and they hated
the French, because their progress indicated a
change of old customs, and the subversion of
institutions which the people regarded with
superstitious reverence, though they neither
enjoyed any benefit from them, nor could offer
the smallest reason for their attachment.

There were many intelligent persons, on the
other hand, who hailed the entrance of the
French with delight, thinking that by the
instrumentality of these invaders, they should
be able to organize their country, and place it
on a respectable footing among nations. Much
indulgence certainly is due to the revolutionists
of Naples, though their patriotism was far from
that purity which in more enlightened parts has
guided the conduct of great and good men in
the arduous work of regenerating states, without having recourse to foreign assistance, or
internal violence.

Such, however, was the wretched condition

of the kingdom, the imbecility of its government, and the poverty of the people, that no
political change could well be for the worse ;
and therefore some excuse may be made for
those who were glad to avail themselves of any
means that offered for bringing in a new system,
by which it was at least possible that the
country would obtain some improvement.
When it is considered that the persons who
entertained these sentiments, and who thought
it their duty to act upon them, were men of the
principal families in Naples, while the adherents
to the old order of things consisted for the most
part of the retainers of the court, and a lawless
rabble, we shall see some cause to respect the
motives of the one, and to pity the folly of the
others. Nor should it be forgotten, that the
revolution in this nation, by which the government was changed from a weak monarchy into
a romantic republic, was neither stained by
regicide, nor disgraced by persecution : and well
would it have been for the cause of humanity,
and the honour of the British character, if the
restoration of the sovereign, which was effected
solely by our navy, had been marked by equal
liberality and moderation.

It was no doubt our duty, as the ally of
Ferdinand, to re-establish him upon his throne,

by freeing his country of the intruders ; but, in doing this, great care and caution became necessary, to avoid meddling between him and any description of his subjects. How this obvious course of policy was regarded, now remains to be shown ; for unfortunately the subject is so necessarily interwoven with these memoirs, that, to have passed it over in silence, or in a cursory manner, would have been inconsistent with truth and justice.

Cardinal Ruffo, the vicar-general of the kingdom, and high in the confidence of Ferdinand, received a commission to use his exertions in raising the Calabrese to arms, for the restoration of the monarchy. His Eminence acted in this business with a zeal well suited to the object which he had in view, and the character of the people whose feelings he was employed to rouse. With the cross in one hand, and the sword in the other, he proclaimed a crusade against the modern infidels ; and so powerful were his exhortations, that he quickly gathered to his standard a motley assemblage, which he dignified with the title of the Christian army ; [1] consisting of peasants, animated by an attachment to their country; priests, fired with

---

[1] Lord Nelson styled Ruffo—" the great devil who commanded the Christian army."

enthusiasm for their religion ; and vagabonds, who had no other principle than the love of plunder. But whatever were the elements of this crew, it cannot be denied that their leader was legally authorized in the measures which he adopted ; and, accordingly, as the representative of his sovereign, he was assisted by the British ships on the coast, together with the Russians and the Turks, who formed part of the alliance against the French republic.

The capture of Naples depended on the surrender of the fortress of St. Elmo, which overawes the town, and of the castles of Uovo and Nuovo, which command the anchorage. The first was in the possession of the French, and the two last were garrisoned by the Neapolitan revolutionists. The forts were all strong by nature, and well furnished with the means of defence ; besides which, it was known that the enemy had a powerful fleet in the Mediterranean, the object of which could hardly be doubted. Under these circumstances, the cardinal felt himself justified in consenting to terms of capitulation with the insurgents, by which their persons and property were secured on condition of surrendering up the castles which they held. To this treaty the Russian, Turkish, and British commanders were subscribing parties ; but, thirty-six hours after the agreement had been signed, and while the flag of truce was yet flying on the *Seahorse* frigate, Lord Nelson appeared in sight with his whole squadron, and, by a signal, annulled the treaty which had been regularly formed, and solemnly ratified.[1]

Thus by a spontaneous movement, without inquiry or deliberation, the British admiral took upon himself to abolish an agreement in which he was not concerned, and over which he had no legal control, even on the supposition that the terms had been injurious to the rights of the Sicilian crown. But, in truth, there was nothing in the treaty itself that could justify this breach of an express contract ; for in shielding the revolutionists from the vengeance of the court, which, like all vicious governments, was as sanguinary in prosperity as it had been abject in its fall, the cardinal acted with a moderation

[1] The greater part of the belligerents in the castles were subjects of the King of Naples, but supporters of the Parthenopeian Republic. On the arrival of Lord Nelson, he, as the representative of Ferdinand, decided that the capitulation could not be carried into effect without the sanction of that sovereign, as Cardinal Ruffo had exceeded his powers, and disobeyed his instructions in granting terms to rebels ; he being empowered to grant no terms but those of unconditional surrender.

which did him honour, and a policy that reflected credit on his understanding. In the
cabin of Lord Nelson's ship, he defended, with
energy, the treaty, which he had full authority,
by his commission, to enter into ; and which
our admiral unquestionably could not abrogate
by any other plea than that of power. A long
altercation took place, in which Sir William and
Lady Hamilton acted as interpreters, but without making any impression on the cardinal, who
could not, on common principles of morality,
allow that the breach of faith was vindicated by
the bad characters of those to whom a pledge
of indemnity had been given. Much abuse has
been thrown on this man, both by the admirers
of Lord Nelson and by the advocates of demo-
cracy ; the one endeavouring to screen the hero
from the reproach which this transaction has
cast on his memory, by the supposed treachery
of the cardinal ; while the others have, with
equal truth, aspersed Ruffo as the unprincipled
tool of a despotic government. But when the
whole of the history is examined with that
calmness which becomes every inquiry into
moral actions, it will appear that the man's
views, in the present instance, were such as
indicated an enlarged mind, equally honest,
humane, and independent. Had the cardinal

13

been of that trimming disposition which he is
described by one party, he would not have
opposed the royal will and Nelson's declaration
in the manner he did ; and if his Eminence was
really the worthless being his enemies have
painted, it was easy for him to have devised
some means to save his interest with the court,
by allowing that he had acted without sufficient
authority. Instead of this, the cardinal adhered
inflexibly to the measure, on the simple ground,
that it could not be departed from without
infamy ; which surely was a strange degree of
obstinacy in a man who is represented as of a
shuffling disposition, and void of all honourable
feeling. But let the cardinal have been as bad as
possible, he conducted himself, in this instance,
with a much more lively sense of just dealing
than those who thought proper to destroy that
treaty which he and three other official persons,
acting as the representatives of their governments, had entered into for the general good.
Should it be said, that too much notice has been
taken of this transaction, which has eclipsed the
reputation of our naval hero beyond the possibility of justification, it is sufficient to observe
that Nelson was now under an influence, which,
unfortunately for his fame, led him aside from
that course of duty, a perseverance in which

would have preserved him from many other
errors. No sooner was the court of Naples in
a state by which it was enabled to exercise its
vengeance, than a sanguinary determination was
formed to sacrifice all who had distinguished
themselves in the revolution ; and, finding that
the chief of these partizans were included in the
amnesty granted by the late treaty, as having
composed part of the garrisons in the two castles
on the bay, it was immediately resolved to re-
peal what had been done, under the pretext that
the measure was contrary to the king's express
command. So far the nefarious business affects
the character of their Sicilian majesties, and their
confidential advisers only ; but in all that follows,
the British ambassador and the admiral were
equally implicated. Lady Hamilton was indeed
at the bottom of the whole ; and the malignity
of her disposition, and the hardihood of her
counsels, appeared conspicuous in every part of
this dark affair. In the cabin of the *Foudroyant*
she conducted herself with extreme violence
towards the cardinal, whose words were so
much perverted by her management and that
of her husband, as to produce considerable
agitation in the mind of Nelson, who naturally
conceived, from the zeal of his Eminence, that
he was adding insult to fraud. When, there-

fore, Ruffo found that all his reasoning and statements were ineffectual, and that, instead of bringing the admiral to conviction, he was only wasting his own patience and inflaming the passions of his Lordship, he withdrew in disgust at the treatment which he had received, and which certainly was such as did no credit to the urbanity or the justice of those who affected to have no other rule of action than the sense of public duty.[1]

The behaviour of Nelson to Captain Foote, who was a subscribing party to this treaty, was marked by circumstances which were far from reflecting any honour on the judgment or the candour of this celebrated commander. That officer could not have acted otherwise than he

[1] The account of this transaction as given in the text is much exaggerated, and has but little foundation in fact. The dispute on board the *Foudroyant* lasted two hours, till Sir W. Hamilton, quite exhausted with acting as interpreter, sat down, and requested his wife to take his place. The change had no effect on the cardinal, who would agree to no proposals; when Nelson concluded the discussion by observing that as he found an admiral was no match for a cardinal in talking, he would try the effect of writing. He then delivered to Ruffo his written opinion that the capitulation ought not to be carried into execution without the sanction of the King of Naples and the English Commander-in-Chief in the Mediterranean, and the interview was at an end.

did, without incurring a severe responsibility,
and laying himself justly open to censure : for
it was not his place to interfere in such regula-
lations as the minister of the Sicilian monarch
thought best to adopt for his master's interest
on the shore of Naples ; and, therefore, in sign-
ing the treaty, he conducted himself strictly
within the line of his professional duty.

Contracts have always been accounted as so
very sacred, even among savage tribes, that,
when they have even proved disadvantageous
and impolitic on the one side, much inconvenience has been commonly endured for a time,
rather than that a specific agreement should be
violated. Many instances might be produced
where chicanery has been practised on the
ignorance and credulity of negotiators, and
others, where agents have exceeded their
powers ; and yet the states whom they represented have rather chosen to endure a considerable inconvenience than set a bad example, by
annulling a formal agreement, on the faith of
which so much dependence has been laid. In
the present case it should be considered, that the
persons who were in possession of these castles
had, on their part, put so much confidence in
the engagement of the allies, as to deprive
themselves of the chance of escape. Now if

these contracting parties to the pledge contained
in that agreement were without authority, they
must have deported themselves to the persons
composing those garrisons in a manner totally
unworthy of the commissions which they bore,
and of the characters which it was their duty to
sustain.   But Lord Nelson, by his abrogation,
directly charged these officers with having exceeded their powers, and promising what they
had no right to grant.   In doing this, it became
his Lordship to have made a strict investigation into the business, and to have shown the
authority by which he presumed to dispose of a
treaty at his own pleasure.   Instead of entering
upon the first, he announced his decree by a
signal, before he had made himself at all
acquainted with the terms of the agreement, the
grounds upon which it had been made, or the
nature of the sanction with which it was clothed.
How he was authorized to take this high office
upon himself, in setting aside an express agreement signed by four persons of competent rank,
has never yet appeared in any other way than
that of an unproved charge against the cardinal,
for having gone beyond the orders of his
sovereign.   But were this allowed, it would not
reach to a justification of the admiral, who had
no right to annul the treaty, merely because he

conceived it to be imprudent in itself, and an unwarrantable proceeding on the part of the Sicilian minister. Such a mode of interpreting the expediency and validity of contracts, would throw the whole code by which nations have hitherto consented to be guided into confusion ; and nothing could be relied upon, in the shape of a written agreement, where the sword should be suffered to determine the legality of the instrument. That it did actually do this, in the present case, cannot be denied ; and the consequences which immediately followed showed too plainly for what purpose the treaty had been set aside. Among other persons of distinction sheltered in one of these castles was the Prince Francisco Caraccioli, a nobleman, nearly seventy years old, who was highly beloved by the Neapolitans, as an excellent officer, having been long at the head of their marine service. This respectable man accompanied the royal family to Sicily ; but when the new republic was established, and an edict was issued, decreeing, that those who did not return within a limited time, should forfeit their estates, Caraccioli unfortunately hastened back to Naples, to preserve his patrimony. There he was soon solicited to take the command of the navy, and with this request he was induced to comply, most

probably from the fear of incurring the resentment of those who had everything at their disposal, and who could, of course, in a moment,
have deprived him of his property and his life.
Caraccioli certainly had many excuses to make
for his conduct ; and even if he had not, the
fact of his having served forty years with credit,
independent of his private virtues, ought to
have weighed as an atonement for the venial
transgression of a few days, during which no
outrage had been committed by his orders, and
when the king's cause could not have been
injured by his being at the head of the marine.
But when a wealthy man has rendered himself
obnoxious to a vicious and despotic government,
he will find that all his merits have no other
effect than that of sharpening the axe by which
his fate is to be determined. Caraccioli, perceiving that his destruction was determined
upon, and seeing that the English commander
had violated the only means by which his life
could have been saved, endeavoured to effect
his escape in disguise. The distribution of
money, however, among the peasantry, and the
offer of ample rewards for the apprehension of
the proscribed revolutionists, quickly brought
this venerable old man within the grasp of those
who thirsted for his blood. He was taken in

the disguise of a peasant, and hurried on board of Nelson's own ship ; which thus became, by a most unnatural act, a jail for the imprisonment of those who were neither subject to our laws, nor could be brought from their own shores to be confined there, without manifest injustice. Whatever might have been the crimes of Caraccioli, he ought not to have been received on board an English ship as a prisoner ; and the very act of doing it was an indelible stain upon our national character, which all the professional merit of the person who allowed it could not efface. But what followed this detestable business can never be palliated by casuistry, nor defaced by splendour. It must for ever stand as one of those spots, which, in the midst of all that is gaudy and dazzling, will obtrude themselves on the memory, to humble the pride of man, and teach him that the greatest of mortals are not those who astonish the world by their heroism, but those who enlighten it by their virtues.

Within an hour from the time that this poor old man was brought on board the *Foudroyant*, a court-martial of Sicilian officers, the president of which was his determined enemy, assembled in that ship by the orders of Lord Nelson, to try the subject of another state for treason.

That Caraccioli was found guilty by this junto,
who had no authority for what they did, was a
matter of course. The court was as complete a
mockery of justice as it was an outrage on
humanity. The wretched prisoner was tried,
but without having the means of defence; for
he had no time to prepare himself, either by
legal advice or the production of witnesses.
The King of Naples, who could alone grant a
commission for his trial, was at Palermo; but
Sir William and Lady Hamilton were on board
the *Foudroyant;* a circumstance that will
sufficiently account for the indecent hurry with
which the proceedings were hastened, and for
the catastrophe which ensued. It was in vain
that Caraccioli alleged, in his excuse, that he
had been compelled to enter into the republican
service, though, if he had proved it by the fullest
evidence, it would neither have operated in his
favour on the trial, nor stayed the execution,
which had been obviously predetermined with
as much certainty and justice as the decree of an
Eastern divan. Caraccioli was found guilty,
and received sentence of death; the report of
which being communicated to the British
admiral, he signed the warrant for its being
carried into effect the same evening, by hang-
ing the prisoner at the yard-arm, on board a

Sicilian frigate. The unhappy prisoner acted
with firmness, though the disgraceful manner
of his death gave him great uneasiness ; and
he solicited to be shot, saying to Lieutenant
Parkinson, who had the charge of him—" I am
an old man, Sir, I leave no family to lament me,
and therefore cannot be supposed to be very
anxious about prolonging my life : but the
disgrace of being hanged is dreadful to me."
The lieutenant, who felt as a man and an officer
on this occasion, went to Nelson with the
request of the prisoner ; but the only answer he
could obtain was to go and mind his duty.
Caraccioli then asked the lieutenant if he
thought that an application to Lady Hamilton
would not be likely to have some effect in
changing the sentence. The lieutenant, anxious
to oblige an unfortunate gentleman, for whom
he entertained a personal respect, went to seek
her Ladyship, who could not be found. This
woman, however, was in the cabin all the time ;
and she knew, as well as Nelson, the intent of
the application ; though she neither had the
civility to hear what the kind-hearted Parkinson
had to say, nor humanity enough to interpose
in favour of one to whom she and Sir William
owed many obligations. But though the
ambassador and his wife could not find it in

their hearts to speak a favourable word in the
behalf of an old acquaintance, they had sufficient
strength of mind to view the last horrible scene
of the tragedy, which was executed at five
o'clock the same evening, at the fore-yard-arm
of a Sicilian frigate, commanded by one of
Caraccioli's bitterest enemies. As if, however,
revenge could not be carried far enough, the
rites of sepulture were forbidden to the body,
which was thrown overboard in the bay of
Naples, when it might easily have been taken
on shore and interred with decency.[1]

---

[1] The account given in the text, of the case of Caraccioli,
is wrong in almost every particular. Far from being a
venerable old man, Caraccioli, at the time of his execution,
was scarcely fifty years old, and instead of " committing
no outrage " while commanding the republican navy,
his gunboats fired on the town of Annunciata, and on the
Sicilian frigate *Minerva*, which ship he had himself commanded in the service of Ferdinand. Captain Troubridge,
as well as Nelson, at first considered that Caraccioli was
forced to act as he did, against his own inclination, but
were compelled by conclusive facts to alter their opinion
of him. On the 1st of May Troubridge wrote to his commander: "Caraccioli, I am now satisfied is a Jacobin." Lord
Nelson had been invested with almost unlimited powers
by the King of Naples, and as Commander-in-chief of
the English and Sicilian ships, had full authority to order
Caraccioli for trial. The prisoner himself admitted this,
by petitioning the English Admiral to grant him another
trial. Count Thurn, the president of the court-martial,

This savage act, which would have disgraced the most barbarous horde in the inhospitable wilds of Africa, was followed by an incident that could not fail to make a deep impression on superstitious minds. Three weeks after the execution, when the king returned from Palermo, a Neapolitan, who had been fishing in the bay, came one morning to the *Foudroyant*, where he assured the officers that Caraccioli had risen from the bottom of the sea, and was coming as fast as he could to Naples, swimming half out of the water. The story of the fisherman, which at first gained little credit, was soon confirmed, for the same day Lord Nelson, indulging the king by standing out to sea, the ship had not proceeded far, before the officers of the watch beheld a body upright in the water, directing its course towards them. Captain Hardy soon discovered that this was actually the body of Caraccioli, notwithstanding

was the senior Sicilian officer present, and instead of being the "determined enemy" of the prisoner, was, according to Captain Brenton, "a man of unimpeachable integrity." The sentence on Caraccioli given at twelve noon, was that he should be hanged in two hours after, at two p.m. The warrant for the execution, issued by Lord Nelson, fixed the time at five in the evening, and neither Sir William nor Lady Hamilton were present as spectators.

the great weight which had been attached to it ; and it became extremely difficult to decide in what manner the extraordinary circumstance should be communicated to the king. This was performed with much address by Sir William Hamilton ; and with his Majesty's permission the body was taken on shore by a Neapolitan boat, and consigned to Christian burial. The coxswain of the boat brought back the two double-headed Neapolitan shot, with a portion of the skin still adhering to the rope by which they had been fixed. These were weighed, out of curiosity, by Captain Hardy, who ascertained that the body had risen and floated with the immense load of two hundred and fifty pounds attached to it.[1]

Another victim to a vengeful despotism was Dominico Cirillo, the king's physician, who had taken a part certainly in the late revolution, but whose age and talents ought to have operated in his favour. This venerable old man, however, was also executed, though it has been said that Lady Hamilton and the queen solicited his pardon on their knees : but they who can believe that these women acted such a part with sincerity, may with equal reason vindicate them

---

[1] Mr. Clarke's Life of Nelson, from the particular communication of Captain Hardy, vol. ii. p, 189.

for their virtue. Ferdinand could not have
resisted the application, either of the one or the
other ; and Lord Nelson, in his note of the
transaction, has admitted that the old man was
sacrificed because he refused to confess his
crime : but the British admiral has not gone
so far as to say that any measures were taken
by him and his friends on the side of mercy.
It is evident, indeed, that all their influence
went a different way, for his Lordship says :
" Eleonora Fonseca had been a great rebel ;
and Dominico Cirillo, who had been the king's
physician, might have been saved, but that he
chose to play the fool, and lie ; denying that he
had ever made speeches against the government,
and that he only took care of the poor in the
hospitals." [1]

Of the part which Lady Hamilton took in
these sanguinary proceedings, no doubt can be
formed by any one who knew her character and

---

[1] Cirillo wrote a pathetic letter to Lady Hamilton, en-
treating her good offices in his behalf, in which he said :
" Milady, you are a sensible and charitable lady, I know
your sentiments of humanity, therefore, you alone may do
everything in my favour. You are the intimate friend of
Lord Nelson, he justly esteems you, and *he has the power
from the King of Naples to dispose of everything.*" This is
conclusive as regards *the authority* exercised by the
admiral in the bay of Naples.

history, for she made no scruple, during her residence in Italy, to exult in the triumph which by her means had been gained over the enemies of the Queen of Naples. But when her Lady-ship returned to a country where these transactions could not fail to be investigated and exposed, she felt great alarm, and made use of every engine in her power to make it appear that she had borne no part in the persecution of the unhappy Neapolitans. Some hireling writers and publishers, who were entertained at her house, received from her papers and oral information for the purpose of elucidating the history of the revolutionary war, and they readily consented to defend the reputation of this female at the expense of truth, though the principles of these very men were at the same time of the most violent republican stamp.

Such was the power of Lord Nelson at this period ; and so predominant was the influence of Lady Hamilton over his mind, that the slightest intimation of their wishes in the cause of mercy must have prevailed : and, therefore, when we contemplate so many executions as took place after the restoration of the monarchy, it is impossible to acquit either her Ladyship or her friend of the charge of having countenanced the tragical scenes, which, by their mediation, might

have been prevented.[1]   It would be a mockery
of the feelings of human nature to allege, in
justification of this neglect, that such an interference with the course of justice at Naples was
inconsistent with the public duties of the British
ambassador and the noble admiral.   We have
seen, indeed, that these persons were not so
scrupulous in sentencing the subject of another
nation to death on board an English ship of
war ; and surely they who could take upon
them to try a foreigner for an offence committed
against his own sovereign, might have been as
laudably employed in endeavouring to render
the monarch popular, by advising him to exercise the highest prerogative of his crown, instead
of remaining silent, when the voice of policy,
no less than humanity, was calling for mercy.
But that divine attribute had no advocate in the
councils of Naples ; and, therefore, though it

[1] The good offices of Lady Hamilton were constantly
requested by prisoners awaiting trial, or under sentence,
to their advantage.   Lord Nelson, in a letter to Mrs.
Cadogan, said of her : " She (Lady H.) is perfectly well,
but has her time so much taken up with excuses from
rebels, Jacobins, and fools, that she is every day most
heartily tired. We are restoring happiness to the kingdom
of Naples, and doing good to millions."   According to
Captain Brenton, (with whom Lady Hamilton was no
favourite) : " Sir William and Lady Hamilton, and Lord
Nelson, saved many."

should be granted that our countrywoman, who
then figured with such splendour at that court,
had no direct concern in promoting the work of
vengeance, which plunged thousands of families
in misery and lamentation, we cannot give her
the credit of having in a single instance dried
up the tears of the afflicted.   No widow experienced her consoling pity — no sorrowful
mother had to thank her for exerting the
influence which she possessed in behalf of a mis-
guided son, whose only guilt was that of having
been carried away by a delusion, which had at
least much in it to deceive the wise as well as
the ignorant, and to impose upon the virtuous,
while it became an instrument of wrong in the
management of the wicked.   It is, therefore,
surprising, that an able writer, who has bestowed
great attention on these events, of which he has
given a very luminous account, should have
thought proper to call in question the part that
was evidently borne by Lady Hamilton in the
cruelties of the Sicilian government ; but while
it is admitted that the wife of our ambassador
had great power with the heads of that state,
and that she feasted her eyes on a spectacle from
which any other woman would have turned with
horror, it is said by way of apology for her
character :—

"Of her being present at the execution of Caraccioli, there cannot be the least doubt, but it is to be hoped, for the honour of her sex, and of her country, that she never directly, or indirectly, encouraged that vindictive spirit which too much pervaded the councils of the king, and the administration of the Neapolitan state junto, after his Majesty had returned to Palermo.

"Emma Lady Hamilton, one of the most extraordinary women of the age, amidst all her faults, was more noted for her general attention and hospitality, than for any deliberate acts of cruelty towards the Neapolitans, by whom she was in general adored. In the voluptuous court of the Sicilian monarch, her fascinating person commanded a very powerful influence; but in a situation of so much delicacy and danger, she never forgot the character that was expected from the wife of an English ambassador, nor was deficient in any of those courtesies and friendly attentions which mark a liberal and humane disposition. From the arrival of the British squadron at Naples, she had exerted herself to support that good cause, for which Admiral Nelson had been detached: and having in this respect rendered some service, the natural vanity of her mind led her to imagine, and to endeavour to make the noble admiral and others believe, that from her alone proceeded the means of performing those great events which threw such a splendour on the favourite object of her idolatry. Her leading passion was the love of celebrity ; and it was this passion, added to the above delusion, which gradually brought on that fatal and highly wrought attachment which she formed for the hero of Aboukir ; for it was the hero, and not the individual, which had captivated her glowing imagination. Its ardour, as it increased, overpowered the natural kindness of her disposition, and eventually involved her in an endless succession of private altercation and public disappointment." [1]

[1] Mr. Clarke's Life of Lord Nelson, vol. ii. p. 188.

CHAPTER XI.

Beauty, though injurious, hath strange
power.   MILTON.

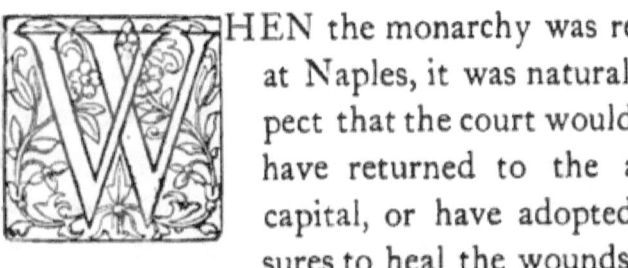

HEN the monarchy was restored
at Naples, it was natural to expect that the court would either
have returned to the ancient
capital, or have adopted measures to heal the wounds which
had been inflicted, by correcting the evils under
which the people groaned. But nothing of
the kind took place, and Ferdinand, instead of
softening the horrors produced by civil war,
and of acting like a magnanimous prince, who
wishes to appear as the father of his family,
hastened back, with the British admiral and the
ambassador, to Palermo, there to enjoy his
sports and follies ; while the persecuted Neapolitans were hunted down by hired blood-
hounds, and hurried to the prison and the

scaffold, without the least compunction or sentiment of pity.   The only security any man had
in that state, from the vengeance of the trium-
phant party, was in his poverty ; but, while he
thus found protection in his misery against the
eagerness of spies and informers, he was, on
the other hand, exposed to the certainty of
perishing by famine, which now began to stare
with a ghastly aspect on the wretched inhabitants
of this beautiful city.

There is a peculiar kind of cruelty in vicious
and effeminate minds, by which, though they
do not imbrue their own hands in blood, they
avoid interposing any good offices to repress the
vindictive spirit of others; and this want of
virtuous feeling for the sufferings of their fellow-
creatures leads them to shun the places where
they would be called to exercise the duty of
humanity.   These persons content themselves
with that negative virtue which consists in
being silent when great oppressions are committed, and in withdrawing from scenes of
horror, which, though their influence could not
have altogether prevented, their presence might
have served to render less painful and disgusting.
They who abandoned the Neapolitans to the
fury of assassins, the rapacity of informers, and
the merciless resentment of an unprincipled

government, probably thought that they were acting with a strict regard to justice, and according to the dictates of sound policy. This frigid indifference to the calamities of mankind would have been, under any circumstances, disgraceful to those who knew the value of a free constitution, and had the experience, in their own country, of equal laws ; but, in the present instance, it was accompanied by a wanton levity, which proved that the distresses of Naples, and the violence of its oppressors, gave little uneasiness to our ambassador and his friends. Lord Nelson, on his return to Sicily, accepted a ducal title,[1] with an estate, from Ferdinand ; yet it has been said that the admiral did not consent to the proposal till it had been urged by Lady Hamilton on her knees. Whether this story rests on a legitimate foundation, can hardly be determined ; since the only authority which it ever had, was the testimony of the person who is said to have exerted herself in so uncommon a manner to aid the grateful intentions of his Sicilian Majesty. Had Nelson been less vain and solicitous of titles than he was the reverse,

---

[1] The Sicilian Dukedom of Brontë, with an estate, worth about £3,000 per annum. The first act of Nelson, after accepting this reward, was to charge the estate with an annuity of £500 for life to his father.

such a tale might have passed without any observation on its improbability; but it certainly becomes doubtful, when it is known that he ever attached an extraordinary value to this distinction, which, when coupled with the character of the personage who conferred it. and the class of nobility with whom it associated our countryman, was far from being an object of congratulation. It would indeed have been creditable to Nelson had he declined this honour; and, resting satisfied with the unpolluted favours of his own sovereign, preserved the independence of his character. By enrolling his name among the nobles of Sicily, and accepting an estate in that island, for having replaced Ferdinand on the throne, this great man tacitly sanctioned the acts of that monarch, and the cruelty which he displayed towards his unhappy subjects. Painful as it is to make these reflections, they are powerfully suggested by the transaction which we have been obliged to record; and the glory of Nelson would unquestionably have shone with greater lustre, if he had resisted with firmness the prostituted titles of an infamous court, at a time when the hand that held out the gift was stained with blood.

On the arrival of the *Foudroyant* at Palermo, the queen came on board, where she embraced

Lady Hamilton, and the same moment hung round her neck a chain of gold, to which was suspended a portrait of her Majesty, superbly set with diamonds, and having, this motto on the back, "Eterna Gratitudini!"

Five days afterwards, while her Ladyship was at the palace with the queen, two coach-loads of costly dresses were secretly sent to the house of the ambassador, with a picture of the king richly set in jewels, worth a thousand guineas, for her Ladyship; and another of her Majesty, of the same value, for Sir William Hamilton. The whole of the presents made by their Sicilian majesties on this occasion amounted in value to six thousand guineas.

On the 3rd of September, an idle piece of mummery was exhibited in the royal gardens at Palermo, to celebrate the recovery of Naples by the exertions of Lord Nelson.

To transcribe the ridiculous account of this childish puppet-show, as given by Lady Hamilton in the life of Nelson published under her authority, would be insulting to the judgment of the reader, since it is impossible that any Englishman could be pleased with the description of the Temple of Fame, erected on that occasion, and of the three wax figures, representing Nelson, the ambassador, and his wife; the latter being, very appropriately, no doubt, in the character of Victory, having on her robe the names of all the heroes who were distinguished at the battle of the Nile. At this silly fête, the queen is said to have expressed herself thus to the Turkish admiral, who was present : "On this day last year we received from Lady Hamilton intelligence of this great man's victory, which not only saved your country and ours, but all Europe ! "

Such was the farce with which their Sicilian majesties thought to obliterate the impression made by the tragedy of Caraccioli, and of the numerous other victims of their revenge at Naples.

In returning to Palermo, the noble admiral committed an error which tarnished his professional reputation as much as it affected his private character. His presence was certainly not necessary at that place, but it was unquestionably wanted in other parts of the Mediterranean. Commodore Troubridge, who had the greatest personal regard for Nelson, was deeply chagrined at being left to conduct the operations on that coast; while his friend was indulging himself in a round of frivolous amusements, and yielding to the dalliance of female allurements. It was impossible that such proceedings could pass without observation ; and they did, in fact, occasion much animadversion both at home and abroad. The Sicilians looked upon the admiral with contempt, and bestowed upon him an opprobrious epithet, characteristic of the influence which Lady Hamilton had gained over the hero : and, so undisguised was this attachment, that many persons of high rank and integrity took the freedom of remonstrating with his Lordship upon the impropriety of his conduct. One naval friend in England expressed his sentiments in this remarkable language : " They say here, my good Lord, that you are Rinaldo, in the arms of Armida ; and that it requires the firmness of an Ubaldo and his brother knight to draw you from the enchantress." This allusion was pointed enough, but the reprehension administered by his friend Troubridge was much more severe : " Pardon me, my Lord," said that honest seaman : " it is my sincere esteem for you that makes me mention it. I know you can have no pleasure sitting up all night at cards : why then sacrifice your health, comfort, purse, ease, everything, to the customs of a country where your stay cannot be long ? Your Lordship is a stranger to half that happens, or the talk it occasions : if you knew what your friends feel for you, I am sure you would cut all the nocturnal parties. The gambling of the people of Palermo is publicly talked of everywhere. I beseech your Lordship leave off. I really feel for the country."

At another time the same valuable officer wrote to the admiral from Naples : and his letter is too descriptive of the two capitals to be omitted in this place.

" I dread, my Lord," said Troubridge, " all the feasting at Palermo. I am sure your health will be hurt. If so, all their saints will be damned by the navy. The king would be better employed digesting a good government. Everything gives way to their pleasures. The money spent at Palermo gives discontent here : fifty thousand people are unemployed ; trade discouraged ; manufactures at a stand. It is the interest of many here to keep the king away ;—they all dread reform ;—their villainies are so deeply rooted, that if some method is not taken to dig them out, this government cannot hold together."

The deplorable condition of Naples at this time, owing to the brutal ferocity of the dominant party, is thus strongly portrayed by the same intelligent observer : " There are upwards of forty thousand families who have relations confined. If some act of oblivion is not passed, there will be no end of persecution; for the people of this country have no idea of anything but revenge; and, to gain a point, would swear ten thousand false oaths. Constant efforts are made to get a man taken up, in order to rob him."

It is to be lamented, however, that these re-monstrances had little effect on the mind of the person to whom they were addressed; and the festivities of Palermo seem, in truth, to have completely overpowered his moral faculties. Of this an extraordinary instance occurred, with respect to two rich Spanish vessels, laden with quicksilver, lying in the harbour of Palermo, when these gaieties where going on there. The value of these ships was duly appreciated; and, at a dinner given by the British envoy, a con-sultation was actually held about the best means of getting possession of them. After various measures were proposed, it was agreed to ask Ferdinand's permission for the boats of the fleet to cut the Spaniards out of the harbour. This arrogant request was accordingly made by Lady Hamilton, in an entire confidence that his Majesty could not refuse so equitable a demand to those who had recovered for him the throne of Naples. But, weak as the king was, he had

not altogether lost his spirit nor his understanding ; so that, turning indignantly from the
dishonourable proposal, he asked " whether they
took him for the Dey of Algiers, by asking him
to allow an act towards a friendly power which
the most barbarous of the African states would
reject with abhorrence."

The persons who could thus solicit Ferdinand
to violate, in their favour, the rights of hospitality and the laws of nations, manifested their
tenderness, about the same period, towards the
suffering people of Malta, who were actually
reduced to the most miserable condition for the
want of food, when the island of Sicily could
have furnished them with abundance. Commodore Troubridge, in a letter to Nelson, dated
New Year's Day, 1800, gives an affecting picture
of the state of Malta, with no very honourable
mention of the gentle feelings of the British
ambassador : " My Lord," says Troubridge,
" we are dying off fast for want. I learn, by
letters from Messina, that Sir William Hamilton
says, Prince Luzzi refused corn some time ago ;
and Sir William does not think it worth while
making another application. If that be the case,
I wish he commanded at this distressing scene
instead of me. Puglia had an immense harvest.
Near thirty sail left Messina before I did, to

load corn : will they let us have any ? If not,
a short time will decide the business. The
German interest prevails. I wish I was at your
Lordship's elbow for an hour : all, all will be
thrown on you, rely on it. I will parry the
blow as much as is in my power: I foresee much
mischief brewing. God bless your Lordship—
I am miserable. I cannot assist your operations
more. Many happy returns of this day to you :
I never spent so miserable an one. I am not
very tender-hearted ; but really the distress here
would move even a Neapolitan." While thousands were starving for want at Malta and
Naples, there was nothing but riotous waste at
Palermo, with continual shows and successive
entertainments on board the English ships in the
harbour.[1] Sometimes the fleet made short trips
to sea; not to look after the enemy, but to
gratify the king and Lady Hamilton ; particularly
the last, who appeared in the admiral's barge
like Cleopatra ; and, in point of extravagance,
she certainly did not fall short of that voluptuous and accomplished woman. One of these
disgraceful scenes is thus described by an eye-
witness : The ships were all decorated with

---

[1] Through the influence of Lady Hamilton, three ships
laden with corn, and £7,000 were sent to the relief of the
Maltese, by the Queen of Naples.

flags, firing salutes, and manning the yards, as
the royal party sailed along, followed by above
one thousand boats, in many of which were
bands of music playing, Nelson and Lady
Hamilton leading the van, in a twelve-oared
barge.   The king, in one of eight oars, was not
paid much attention to : but he amused himself
with the princely sport of shooting sea-gulls.
The whole party visited the *Minotaur* commanded by Sir Thomas Louis, where they partook of a cold collation, and returned in proces-
sion to the *Foudroyant* ; on reaching which ship,
royal salutes again were fired.   The dinner on
board was served on tables reaching the whole
length of two decks ; the cannon being even
removed to make way for fruit and chocolate
tables on each side.   This degrading spectacle, so
unbecoming a British ship of war, affected Lord
Nelson very seriously, and he could not help
showing his feelings, though unfortunately his
resentment was soon dispelled by that charm
which then bound him in spite of his understanding.   He left the dinner party very early ;
and, taking a turn or two upon the quarter-deck
with one of his officers, appeared, for a little
while, extremely agitated ; and, at last, as he
looked at the strange scene before him, he mut-
tered, " Curse upon such doings ! I wish there

was an end of them. My ship looks for all the
world like a pastry-cook's shop !" When Lady
Hamilton perceived his thoughtful manner, she
arose immediately from the table, and, hastening
to the hero, conducted him lovingly back to the
company ; where, by her arts, he soon appeared
to have lost his uneasiness. When the evening
came on, the ships were illuminated, and salutes
were fired at the drinking of every toast, which
were repeated from the forts on shore.

Another remarkable instance of the folly into
which great men can fall, when they suffer
themselves to be led away from the path of
duty by the allurements of pleasure, happened
shortly after the expensive entertainment which
has just been described. One of Nelson's
favourite amusements was to go about the
streets in disguise, accompanied by Lady Hamilton, who could adopt any character, and perform
it to great advantage.[1] Having taken a cheerful glass on a fine evening, he proposed to his
dulcinea to take a ramble about the city, which
was acceded to, and they accordingly sallied
forth, laughing at all they met, but without

[1] According to Mitford, who apparently was an eye-wit-
ness, "Lady Hamilton at Palermo frequently accompanied Nelson in nocturnal rambles, dressed in sailor's
clothes."

being known until they entered a house of entertainment, where a party of English officers were enjoying themselves with their ladies. Here our hero and his friend indulged in the humours of the place, thinking that they were undiscovered ; but it chanced that the boatswain of the *Foudroyant* looked into the room with a midshipman, and recognized the admiral. The boatswain, being a man of pleasant manners and address, contrived to watch his Lordship and his companion from place to place, till they reached the ambassador's house, after which, the two shipmates, out of a frolic, went to court, which was very easy of access to British officers. There the boatswain attracted the notice of the king, who entered into conversation with him, which ended by conferring on the man one of the honours of knighthood. This afterwards became known to Lady Hamilton, who followed the unfortunate chevalier with inexorable vengeance, and the admiral, at her instigation, turned the boatswain, notwithstanding his new dignity, before the mast ; but the midshipman escaped with a reprimand for having been a party in a frolic, which, to say the most of it, was far from deserving censure, and least of all from those who were guilty of exhibiting in their own conduct an unpardonable degree of levity and indiscretion.

A volume would not suffice to narrate the disgusting circumstances which occurred at Palermo ; but though the dissipation daily witnessed there gave just offence to every man who felt for the honour of his country, and the sufferings of those who were injured by these proceedings, there was still more to be deprecated in them than the mere waste of time and money with which they were attended. The service itself was materially affected by the influence of Lady Hamilton, who had so much command over her admirer, as to interest herself in the promotion of some persons who did little honour to the recommendation.

It is also a fact, that vessels were purchased for the use of the fleet, which proved of no other utility than that of increasing this woman's patronage. Such proceedings could not escape public observation, and to have permitted the continuance of them would have been a criminal negligence on the part of the administration. The obvious mode of remedying the evil without animadverting on the conduct of the admiral, was that of recalling the ambassador, a measure which ought to have been adopted long before, in which case probably many evils would have been prevented, and the glory of our great hero would have remained unsullied. Mr.

Arthur Paget was appointed to supersede Sir
William Hamilton, very much to the disquietude
of his lady, and the mortification of Lord Nelson,
who saw in the proceeding a marked disapprobation of the line of conduct which he and his
friends had pursued on this station. But instead
of considering the matter in the only proper
light, as an act of imperious necessity at an
eventful period, when every sacrifice for the
public good became indispensable on the part of
individuals, no less than of government, his
Lordship immediately came to the resolution of
giving up his employment, and of returning to
England with his friends ; and such was their
patriotism, that they gladly encouraged him in
this design.

Lady Hamilton, however, had some consola-
tion in the midst of this disgrace, by receiving
from that strange monarch, the Emperor Paul,
the cross of the order of Malta, being the first
Englishwoman on whom that distinction was
ever bestowed, and the last perhaps that ever
would have desired it. Leave was solicited of
our court to confirm the honour by a special
grant to wear it ; but though much was done
for this purpose, the application was treated
with dignified silence.

Another remarkable instance of royal favour

with which this extraordinary woman was distinguished, cannot be passed over; though it was one that did little credit to her sensibility or that of her husband. The King of Naples requested that her Ladyship would consent to suffer a model of her to be taken in a perfect state of nature, as large as life; and this was actually done to gratify the taste of the monarch and the vanity of the lady, whose marble figure adorned the royal apartments with all the elegance of Venus.

But these honours could not allay the disquietude which was occasioned by the mandate of recall, a circumstance that gave all the parties concerned in it so much uneasiness as to lead them to commit an act of the most unkind and indecorous nature against an individual who had done them no wrong. When Mr. Paget arrived in Sicily, Sir William Hamilton, instead of paying him proper attention, and entering upon such explanations as were requisite for his particular guidance, and the benefit of the nation, hastened with his wife on board the *Foudroyant*, and sailed for Malta. Soon after their return to Palermo, the whole party, accompanied by the queen, with three of the princesses, and Prince Leopold, embarked for Leghorn, where they landed on the 16th of June, 1800.

Here her Sicilian Majesty presented to the admiral a picture of the king set in diamonds and emeralds ; while to Sir William Hamilton she gave a snuff-box of gold, with the pictures of the king and queen on the lid, set round with diamonds ; and his lady received, at the same time, a superb diamond necklace, with the cypher of the names of all the royal children.

After remaining about a month at Leghorn, an alarm was spread that the French were advancing, on which the populace arose, armed themselves from the arsenal, and demanded that Lord Nelson should lead them against the enemy. Here, as we are told, the eloquence of Lady Hamilton succeeded in prevailing upon the whole of the infuriated mob to return their arms to the place from whence they had been taken. Notwithstanding this extraordinary gallantry in the people of Leghorn, their royal and noble visitors thought it most prudent to set off early the next morning for Florence, where they remained two days, and received the most respectful attentions. After continuing at Ancona about a fortnight, they embarked in two Russian frigates for Trieste, from whence the queen immediately proceeded for Vienna, followed by Lord Nelson, and Sir William and Lady Hamilton. In this capital they remained

six weeks, partly on account of the weakness to
which the travelling had reduced Sir William,
and partly out of compliance with the urgent
entreaties of the Queen of Naples, who, as the
mother of the Empress, wished to do all the
honours that lay in her power to the companions
of her journey.

Among others who were eager to entertain
the English visitors, the Prince and Princess of
Esterhazy distinguished themselves greatly by
their hospitality, as well out of respect to
Nelson, as in return for the civilities which they
had experienced at Naples from our ambassador.
The strangers were received with uncommon
marks of distinction at the palace of Eisenstadt,
belonging to the prince; and during a stay
there of four days, a hundred grenadiers, each
six feet in height, constantly waited at table,
where every delicacy was served up in profusion.
A grand concert was also given in the chapel,
under the direction of Haydn, whose oratorio
of the Creation was performed in honour of
the guests.

It is said that the Queen of Naples was very
solicitous that Lady Hamilton should return
with her to Italy; and that when she could not
prevail, her Majesty made an offer of settling
upon her Ladyship an income of one thousand

pounds a-year, which was refused by Sir William
and his wife, on the ground that the acceptance
would subject them to suspicions at home.
This story is much of a piece with some others
which we have been obliged to notice; and
though the relation of it was designed to display
the disinterested character and delicate sentiments of the parties, who are represented acting
in a manner so very unlike themselves; yet
when it is known that Lady Hamilton
afterwards made applications to the queen for
pecuniary aid, without receiving even an
answer to the request, some doubts may reason-
ably be entertained of the truth of the narrative.
From Vienna the travellers proceeded by invitation to see the Archduke Charles, who was then
at Prague, and after a splendid reception there,
they departed for Dresden, where they took
water,[1] and thus pursued the remainder of their

---

[1] Mrs. Trench, who at this time was residing at
Dresden, and intimate with Mr. Elliot, the British
Minister there; has recorded in her diary the impressions
made on her by Sir W. and Lady Hamilton, Lord Nelson,
and their fellow-voyagers, Mrs. Cadogan, and Miss Knight.
She evidently regarded all of them as very odd and
eccentric persons, and her account of the departure of the
party from Dresden on October 10th, is very diverting.
"The moment they were on board, there was an end of
the fine arts, of the attitudes, of the acting, the dancing,

journey to Hamburg; at which city the hero
of the Nile was welcomed with universal
acclamations; and some very singular anecdotes
have been related of the enthusiastic veneration
in which he was held by the people of Germany.
One of these is too remarkable to be omitted in
this place, though some particulars in it have
the appearance of being apocryphal. A wine
merchant of Hamburg, who was above seventy
years of age, one day requested to speak with
Lady Hamilton, and informed her that he had
some excellent old Rhenish wine, of the vintage
of 1625, of course one hundred and seventy-
five years old, which, as he said, had been in his
own possession above half a century. This, he
observed, had been preserved for some very
extraordinary occasion; and one had now arrived
far beyond any that he could have expected.
The old gentleman, therefore, who had been so
careful of his wine for an indefinite time and

and the singing. Lady Hamilton's maid began to scold
in French about some provisions which had been forgot,
in language quite impossible to repeat, using certain
French words which were never spoken but by men of
the lowest class, and roaring them out from one boat to
another. Lady Hamilton began bawling for an Irish
stew, and her old mother set about washing the potatoes,
which she did as cleverly as possible. They were exactly
like Hogarth's actresses dressing in a barn."

purpose, requested her Ladyship to exert her good offices to prevail on Lord Nelson to accept of six dozen bottles, that, as he said, " part of this extraordinary liquor might have the honour of flowing with the heart's blood of the immortal hero, a reflection which could not fail to render the donor the most fortunate man in existence during the remainder of his days." His Lordship being informed of this curious application, came into the room, and took the old gentleman very kindly by the hand, though at the same time he declined the present. He was, however, prevailed upon at last to accept of six bottles, on condition that the merchant should dine with him the next day. This was cheerfully acceded to, and a dozen bottles were sent; on which the admiral remarked, that as he yet hoped to have six more victories, he would keep that number of his friend's wine on purpose that he might drink a bottle after each. This his Lordship did not fail to remember on coming home after the battle of Copenhagen; when he devotedly drank the health of the old wine merchant.

On the arrival of the party at Hamburg, Lord Nelson wrote home for a frigate to accommodate himself and his friends; but this not being granted as promptly as it had been expected, a packet was hired at Cuxhaven, which, after a rough passage of five days, entered Yarmouth on the 6th of November. Three days afterwards, his Lordship, accompanied by Sir William and Lady Hamilton, reached London, but instead of separating, as they ought to have done for a little while, out of respect to private feeling and public decorum, all three proceeded to take up their residence at the same hotel, where Lady Nelson and the venerable father of the admiral already occupied apartments. It is impossible to account for so flagrant an indecorum on any other ground than an absolute intention of giving offence to the sensibility of a wife, knowing, as Lady Hamilton did, that the notoriety of her connection with Lord Nelson had been long and loudly talked of, not only in Italy, but in England. She had, indeed, received many communications on the subject from some of her correspondents, and particularly from her old protector, Mr. Greville, who apprised her of the rumours which were in circulation to her disadvantage. Any woman, therefore, who had the smallest regard for her own character, or respect for the feelings of a wife and a father, would have avoided the slightest occasion of giving them uneasiness, at the very first interview between them and their

gallant relative.[1]   But, as if Lady Hamilton
had lost all idea of propriety in the climate
where she so long danced the circle of pleasure,
the sober customs of England were treated by
her with utter contempt ; and she evinced also
such a total insensibility to the mental wounds
which her presence inflicted, as showed but too
clearly a determinate plan to effect that fatal
breach, which shortly afterwards she was
enabled to accomplish.

[1] On the arrival of Lord Nelson and his fellow-
travellers in London, November 9, 1800, the party
separated ; Sir William and Lady Hamilton going to Mr.
Beckford's house in Grosvenor Square, which had been
placed at their service, and Nelson to his wife and
father, at Nerot's Hotel, King Street, St. James's.

CHAPTER XII.

Bright characters lose much of their
splendour at a nearer view; and many,
who fill the world with their fame,
excite very little reverence amongst
those that surround them in their
domestic privacies.

JOHNSON.

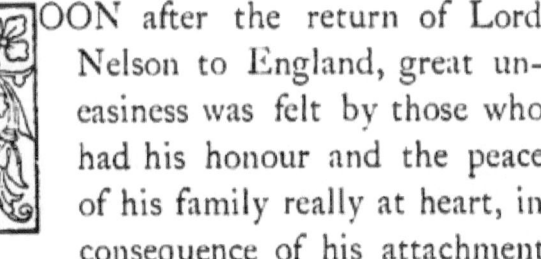

OON after the return of Lord
Nelson to England, great uneasiness was felt by those who
had his honour and the peace
of his family really at heart, in
consequence of his attachment
to Lady Hamilton, and her treatment of his meek
and accomplished partner. An instance of this
occurred within a fortnight; and it was of so disgusting a nature, that if the relation were not
calculated to throw a light on the characters, the
scene should be buried in oblivion. A house
having been taken for his Lordship in Dover

Street,[1] he had of course many visitors of distinction, among whom, one day, was a lady of
very high rank, who paid him and Lady Nelson
much polite attention, but without deigning to
notice Lady Hamilton, though the admiral endeavoured to bring the latter forward as his
particular friend. This circumstance was not
likely to pass unobserved, and when the duchess
retired, much contemptuous language ensued on
the subject of her behaviour, in which abuse
Lady Nelson did not concur, but preserved an
absolute silence ; for which she drew upon herself some very opprobrious epithets from her
husband. That day the company at dinner
happened to be numerous, and during the entertainment, Lady Hamilton conducted herself with
a marked malignity towards Lady Nelson, in
which the admiral was weak enough to participate. At length the cunning woman, whether
from real illness, repletion, or vexation, withdrew to her own room ; and when Nelson
perceived that she remained absent longer than
common, he harshly demanded of his wife
where Lady Hamilton was, and who was with
her. Lady Nelson mildly replied, "that her
own woman had been sent to attend her Ladyship ;" on which his Lordship flew into a

[1] Arlington Street.

violent passion, and insisted that she should
instantly go and wait upon Lady Hamilton
herself. Without resenting this rudeness and
want of feeling, Lady Nelson arose from table,
and went as she was directed ; but soon afterwards the impatient hero hastened also to the
apartment, where he found one lady very sick,
and the other holding the basin for her accommo-
dation. Instead of being affected, as he ought
to have been, by this act of condescension, his
Lordship became more furious, and directly
charged his gentle partner with being the cause
of the distressing state in which he found his
favourite. On being asked the reason for this
accusation, he inveighed bitterly against his wife,
as having injured the virtuous sufferer, by
calumniating aspersions and jealous insinuations ;
on which, Lady Nelson instantly applied to
Lady Hamilton, and asked " whether there was
anything in the treatment which she had received since her arrival in England that could
justify what she then heard ? " This appeal was
so powerful, as to have for the moment the
effect of eliciting a frank confession that there
was no ground for what had been so harshly
alleged : on which, the astonished Nelson,
turning to the speaker, exclaimed : " that her
soul was as black as hell ; for that she had con-

tinually been poisoning his mind with stories
of Lady Nelson's jealousy and illiberality."
Roused at this keen reproach, the sick lady
started up, and swinging poor Lady Nelson by
the arm round the room, she tauntingly said :
" There, madam, only serve him as I have done
you, and he will know better how to behave
himself." [1] It might have been expected, that
after this discovery of the treachery of the
woman who had allured him by her wiles, Lord
Nelson would have broken the fatal chain in
which he was held. This, however, he wanted
resolution to perform ; and, on the contrary, he
became more enchanted than ever ; which is
accounted for by the fact that the fair companion of his cruises and his travels was now
in a state which indicated the appearance of an
evidence that their friendship had been somewhat more than platonic. The prospect of this
living witness excited no other uneasiness in the
parties than that which arose from the sense of
their being unable to give a legitimate name to
the fruits of their intercourse. Though they
were both married, Lady Hamilton had reason
to think from the age of her husband that the day
of her emancipation could not be far distant :
but the case was otherwise on the opposite side.

---

[1] This story must be taken *cum grano salis.*

where little chance appeared of a dissolution by the death of the wife, and none at all of a separation being effected by her indiscretion. To this may be ascribed the rancorous hatred which Lady Hamilton conceived against the woman whom she had so cruelly injured, by alienating from her the affections and civilities of her husband. In Italy the impediment to her ambition might have been removed without much difficulty ; but in England, the only thing that could be done, was to widen the breach, and to triumph in the wrong. Sir William Hamilton being far advanced in years, was easily imposed upon by fictitious ailments, which were devised as the occasion of frequent sickness, and other symptoms that required seclusion. He and his lady were now settled in a house in Piccadilly,[1] overlooking the Green Park : and here Lord Nelson was much oftener to be found than at his own home, of which a curious testimony has been kindly imparted to the editor by the professional gentleman who was employed in preparing the lease of the premises. " At the time," says he, " when I went over the house with the upholsterer and a servant, who showed us the rooms for the purpose of taking

---

[1] No. 23, Piccadilly, to which the Hamiltons removed from Grosvenor Square.

a schedule of the fixtures, I observed an emaciated weather-beaten person, rather shabbily dressed, follow us from room to room with seeming anxiety. At length he said, ' Pray, gentlemen, what is it you are about ? ' I answered, ' We are taking a list of the fixtures in the house, to annex by way of schedule to the lease.' ' Oh, oh,' he replied, ' if that be the case, I think you should include me in the list.' He then seemed satisfied and left us. After his departure I inquired of the servant who this person was, when, to my great surprise, he told me it was Lord Nelson. I had looked but cursorily at him, and from the old crumpled hat he wore, and the striped old brown great coat thrown over his shoulders, and his general appearance, I took him for some foreign refugee and hanger-on of Sir William's, as he had much the appearance of the French priests with whom the streets at that time were crowded. I tried afterwards, and made excuses, to go into several rooms to correct the list, in order to get another look at the veteran, but without effect."

The great object which his Lordship had now in contemplation was a separation from his wife, and to become a fixed resident in the same house with the woman who had contrived to seduce him from the paths of peace. This last business

required some little management, and the way
in which it was effected did no more credit to
the ingenuity of the contrivers, than the motives
by which they were actuated did honour to
their morality. It was represented to Sir
William Hamilton, that his noble friend was
actually driven from his domestic comforts by a
series of persecutions and reproaches, which had
completely destroyed his tranquillity. These
complaints were heightened from day to day,
sometimes by his Lordship, and at others by the
artful Emma, who had cunning enough to excite
the resentment of her husband against Lady
Nelson, by the reports of insults that were
never offered, and of calumnies which were
never uttered. At length his Lordship surprised his old friend one day with the declaration
that he had no longer a house to put his head in,
as he chose to express himself ; on which Sir
William, turning to Emma, exclaimed : " Do
you hear what Lord Nelson says ? Our house
is large enough : shall we give him the use of
it ? " As this was what her Ladyship expected,
she at once signified her assent ; but the hero
observed, that such a proceeding would in all
probability make the world talk, and therefore
must be avoided. " A fig for the world,"
replied the knight. " I have lived too long to

mind what the world either thinks or says on
such matters ; so you have no more to do than
to plant yourself here without further scruple
or delay." [1] Such was the friendship of Sir
William, and in this magnanimous contempt of
public opinion he was supported by his lady,
who certainly through life never manifested
much respect for those sentiments which have
usually been considered as the rule of good
manners.

Nothing could be more ridiculous than to
describe the admission of Lord Nelson into the
family of Sir William Hamilton as an act of
charity, and yet so it has been represented by
some impudent panegyrists of the insidious betrayer of an aged husband's honour, and the
destroyer of a virtuous woman's happiness. If
Lord Nelson had really any cause for dissatis-
faction in his own habitation, he was far from
being under the necessity of seeking an asylum
elsewhere ; but least of all should he have accepted the invitation of the man, with whose
wife he was more than suspected of carrying on
a scandalous intercourse. The parties were all

[1] Lord Nelson did not make the house of the
Hamiltons his home when in London, till after the birth
of his daughter Horatia, and his return from the Baltic in
1801.

acquainted with what people said, both in England and everywhere else ; this outrage, therefore, upon public decency, the utter disregard of private feeling, afforded too plain a testimony of their want of sensibility, who were so far from being careful to avoid giving offence, that they were not even guided by common prudence in preserving appearances. The father of Lord Nelson, then on the verge of eighty, still continued his kind attentions to his daughter-in-law, with whose virtues he had been so long acquainted, and in whose sorrows he could not fail to participate. Uncommon exertions indeed were made by his Lordship, and those who courted his favours by flattering his follies, to remove the ill impressions which this connection had produced on the mind of the good old man. But though he bore his faculties meekly, and at length ceased to complain, because he saw that it would be useless, nothing can be farther from the truth than the assertion that he was rendered easy by the arts which were used to lull his suspicions. Other branches of the family, indeed, took little pains to satisfy themselves on the subject, and the consciences of some were made of such flexible stuff, that the strange fact of Lord Nelson's living under the roof of a man, whose honour was not much respected by the circumstance, was so far from giving them any concern, that they quickly transferred to the lady of the mansion those attentions which they had been accustomed to pay to their own amiable, but now insulted and deserted, relative.

It has been falsely said that this excellent woman was totally indifferent to her husband's glory, and yet that the rank to which she had been elevated produced such an effect upon her mind, as to prove extremely mortifying to the rest of the family ; both which accusations could not be true ; for if she was so proud of her title, as she is stated to have been, she must also have felt some satisfaction at the means by which it had been acquired. But, in reality, no woman ever deported herself with more humility, in all the changes which she passed through, from the time when she refused the most advantageous offers for the sake of Nelson, and placed her property at his disposal, to the period when by a cool, and still more cruel act, he succeeded in prevailing upon her to sign a deed of separation.[1]

---

[1] There was no formal deed of separation. On the arrival of Lord Nelson and his friends in London, Lady Nelson soon saw with her own eyes more than enough to confirm all the rumours that had reached her of the attachment of her husband to Lady Hamilton. One evening,

Let it, however, be remembered, when all the
aspersions of sycophants and liars are consigned,
with the authors of them, to the regions of in-

a day or two after his return, being with him and the
Hamiltons at a theatre, Lady Nelson, unable to control
her feelings, fainted in the box in which they were sitting.
On December 19th, leaving Lady Nelson in London to spend
her Christmas alone, Nelson, with Sir W. and Lady Hamilton, set out for Fonthill in Wiltshire, on a visit to *Vathek*
Beckford, who was a cousin of Sir W. Hamilton. Their
journey was a kind of triumphal progress; they were
fêted at Salisbury, and escorted to Fonthill by Yeomanry,
Volunteers, and bands of music. Nelson returned to
London December 29th, and in about a fortnight afterwards the final rupture between him and his wife took
place, and they never lived together again. He probably
saw Lady Nelson for the last time on January 13, 1800, the
day he started for Plymouth to sail with the expedition to
Copenhagen. His last letter was written to her on board
the *St. George*, off Copenhagen, March 1, 1801. During
his absence in the Baltic, March to June, 1801, the breach
between the pair seems to have widened, and Nelson
resolved to make the separation final. On April 25th he
wrote to his agent and friend, Alex. Davison : "My dear
Davison,—You will, at a proper time, and before my arrival
in England, signify to Lady N. that I expect, and for
which I have made such a very liberal allowance to her
(£1,600 per year), to be left to myself, and without any
inquiries from her, for sooner than live the unhappy life
I did when last I came to England, I would stay abroad
for ever. My mind is fixed as fate ; therefore you will
send my determination in any way you may judge proper ;
and believe me ever your obliged and faithful friend,
Nelson and Bronte."

famy, that the man who, in the height of his
splendour, cast off the partner of his humbler
days, and the sharer of his obscurity, for an
extravagant and wheedling wanton, bore this
candid testimony to the dignity of virtue, on
the day of separation, which was the 13th
of January, 1801 : " I call God to witness
there is nothing in you, or your conduct, I wish
otherwise."   After this last interview, his Lordship, accompanied by his reverend brother, set
off for the west of England, on which route a
regular correspondence was kept up with Lady
Hamilton, who at this time was troubled very
much, as her husband informed his noble friend,
with " convulsive complaints in the stomach,
and vomitings, which required some confinement,
and obliged her to take a little tartar emetic ! "
This was written on the 20th of February, and
at the beginning of the following month Sir
William says, " Emma is certainly much better,
but not quite free from bile."

It was in this interval that the child was born,
about whose origin so much mystery is supposed
to exist.[1]   The birth took place in Sir William

---

[1] This infant was born about the 30th or 31st of January
1801, at 23, Piccadilly. In less than a fortnight after its
birth it was taken by night to 9, Little Tichfield St., Marylebone, and delivered to a Mrs. Gibson, who had the care

Hamilton's own house, where every care and precaution had been adopted to keep the matter as secret as possible from him, and from one or two prying members of his own family, though less scruple was observed with respect to another, that had at least an equal interest in the event. Professional attendance was not necessary, where a well-practised mother resided on the spot : and as soon as the patient was capable of moving about, which, owing to her remarkable constitution, was tolerably early, the infant was conveyed by her in a large muff, and in her own carriage, to the house of the person who had been provided to take charge of it in Little Tichfield Street. On this occasion her Ladyship was accompanied by Lord Nelson's confidential agent, Mr. Oliver, who had been brought up from the age of twelve years in the house and under the protection of Sir William Hamilton at Naples. The condition of the infant, when brought to the appointed nurse, plainly showed the hurried process by which it came into the world ; and from all these circumstances the reader may judge whether any one but a mother

of the child for some years, during which time (according to the testimony of Mrs. Gibson's daughter) Lord Nelson "often came alone, and played for hours with the infant on the floor, calling her his own child."

would have conveyed a new-born babe in her own carriage, to the house of a woman with whom she had no acquaintance, and that too accompanied by an old confidential steward?

But should any doubt still be started on the subject, the subsequent acknowledgment of the infant by the parties who were most concerned in the history of her origin must wholly remove the smallest shade of scepticism from the mind of the incredulous. That Lady Hamilton made no scruple of admitting the relation, after the death of her husband, can be easily proved; and in what estimation the noble lord regarded the infant the world has not to learn.[1] It has been

---

[1] The most conclusive evidence on the subject is a letter written by Lord Nelson to Lady Hamilton direct, without any of the Mrs. Thomson mystification, March 1, 1801, which contains the following: "Now, my own dear wife—for such you are in my eyes, and in the face of Heaven—I will give full scope to my feelings, for I dare say Oliver will faithfully deliver this letter. You know, my dearest Emma, that there is nothing in this world that I would not do for us to live together, and to have our dear little child with us. I never did love any one else. I never had a dear pledge of love till you gave me one; and you, thank my God, never gave one to anybody else." The letter, which is unquestionably genuine, concludes with this postscript: "Kiss and bless our dear Horatia—think of that." It shows the confiding and unsuspicious nature of Nelson, and how little he knew of the early history of his "dearest Emma," that he believed

said, indeed, that being his godchild, and adopted by him on that account, his affection for her became ardent to a degree of paternal fondness. But the truth is, that in the proper sense of the word, she was not his godchild, for he neither appeared at the font in person, nor by proxy. About a fortnight after the birth, indeed, and when the child was rendered an object fit to be seen and removed, she was taken in a coach to Sir William Hamilton's house, to be shown to Lord Nelson, who came to town for the purpose. At this time also the child certainly was privately baptized, but not by the curate or minister of the parish. That ceremony, by whom or in whatever way performed, could not authorize a

himself to be the father of the only child she ever had. The letters Nelson received from Lady Hamilton in the early part of 1801 he carefully destroyed, and in a letter to her, dated March 1st of the same year, he says : "I burn all your dear letters because it is right for your sake, and I wish you would burn all mine—they can do no good, and will do us both harm, if any seizure of them, or the dropping even one of them, would fill the mouths of the world sooner than we intend."

On October 21, 1803, when off Toulon, Nelson wrote to the child : "My dear Child,—Receive this first letter from your most affectionate father," and ending with, "Be assured that I am, my dearest Horatia, your most affectionate father, Nelson and Bronte." Other letters of a similar character could be quoted, but the specimens given are perhaps enough. (*See note at end of volume.*)

registry of the fact; and, therefore, it was found expedient, about two years afterwards, to have the rite duly solemnized in the parish church of St. Marylebone, where a curious difficulty occurred for the want of proper instructions being given to the person who had the charge of the infant.[1]

When the usual question was asked by the officiating minister, he received for answer, that the name of the child was " Horatia Nelson," by which he accordingly baptized her, though it

---

[1] The child was baptized at Marylebone Church, May 13, 1803, and entered in the register (falsely) thus: " Baptisms 1803. May 13. Horatia Nelson Thompson, B. 29 October, 1800." On February 5, 1801, Nelson wrote to Lady Hamilton, addressing her as Mrs. Thomson : " My dear Mrs. Thomson,—Your dear and excellent friend has desired me to say that it is not usual to christen children till they are a month or six weeks old, and as Lord Nelson will probably be in town as well as myself, before we go to the Baltic, he proposes then, if you approve, to christen the child, and that myself and Lady Hamilton should be two of the sponsors. It can be christened at St. George's, Hanover Square, and, I believe, the parents being at the time out of the Kingdom, if it is necessary, it can be stated —born at Portsmouth, or on the sea. Its name will be *Horatia, daughter of Johem and Morata Etnorb.* If you read the surname backwards, and take the letters of the other names, it will make, very extraordinary, the names of your real and affectionate friends Lady Hamilton and myself, but, my dear friend, consult Lady Hamilton."

was intended by her friends that the first should have been the Christian, and the latter the surname. At the time of the registry this error was discovered when too late, and as the parents could not be stated with safety, the entry presents the insulated peculiarity of a child regularly baptized, and registered without the name of either father or mother.

The name of Thomson, which was afterwards added to the baptismal one of Horatia Nelson, was merely adopted from necessity, to complete the register ; and how it came to be assumed in this instance it will be proper to explain. Apprehensive that something of a very delicate nature would necessarily occur in their correspondence, Lord Nelson and Lady Hamilton agreed to write to each other under the fictitious characters of Mr. and Mrs. Thomson, and the letters so designated always passed through the hands of their confidential agent. But as an epistolary intercourse with Lady Hamilton had been kept up, ever since their first acquaintance, with the knowledge of Sir William, it was still continued at the time when this secret one was conducted ; and in some of those letters his Lordship occasionally mentioned Mrs. Thomson and her child, in terms of great affection, but in such a way as to prevent any suspicion or discovery.

Thus, shortly after the circumstance took place in the house of Sir William Hamilton, his Lordship, in writing to Emma from Deal, has these remarkable expressions, pointed plainly enough to her, though sufficiently cautious and circuitous to deceive the knight :—

" You cannot think how my feelings are alive towards you ; probably more than ever ; and they never can be diminished. My hearty endeavours shall not be wanting to improve and to give us NEW TIES of regard and affection. I have seen and talked much with Mrs. Thomson's friend. The fellow seems to eat all my words when I talk of her and his child ! He says he never can forget your goodness and kind affection to her and his dear, dear child. I have had, you know, the felicity of seeing it, and a finer child never was produced by any two persons. It was in truth a love-begotten child ! I am determined to keep him on board ; for I know, if they got together, they would soon have another. But after our two months' trip, I hope they will never be separated ; and then let them do as they please."

At the time when his Lordship saw the child, an incident occurred, which proved for what purpose the name of Thomson had been assumed. The nurse, who had charge of the

infant, on entering the house, was met by Sir
William Hamilton, who inquired her name and
business. The housekeeper being present,
immediately answered that this was Mrs.
Thomson with her child, who had come to wait
upon Lord Nelson, by appointment, to solicit
his favour. On hearing this, the poor old
gentleman kindly expressed his wishes for her
welfare, and his admiration of the infant which
she held in her arms. Now, as this woman's
name was not Thomson, and she neither bore
any relation to the child, nor had a petition to
present, the whole fabrication was obviously
intended to deceive Sir William, and of course,
the assumption of the appellation was altogether
a trick, to cloak an improper connection.

While Nelson lay in the Downs, at the time
of the expedition against Boulogne, he wrote as
follows to his "dearest Emma" :—

"You need not fear all the women in this
world ; for all others except yourself are pests
to me. I know but one ; for who can be like
my Emma ? I am confident you will do
nothing which can hurt my feelings; and I
will die by torture, sooner than do anything
which could offend you. Give ten thousand
kisses to my dear Horatia.

"Yesterday the subject turned on the cow-pox. A gentleman declared, that his child was inoculated with the cow-pox ; and afterwards remained in a house where a child had the small-pox the natural way, and did not catch it. Therefore, here was a full trial with the cow-pox. The child is only feverish for two days ; and only a slight inflammation of the arm takes place, instead of being all over scabs. But do you what you please."

Notwithstanding this opinion in favour of vaccination, the child was inoculated at the close of the summer, for the small-pox, by the advice of Dr. Rowley ; and during the disease, a furnished house was taken, purposely for the nurse, in Sloane Street, by Mr. Oliver, who also resided there, till the recovery was complete.

Trifling as this may appear, it proves the tenderness of the relation, and the absolute conviction which Nelson had that the child was his own; and how he regarded the mother, is manifest from the following expressions in a letter written at Deal, the 18th of August, this year.

" May Heaven bless me very soon with a sight of your dear angelic face. You are a nonpareil ! No, not one fit to wipe your shoes. I am, ever have been, and always will remain, your most firm, fixed, and unalterable friend."

LORD NELSON.

From an engraving by Turner after R. Bowyer

If anything could aggravate the inhumanity with which Lady Nelson was treated, through the whole of this eventful year, it was the painful consideration, that the woman who had robbed her of peace was entrusted with the office of separating her wardrobe from the things belonging to his Lordship, in Norfolk ; and after ransacking the whole, sending her what she pleased. A man of truly liberal sentiment would have shuddered at such an act of indelicacy ; and had Lady Hamilton possessed the smallest degree of shame, she would have declined the commission, with a recommendation that it should be performed by some of his Lordship's female relations. Instead, however, of being actuated by anything like sensibility, this unfeeling woman exulted in the conquest which she had made, and gladly did she seize every opportunity that her ascendency over the mind of Nelson afforded of inflicting a fresh wound in the heart of his wife.

This summer, Sir William Hamilton, at the desire of his noble friend, completed the purchase for him of Merton Place, in Surrey, about eight miles from London ; and the object which his Lordship had in this acquisition was to accommodate all the parties under one roof, and to leave the estate as a testimony of his friendship to Emma. Here was another instance of Sir William's excessive meanness ; for while he readily acceded to his friend's wishes, he took care to modify his own will accordingly ; and knowing that his widow would be thus comfortably settled, he bequeathed her only seven hundred pounds a year,[1] leaving all the rest of his property, which was considerable, to his nephew, and other relations.

In the whole of this business, and the improvements which were made on the farm, Lady Hamilton had a principal concern, as, indeed, her interest, and that of the child, had been the sole inducement to the purchase. Though his Lordship had not seen this estate, he was resolved to be pleased with the situation, and with all that was done to render the house and grounds agreeable, merely because the place was adorned by the presence and talents of his charmer.[2]

---

[1] Sir W. Hamilton left his widow an immediate legacy of £800, and an annuity of £800 for life, charged upon his Welsh estate.

[2] On October 16, 1801, Sir William Hamilton wrote from Merton to Lord Nelson : "My dear Lord,—We have now inhabited your Lordship's premises some days, and I can now speak with some certainty. I have lived with our dear Emma several years. I know her merit, have a great opinion of the head and heart that God Almighty has been

"You may rely upon one thing," says he, "that I shall like Merton; therefore do not be uneasy on that account. I have that opinion of your taste and judgment, that I do not believe it can fail in pleasing me. We must only consider our means; and for the rest, I am sure you will soon make it the prettiest place in the world." Adverting then to the child, who naturally engrossed much of his thoughts, he says :—

"Whatever, my dear Emma, you do for my little charge, I must be pleased with. Probably, she will be lodged at Merton ; at least, in the spring, when she can have the benefit of our walks. It will make the poor mother happy, I am sure."

The following passage in the same letter cannot be passed over without observation. "Have we," inquires his Lordship, "a nice

pleased to give her, but a seaman alone could have given a fine woman full power to choose and fit up a residence for him without seeing it himself. You are in luck, for in my conscience I verily believe that a place so suitable to your views could not have been found, and at so cheap a rate—you might get a thousand pounds to-morrow for your bargain. It would make you laugh to see Emma and her mother fitting up pig-styes and hen-coops." At Merton, Nelson spent the greater part of the time he was in England, from October, 1801, to May, 1803.

church at Merton? We will set an example of goodness to the under parishioners." Thus, like many who flatter themselves that an external respect for the forms of religion will be admitted as an equivalent for the observance of its precepts, this great man imagined that his rank and character would give so much effect to his constant attendance at church, as to render his private obliquities of no moment to society. Such an " example of goodness to the under parishioners " was very proper as far as it went ; but if any of those persons made an inquiry into the manners of the family at Merton Place, they would have been very little edified by the appearance of his Lordship and his friends at the parish church. It is to be lamented, that this letter should contain a melancholy evidence of the noble writer's notions of that purity of heart which can alone render worship acceptable, or example effica- cious ; for thus he speaks of his aged parent, and his virtuous wife :—

" I had yesterday a letter from my father : he seems to think that he may do something which I shall not like. I suppose he means going to Somerset Street. Shall I, to an old man, enter upon the detestable subject : it may shorten his days. But I think I shall tell

him that I cannot go to Somerset Street to see
him. But I shall not write till I hear your
opinion. If I once begin, you know, it will
all out about her, and her ill-treatment to her
son. But you shall decide."

This subservience to the will and counsels
of the deceiver showed the weakness to which
his Lordship was now reduced ; and it is a
fact, that while to every one else the artful
woman represented Lady Nelson as endeavouring to sacrifice the interests of her husband's
relations to the aggrandizement of her son,
she filled the mind of the admiral himself
with the grossest falsehoods of her Ladyship's
cruelties to her own child. Let it not be forgotten, however, that Nelson's letters to his
wife, and his last solemn asseveration, made at
the time of their separation, completely refute
any insinuation to her disadvantage ; while at
the same time it must be admitted that his
writing in the way he did was neither a proof
of his candour nor magnanimity. It was yet
within remembrance when the language of the
hero to his lady was like his conduct, warm,
manly, and liberal; indicating a heart wholly
uncorrupted, and animated by the sentiments
of honour and love. Greatly, therefore, is it
to be lamented, that he should now have fallen

so low as to asperse the same woman with the coarsest epithets when writing to another man's wife, whom he scrupled not to flatter in this fulsome manner : " I assure you, my dear friend, that I had rather read and hear all your little story of a white hen getting into a tree, an anecdote of Fatima, or hear you call, ' Cupidy, Cupidy ! ' than any speech I shall hear in Parliament : because, I know, although you can adapt your language and manners to a child, yet that you can also thunder forth such a torrent of eloquence, that corruption and infamy would sink before your voice, in however exalted a situation it might be placed."

In October his Lordship joined his friends at Merton, between which place and Sir William's house in Piccadilly the winter was divided with considerable gaiety, and a perpetual round of visitors, among whom were several of the Nelson family, particularly the present head of that house, who unquestionably was far from being deficient in his attentions to the idol of his brother's devotions. This noble Lord cannot be accused of having displayed any zeal against the ascendency of Lady Hamilton over the mind of his illustrious relative ; nor did he ever show the least disapprobation of that authority which she exercised, where the presence of a wife would have been a more graceful object.

In the summer of 1802 Lord Nelson, accompanied by his brother, with Sir William and Lady Hamilton, made a tour through the midland counties into South Wales ; but at Blenheim the party experienced considerable mortification in the slight that was put upon them by the noble family, none of whom condescended to make their appearance, while these visitors were viewing the mansion. This apparent contempt gave so much offence to the hero of the Nile, that he refused the refreshments which were offered ; and his Cleopatra, putting on one of her high airs, said, " I told Nelson that if I had been a queen, after the battle of Aboukir, he should have had a principality, so that Blenheim Park should have been only as a kitchen garden to it."

At this extravagant flight, it is said that the gallant chief shed tears, and in an impassioned tone of resentment, occasioned by the reception which he and his companions had experienced, he observed, " That he had yet more beds of laurel to gather." Now had this great man duly reflected on the character and dignity of the house of Spencer, he would have seen more to admire than to censure in their conduct on the present occasion ; since whatever inclination the members of that family might have to show their respect for so distinguished a commander, it was evident that they had more for the interests of virtue. The noble inhabitants of Blenheim would very gladly have welcomed Nelson under their roof ; but when they found him so accompanied, that a particular attention could not be paid to him without giving some countenance to an improper connection, they prudently retired from observation. If his Lordship had brought Lady Nelson with him, instead of the woman who had supplanted her in his affections, he would have met with different treatment ; and, therefore, when he proudly declined the proffered refreshments, he ought to have considered whether, in fact, he had not himself committed a much greater offence than that which he resented. There were other persons of distinction, in the course of this tour, who felt themselves bound to withhold their personal attentions from the noble admiral, out of a sense of superior duty, and a persuasion that they ought not to sanction, by their complaisance, the presence of unblushing infidelity. Is it to be endured, that because a man has rendered uncommon services to his country, and gained a splendid name by his talents, he may, therefore, dispense with the ordinary forms of civil life, and set at defiance those rules of action which constitute the vital spring of social order ? Shall valourous deeds, and extraordinary powers, atone for the violation of private duty, or be admitted as an apology for the breach of those institutions which all ages have concurred in pronouncing sacred?

Though Lady Hamilton found some pliable dispositions in England, of both sexes, who were ready enough to favour her with their company, because they wished to court the friendship of her admirer, she had the mortification of seeing that the public feeling was of a much sterner cast, and that the body of the people, while they followed the hero with their acclamations, pitied him for his weakness as a man. Of this mixed sentiment the party experienced many instances during their journey through the Principality, as well as in various parts of England ;[1] but they had been so long used to

---

[1] The party consisted of Nelson, his brother the Rev. Dr. Nelson and his wife, and Sir W. and Lady Hamilton. They first went to Oxford, where Nelson and Sir W. Hamilton were honoured by the degree of D.C.L. ; then to Gloucester, Monmouth, Brecon, and Milford Haven ; fêted, cheered, and escorted at every place. The

the dissolute manners of Italy, as to "care for none of these things." At all the entertainments which were given, by corporate bodies, and other public assemblies, in honour of the admiral and his companions, Lady Hamilton never failed to enliven the festive board by her vocal powers, the charming effects of which were constantly trumpeted to the world through the medium of the newspapers.

At the beginning of September, the travellers returned to Merton, where, for the most part, they continued to reside during the following winter ; but in March, Sir William Hamilton, being taken seriously ill, was conveyed to his house in Piccadilly, where he died on the 6th of April, in the presence of his wife and Lord Nelson. In his last moments, he is reported to have addressed himself to his Lordship in

object of the journey was to see the improvements on Sir W. Hamilton's Welsh estate, and the development of the harbour at Milford, which had been effected by Sir William's nephew, Mr. C. Greville, under Parliamentary authorization. On August 1st, the anniversary of the Battle of the Nile, there was a grand dinner and great rejoicings at Milford Haven. From Milford the party went to Swansea, thence to Monmouth, Ross, and Hereford ; from Hereford, to Worcester, and from Worcester to Birmingham (where medals were struck to commemorate the visit) and from thence to Coventry and Warwick, on their way home.

these words : " Brave and great Nelson ! our
friendship has been long, and I glory in my
friend. I hope you will see justice done to
Emma by ministers, for you know how great
her services have been, and what she has done
for her country. Protect my dear wife ; and
may God bless you ; and give you victory, and
protect you in battle ! " Then turning to his
Lady, he said, " My incomparable Emma, you
have never in thought, word, or deed, offended
me ; and let me thank you again, and again,
for your affectionate kindness to me, all the time
of our ten years' happy union."

By a codicil to his will, made about a week
before his death, Sir William bequeathed to his
noble friend a picture of Emma in enamel ;
and his Lordship, in a strain of uncommon
generosity, settled upon her, two months afterwards, an annuity of twelve hundred pounds,
to be paid in monthly portions. This was
equivalent to the pension which had been granted
to Sir William at the expiration of his embassy,
and the continuance of which was solicited in
vain by his widow. There was a striking
contrast between the conduct of Nelson, and
that of Sir William's family, particularly the
nephew, who compelled her Ladyship to quit
the house in Piccadilly within a month after

the death of her husband. Thus she found the instability of that friendship which is cemented by selfish motives ; and she might, if prudence had been admitted to her counsels, have learnt from hence, that the admiration which is not excited by virtue has never any chance of being matured into esteem. This harsh treatment on the part of her oldest acquaintance and protector was embittered by the silent contempt thrown on her memorial for a pension, as the relict of an ambassador, and as one who had particular claims of her own for a liberal allowance from Government. But it was so well known by the cabinet, that the Sicilian embassy had neither been honourable in the management, nor economical in the expenditure, that no regard was paid to the petition of her Ladyship, though it was supported by the powerful exertions of her noble friend, whose recommendation of her claims brought with it so many unpleasant recollections, as tended, in a great measure, to defeat the object which the parties had in view.

It has been said that Lord Nelson, on the death of Sir William, removed into private lodgings, being actuated by a delicate regard to the widow's reputation, and a laudable care to avoid giving any handle to a censorious world. The motive, had it existed, was certainly proper, but it is strange that the mind in which it arose should not have seen the necessity of observing the same line of conduct in the country as in London, since if there was anything wrong in his continuing under the roof of Lady Hamilton in Piccadilly, after the death of her husband, there was just as much in her living with him at Merton. It is much to be lamented that this wish to avoid giving occasion for the surmises and rumours of the ill-disposed part of mankind, did not result from the conscientious principle of having endeavoured to merit the confidence of the good, which would have led the hero, and the object of his admiration, to study such a line of conduct as might have placed them, like the wife of Cæsar, above all suspicion.

CHAPTER XIII.

This then is liberty, the truth to tell;
To our dear country wishing all things
well.   EURIPIDES.

OON after the death of Sir
William Hamilton, his widow
took a house in Clarges Street,
between which and Merton her
time was divided ; but within a
few weeks she was deprived of
the company of her noble friend and admirer,
in consequence of his being appointed to the
command of the fleet in the Mediterranean.[1]
In a letter written to her from thence, his Lordship gave this extract from one which he had
sent just before to the Queen of Naples : " I
left Lady Hamilton the 18th of May ; and

[1] Lord Nelson was appointed Commander-in-chief in
the Mediterranean, May 16, 1803, and sailed from Portsmouth in the *Victory*, in company with the *Amphion*, Captain T. M. Hardy, May 20th following.

so attached to your Majesty, that I am sure
she would lay down her life to preserve yours.
Your Majesty never had a more sincere,
attached, and real friend, than your dear
Emma. You will be sorry to hear that good
Sir William Hamilton did not leave her in such
comfortable circumstances as his fortune would
have allowed. He has given it amongst his
relations. But she will do honour to his
memory, though every one else of his friends
call loudly against him on that account."

In all this, however, the noble writer judged
wrong ; for when the rise of this woman is
considered, the settlement of seven hundred a-
year will hardly be thought by any reasonable
person to have been an inadequate provision.
Besides, as economy had never been one of her
virtues, Sir William knew well enough that a
larger annuity would only have increased her
extravagance ; and the event proved that he
acted with judgment in this disposal of his
property. What honour she did to the
memory of the man who had elevated her from
a low situation, and one, indeed, that was worse
than servile, to affluence and dignity, will appear
from the fact that she declined the publication
of his papers, letters, and memoirs ; though
when Nelson fell, her first consideration was

that of hiring a mercenary scribbler to write such a history of the hero as should set forth her virtues and talents, in unison with his merits, to the best advantage. A literary friend of Sir William Hamilton urged the propriety of giving to the world a biographical account of one who had so eminently distinguished himself, not only in a diplomatic capacity, but as an antiquary, and a scientific observer. This suggestion having been treated very disrespectfully, induced the person who made it to write rather freely to her Ladyship on the subject ; and then, with her usual address, she endeavoured to recall the words which had been uttered in contempt of a civil and disinterested proposal. The letter which she wrote by way of apology was as follows :—

"Clarges Street, April 23rd, 1803.

"Sir,

"I was very much surprised on receiving your letter this morning, as I cannot think what you mean by my being offended, nor who could have told you so. Mr. O. spoke to me about your wish to have some information about Sir William's pursuits, whilst on his embassy at Naples, which, I said, I should be very glad to give you myself, as many persons had asked me

the same ; but I had been so very unwell, I had
not either health or spirits to enter on the subject with strangers.   But I told Mrs. G. if you
would do me the favour of calling in Clarges
Street, I should be very glad to see you, and tell
you myself many very interesting anecdotes of
that great and good man.   This is all that
passed on the occasion, nor can I account for
what you wrote me, as I never spoke to any one,
but merely to give the message to Mrs. G. as I
thought by so doing I might have been of
service to you and Mrs. W. to whom I beg my
compliments, and am,

        " Sir, your obedient

          " humble servant,

            " EMMA HAMILTON.

" P.S.   If you will let me know by a line any
morning, you will favour me by calling, I will
be at home."

Now this was all mere duplicity and affectation, for nothing more was recommended to her
Ladyship than the publication of her husband's
life, and correspondence, as far as related to his
literary connections and philosophical researches ;
instead of which, she contented herself with
communicating orally some trifling stories and
amusing incidents, and thus the business ended ;

nor has any memoir of this remarkable character yet appeared, though it is evident, from
the length of his residence in Italy, the variety
of his engagements, and the extent of his
acquaintance, that such a work would have been
highly acceptable to the world of letters. But
the truth is, she felt so much hurt at the
manner in which the property of Sir William
had been bequeathed, that she cared as little for
his honour after his death, as she had been
mindful of it in his lifetime. In the attentions
of the Nelson family, however, she became consoled for the supposed neglect with which she
had been treated by her husband and his friends.
The niece of the noble admiral was settled in
the family of her Ladyship, that she might
profit by the instructions and example of such
an accomplished person. This was certainly a
very extraordinary proof of friendship and confidence on the part of the young lady's parents,
though there were not wanting persons who
looked upon it in a light not at all flattering to
the discretion of his Lordship's relations. Dr.
Nelson, having obtained through his brother's
interest, a prebendal stall in the church of
Canterbury, was very assiduous at this period in
his respects to Lady Hamilton, who spent part
of the summer with him at that city, accom-

panied by Mrs. Billington.[1] The inhabitants
of Canterbury were not a little surprised at the
appearance of such visitors in the house of one
of their reverend dignitaries; and more so,
when it was proposed that these enchanting
females should delight and edify the frequenters
of the cathedral with a sacred duet. This offer,
however, was far from being relished by the
guardians of that venerable fabric; and the
respectable citizens had so much Bœotian dul-
ness, that at the end of their cards of invitation
to the new prebendary and his family, they
made it a point to subjoin this curious condition, "But not Lady Hamilton." These old-
fashioned people in the country seem to have
fancied that when the voice of the world was
loud respecting the dominion of this woman
over the mind of the hero, his nearest friends
ought to have discountenanced the rumour by
treating her with distant respect. It undoubt-
edly did wear a strange aspect, that while an
amiable wife was discarded for no offence, all
the relations of the admiral, and particularly
his brother, whose station in the Church called
for the greatest circumspection, should be
diligent in cultivating the acquaintance of the
person who had made such an inroad on the

[1] The well-known actress.

harmony of their family. That they were ignorant of the interest which Lady Hamilton possessed in the affections of their noble relative, can hardly be supposed ; and to the sentiments of the public on that unhappy connection, it was impossible for them to have been strangers.

Not long after the sailing of Nelson, another female infant made its appearance at Merton, which obtained the name of Emma ; but it died early the following year, in a convulsive fit.[1] From the letters which his Lordship wrote to the mother, while he was employed off Toulon, it is necessary to make a few extracts, as confirming, beyond all doubt, his absolute devotedness to Lady Hamilton, and showing that the footing on which they lived was perfectly well known to his most intimate friends. " I rejoice," says he, " that you have had so pleasant a trip into Norfolk ;[2] and I hope one day to

[1] This second " Little Emma " died in March, 1804.

[2] The trip to Norfolk was made in the summer of 1803, and in the following year Lady Hamilton visited the Boltons (Nelson's sister and her husband) at Bradenham Hall, Norfolk. In the same year, 1804, she spent some time with Nelson's brother, the Rev. Dr. Nelson, at Canterbury. The doctor's daughter, Charlotte, afterwards Lady Bridport, resided for months with Lady Hamilton in London, and at Merton, till the death of Nelson in 1805.

carry you there by a nearer TIE in law, but not in love and affection, than at present." Then alluding to his excellent wife, who had been aspersed, as usual, in one of her rival's ensnaring epistles, his Lordship adds, " I wish you would never mention that person's name. It works up your anger for no useful purpose. Her good or bad character of me or thee no one cares about." Thus the completest evidence is afforded not only of the entire control which Lady Hamilton had over the mind of Nelson, but of her baseness in calumniating the woman whom she had supplanted. Had the hero felt as became him, he would have resented the malignant arts which were made use of to inflame him against the person who, of all others, had the strongest claim upon his gratitude and protection. But if anything could add to the severity with which his injured lady was treated at this period, it was the cruel neglect of those branches of the family who had formerly courted her company, and been pleased with her correspondence. Finding that such an intimacy would be no longer agreeable to their illustrious relative, and that, on the contrary, the only sure method of securing his favour lay in flattering the object of his admiration, these persons took special care to avoid giving him

any reason to complain of a want of courtesy
where they knew it was most acceptable.   They
were indeed plainly assured by his Lordship,
"that in manifesting their kind attentions to
Lady Hamilton, they would be sure of a warm
place in his heart."

After the death of Sir William, he conducted
himself towards her as his wife, they having
actually pledged their faith to each other in that
capacity ; and in the month of August the
same year he wrote to her in these strong terms,
when anticipating a speedy blessed meeting :
" The thoughts of such happiness, my dearest
only beloved, makes the blood fly into my head.
The call of our country is a duty which you
would deservedly in the cool moments of
reflection reprobate, was I to abandon it : and
I should feel so disgraced, by seeing you
ashamed of me, no longer saying, ' This is the
man who has saved his country ! this is he who
is the first to go forth to fight our battles, and
the last to return, and then all these honours to
reflect on you !' Ah ! they will think, what a
man !   What sacrifices has he not made to
secure our homes and property ; even the
society and happy union with the finest and
most accomplished woman in the world. As you
love, how must you feel !—my heart is with

you : cherish it. I shall, my blessed beloved, return—if it pleases God—a victor ; and it shall be my study to transmit an unsullied name. There is no desire of wealth, no ambition that could keep me from all my soul holds dear. No ; it is to save my country, my wife, in the eye of God, &c."

About two months afterwards, his Lordship expressed himself in these terms : " As for old Queensberry, he may put you into his will, or scratch you out, as he pleases : I care not. If Mr. Addington gives you a pension, it is well ; but do not let it fret you. Have you not Merton ? It is clear—the first purchase—and my dear Horatia is provided for ; and I hope one of these days that you will be my own Duchess of Bronte; and then a fig for them all !—I am glad to find, my dear Emma, that you mean to take Horatia home. Aye! she is like her mother ; will have her own way, or kick up a devil of a dust. But you will cure her : I am afraid I should spoil her ; for I am sure I would shoot any one who would hurt her."

It appears that Lady Hamilton at this time had formed the romantic scheme of leaving England, accompanied by the niece of Nelson, Horatia, and Oliver, with the view of being

received on board the *Victory*; but much as
the admiral desired a meeting, he had too much
good sense to accede to so imprudent a measure,
especially as he had himself given orders that
no women should be carried to sea in his ship.
His remonstrance on this subject was tender, but
firm and judicious. "I know my own dear
Emma," said he, "if she will let her reason have
fair play, will say I am right : but she is, like
Horatia, very angry if she cannot have her own
way. Her Nelson is called upon, in the most
honourable manner, to defend his country!
Absence to us is equally painful : but if I had
either stayed at home, or neglected my duty
abroad, would not my Emma have blushed
for me? She could never have heard of my
praises ; and how the country looks up. . . .
I am writing, my dear Emma, to reason the
point with you ; and I am sure you will
see it in its true light."

These sentiments did credit to the understanding of the writer, and it would have been
happy if he had acted with equal steadiness in
every instance where his judgment had to
contend with his passions. Lady Hamilton led
a life of such extravagance at this period, that
the allowance which she enjoyed from his
Lordship, and the annuity derived from the

will of her husband, proved inadequate to the supply of her wants. Surrounded by a set of needy parasites, both her house in town, as well as that in Surrey, exhibited a continual round of luxury and gaiety, that could not be supported even by the liberal means which she possessed, and the occasional presents she received. His Lordship frequently gave her some gentle monitions on the necessity of economy, and the propriety of living more at Merton than in London, because it would be attended with less expense. The watering-places also, to which her Ladyship was in the habit of going in the summer months, gave him some uneasiness, on account of the charges which attended these excursions : but so long as they did Emma service, he consoled himself under the pressure, at the same time observing that "it was expedient to be great economists, to make both ends meet, and to carry on the intended improvements at Merton." The following is a good remark, but it was lost upon the person to whom it was addressed : "Your good, angelic heart, my dearest beloved Emma, will fully agree with me : everything is very expensive ; and even we find it, and will be obliged to economize, if we assist our friends : and I am sure we should feel more comfort in it than in

loaded tables, and entertaining a set of people
who care not for us."

But his fair angelic friend was of a very
different opinion, and all his moralizing on
order and frugality was wholly thrown away,
as he found to his vexation, though nothing
could operate upon his infatuated mind to lay
any restraint upon her conduct. He saw,
however, enough in this imprudence of the
mother to make it necessary to provide a
permanent settlement for the child, that she
might not be too great a sufferer by parental
folly.   His Lordship thus mentions the subject
in March, 1804: "I shall, when I come
home, settle four thousand pounds in trustees'
hands for Horatia ; for I will not put it in my
own power to have her left destitute : for she
would want friends, if we left her in this world.
She shall be independent of any smiles or
frowns ! "

This resolution he was happily enabled to
accomplish, and thus the child of his dearest
affections was secured from that misery into
which she would most probably have fallen but
for this moderate provision ; since from the
liberality of the family to which she had an
equivocal relation she could hardly hope for any
support.   It would have added to the prudence

of the measure if Nelson had taken care also
to preserve Merton for the child ; and no
doubt it was his opinion that by this purchase
he had effectually provided an asylum for her
in the event of losing her parents. The manner
in which Lady Hamilton deported herself, and
the company she kept, might have taught him
the propriety of some proceedings for this
purpose ; but whenever demands were made
upon him, he found it impossible to resist them,
though he fretted within himself, and vented
his murmurs of disapprobation to the person
who, while she occasioned his embarrassments,
had no feeling for his uneasiness.

One method which she had of gaining her
point was by alarming the fears of Nelson with
insinuations concerning the great offers that
she pretended to have received from noblemen
of high distinction. These intimations, which
were the mere coinage of her invention, had
the effect desired on his Lordship's mind, and
made him still more dutiful and attentive to
the commands of this artful and rapacious
woman. Among others whose civilities she
contrived to turn to an advantage in this
manner was the late Duke of Queensberry,
who followed her, as he did every handsome
woman that came in his way, with as much

assiduity as if he had been in the prime of his days. At Merton and in Piccadilly this silly old man was quite delighted with the enchanting attitudes and vocal powers of the lively widow, who on her part was not backward in using every art to please the amorous dotard. Nelson, however, had discernment enough not to be afraid of any serious proposal coming from that quarter, for he knew that the Duke, whatever might be his propensities, was a determined enemy to matrimony, of which institution he generally spoke with contempt. But the presents which were made to this nobleman, with the express view of propitiating his good graces in behalf of Lady Hamilton, and to secure the remembrance of her in his will, did little honour to the persons from whom they came, and who in their correspondence treated him with unmeasured ridicule.[1]

While Nelson was in the Mediterranean, he discovered, what he might have found out long before, if his passion had not blinded his judg-

[1] On April 9, 1804, Nelson wrote to Lady Hamilton : " I have wrote to the Duke ; but, by your account, I fear he is not alive. I write because you wish me, and because I like the Duke, and hope he will leave you some money. But for myself, I can have no right to expect a farthing; nor would I be a legacy hunter for the world ; I never knew any good come from it."

ment, that there was no real principle of friendship in the Queen of Naples for his beloved
Emma, though her Majesty had vowed towards
that lady "eternal gratitude." To all his letters
on the subject of the necessities of Lady Hamilton, and the strong claims which she urged on
her behalf, the Queen returned very ambiguous
answers, which drew from his Lordship some
severe observations on her character and conduct ;
while Lady Hamilton avenged herself by relations of the Queen's amours, in doing which
she had not wit enough to perceive that she was
at the same instant bringing her own reputation
under suspicion, for having been so long associated with a personage of that description.

But during this year she had various causes
of vexation, and multiplied evidences that the
esteem of Nelson could not secure the attachment of her old friends ; for a violent quarrel
arose between her Ladyship and Mr. Greville
about the construction of his uncle's will, and
the payment of her annuity. The business was
indeed settled, but not much to the satisfaction
of her Ladyship ; and the admiral was so greatly
provoked at the intelligence, that he was almost
tempted to urge a suit at law.

But one of the most extraordinary instances
of human weakness appears in the following

letter, which Nelson at this time wrote to his
child, who was then only three years old :—

                    " *Victory, April* 13*th*, 1804.

" My dear Horatia,
" I send you twelve books of Spanish dresses,
which you will let your guardian angel, Lady
Hamilton, keep for you when you are tired of
looking at them.   I am very glad to hear that
you are perfectly recovered, and that you are a
very good child.   I beg, my dear Horatia, that
you will always continue so ; which will be a
great comfort to your most affectionate
            "NELSON AND BRONTE."

At the same time he sent a letter to his niece,
in which he mentions this child in the following
manner : " I feel truly sensible of your kind
regard for that dear little orphan, Horatia.
Although her parents are lost, yet she is not
without a fortune : and I shall cherish her to
the last moment of my life ; and curse them who
curse her, and Heaven bless them who bless her !
Dear innocent ! she can have injured no one.
I am glad to hear that she is attached to you ;
and, if she takes after her parents, so she will to
those who are kind to her."
There was certainly a degree of duplicity in

writing thus to a female relation, on a subject which did not require any correspondence at all ; but there was a much greater meanness in suffering this young lady to reside in a dependent capacity with Lady Hamilton, whose dissipated turn of mind was well known to all the visitors at Merton. Whatever were the accomplishments of her Ladyship in other respects, few persons, who had any regard for the substantial attainments which constitute the great excellence of the female character, would for any consideration have placed a favourite daughter in such a family.

The company at this place was of a description not very likely to improve the morals or to enlarge the mind of a young person ; for here might be found Italian singers and English performers, newspaper editors, and miserable poetasters, adventurers without character, and ladies whose names were no recommendation at court. Much has been said of the great loyalty of Lady Hamilton ; and her advocates have expatiated on this supposed virtue ; but if she really merited the encomiums which have been so extravagantly paid her on this account, she would hardly have encouraged the most rancorous party writers, virulent satirists, and determined republicans, at her table.

The names of these persons could easily be mentioned, and the author of this memoir is neither
unacquainted with the freedom of the conversation which took place at the orgies of Merton
Place, nor with the communications which were
there made on political subjects.

At the beginning of the year 1805, this
woman had the vanity and impudence, when
writing to Mr. Alexander Davidson, to subjoin
what she properly enough called "some of her
bad verses on her soul's idol!" Disagreeable
as it is to dwell upon this shocking connection,
to which so many persons gave their countenance, whose situations in life called for another
line of behaviour, the present volume would be
incomplete without this specimen of Lady
Hamilton's poetical talents, and of the delicacy
of her moral principles, for both which she has
been celebrated by her flatterers :—

EMMA TO NELSON.

I think I have not lost my heart,
  Since I with truth can swear,
At every moment of my life.
  I feel my Nelson there !

If from thine Emma's breast, her heart
  Were stolen, or flown away,
Where, where, should she my Nelson's love
  Record, each happy day ?

If from thine Emma's breast, her heart
  Were stolen, or flown away,
Where, where, should she engrave, my love !
  Each tender word you say ?

Where, where, should Emma treasure up
  Her Nelson's smiles and sighs ?
Where mark with joy each secret look
  Of love from Nelson's eyes ?

Then do not rob me of my heart,
  Unless you first forsake it ;
And then so wretched it would be,
  Despair alone will take it.

CHAPTER XIV.

Fair laughs the morn, and soft the
zephyr blows,
While proudly riding o'er the azure
realm,
In gallant trim the gilded vessel goes ;
Youth on the prow, and pleasure at
the helm ;
Regardless of the sweeping whirlwind's
sway,
That hush'd in grim repose expects
his coming prey.

GRAY.

HEN Lord Nelson arrived at
Portsmouth, after his unsuc-
cessful pursuit of the combined
French and Spanish fleets, in
August, 1805, Lady Hamilton
was at Southend with Mrs.
Billington and Horatia ; but on receiving the
agreeable intelligence, she hastened to Merton,
where the rest of his Lordship's family also
assembled to welcome the hero. One person,
indeed, was wanting ; nor did any mediating

voice offer a soothing word to induce the gallant
admiral to see his lady, even as an old acquaintance ; and it is a melancholy fact that she never
had a single interview with him during his last
residence in England. But at Merton all was
gaiety on this joyous occasion, and crowds of
visitors went thither every day to pay their
respects to his Lordship, and the ascendant who
ruled his affections. Such was the morality
which distinguished the zealous admirers of this
great man, that they appeared to have laid aside
in his presence those feelings which usually
actuate honourable minds, on witnessing scenes
of impurity, and being obliged to endure, for a
moment, the company of women who have lost
all sense of shame. That any of the persons
thus admitted to a familiar intercourse with the
noble owner of Merton Place, and the lady
who presided at his table, could be ignorant of
the attachment which subsisted between them,
cannot be supposed, since it is well known that
neither of the parties took the precaution of
casting the slightest veil over their connection.
On the contrary, they both gloried in it, and
it was customary for his Lordship, at receiving
his visitors, to introduce them to the mistress of
the place, " who unfortunately," to use his own
phrase, " was not yet Lady Nelson."

When this brave man was at Naples, he expressed his contempt of that court as being the "seat of fiddlers and poets, whores and scoundrels;" yet it is no less strange than true, that his house at Merton exhibited frequently groups of characters not a whit more respectable than those whom he so emphatically described in Italy. Opera singers and ballad makers, foreign noblemen and their mistresses, with English players, gamblers, and musicians, were the favourite guests of Lady Hamilton; though no doubt the qualities and pursuits of some of these personages were studiously concealed from the knowledge of his Lordship. It may, however, well excite surprise, that he should not have felt disgusted at the sycophants who surrounded his table, and whose manners, for the most part, were as coarse as their principles. But so long as Emma was gratified by the adulation which she received, her noble friend appeared to be under an obligation to the persons who bestowed it, especially as he enjoyed a large portion of the incense.

Among other persons who were entertained at Merton was Dr. Wolcot, generally known by his poetical appellation of Peter Pindar. This eccentric character, having indulged rather freely one evening in his favourite potation, set fire

to his night-cap on going to bed.   The cap
belonged to Lord Nelson, and the next morning
the bard pinned a paper to it with these lines :

> Take your night-cap again, my good Lord, I desire ;
>   For I wish not to keep it a minute :
> What belongs to a Nelson, where'er there's a fire,
>   Is sure to be instantly in it.

It had long been the desire of Nelson that
Lady Hamilton should take Horatia home to
live with her ;[1] and this she not only engaged to
do in her letters, but she actually informed him
that the child was settled at Merton, which
circumstance did not happen till his return,
because her Ladyship was unwilling to have
such a restraint on her amusements as this
charge would necessarily have occasioned.   But
at this period, the child was fixed with her, and
a small settlement was made for life on the
person who had brought her up.   Insignificant
as such circumstances may seem, they serve to
throw light on the history of this extraordinary
connection, as well as on the characters of those

---

[1] In a letter already quoted, Nelson says to Lady
Hamilton : " I am glad you are going to take her
(Horatia) home ; and if you will take the trouble with
Eliza and Ann " (the children of his sister, Mrs. Bolton),
" I am the very last to object."

who were the depositories of the hero's confidence.

The present Earl perhaps may recollect who
it was that, after the death of his brother,
ordered the nurse to hand over to him the
instrument by which the annuity was settled
upon her, and the bitterness with which the
poor woman was treated for bringing only a
copy of the deed, which, on receiving, he hurried
out of the room ; but when he discovered that
this was not the original, he hastened back, and
behaved with such outrage as to hurt the feelings
of his own wife, who was insulted by him for
taking the poor woman's part.

That document was framed under Lord
Nelson's inspection by his own solicitor and
executor ; its validity therefore required no
proof : nor was it doubtful for what services the
grant had been made. This of course is an
additional testimony to the fact that the child
was admitted by the admiral to be his own ;
though, if the slightest shade of uncertainty
could be supposed to exist in the mind of any
unbiassed person, it must be removed by this
codicil to his will : " I give and bequeath to
Miss Horatia Nelson Thompson, who was baptized on the 13th of May last, in the parish of
St. Mary-le-bone, in the county of Middlesex,

by Benjamin Lawrence, curate, and John Wil-
lock, assistant clerk, (and who I acknowledge as
my adopted daughter)the sum of £4,000 sterling
money of Great Britain, to be paid at the expiration of six months after my decease, or
sooner, if possible ; and I leave my dearest
friend Emma, Lady Hamilton, sole guardian of
the said Horatia Nelson Thompson, until she
shall have arrived at the age of eighteen years ;
and the interest of the said £4,000 to be paid to
Lady Hamilton, for her education and maintenance. This request of guardianship I
earnestly make of Lady Hamilton, knowing
that she will educate my adopted child in the
paths of religion and virtue, and give her the
accomplishments which so much adorn herself,
and, I hope, make her a fit wife for my dear
nephew, Horatio Nelson, who I wish to marry
her, if he proves worthy, in Lady Hamilton's
estimation, of such a treasure as I am sure she
will be."

Infatuated as this extraordinary man unquestionably was by the delusions which were
so cunningly cast over his mind, still it is clear
from this expressive declaration of his sentiments, that in truth he regarded the child in the
nearest possible light ; for, had she been an
orphan cast upon his bounty, he would have

stated who were her parents ; and, if she had been the offspring of any obscure persons, he would hardly have recommended her in the way he did to his nephew, of whom he was always very fond. The impudent writer of the memoirs of Lord Nelson, composed under the inspection of Lady Hamilton, allows plainly enough that this was his Lordship's child ; though he insinuates at the same time that the mother was dead at the time when that scandalous account was published. But if this was the case, why was not the name of the woman mentioned ; and how happened it that no one ever claimed any parental relation to the infant, from the time of its birth, except Lord Nelson and Lady Hamilton ? But to put this matter beyond all doubt, a passage from one of his Lordship's last letters to the woman who had alienated him from his connubial duties will show the entire conviction which he had that this child constituted the link that united him to the object of his admiration. " I entreat, my dear Emma," says he, " that you will cheer up : and we will look forward to many, many happy years, and be surrounded by our children's children. God Almighty can, when He pleases, remove the impediment."

Shocking and profane as the last observation is, for it could have only one meaning, that

which precedes it is an express acknowledgment
that there was then existing a living pledge of
their mutual attachment ; for, otherwise, the
language is absolute nonsense. In speaking of
children, his Lordship could not allude to the
distant prospect of a union after the death of
his wife ; for both he and Lady Hamilton were
now arrived at a period when issue was hardly
to be expected. His cheering remark, therefore,
must have been grounded on the object which
they already enjoyed, and the fond hope that
the honours of Nelson would descend to the
fruits of that alliance which his Lordship had
projected between his nephew and the child
whom he called his adopted daughter.

The author of the scandalous memoirs has
spoken of the loves of these persons in terms of
admiration ; though he allows that had Lady
Nelson died, their marriage would certainly
have taken place. Now this hireling knew, for
he had the documents before him at the time,
that, while Sir William Hamilton was living, a
correspondence was carried on between his lady
and Nelson, which went far beyond the limits
of innocent esteem and virtuous friendship.

Here we are compelled reluctantly once more
to notice that abominable insult upon all truth
and modesty, because it exhibits another atro-

cious instance of her Ladyship's utter want of
integrity and delicacy, even where the honour
of her hero was particularly affected by the story
which she invented. Not content with evincing
the unqualified supremacy which she had over
the heart of Nelson, this intriguing woman was
resolved to participate in the glory which ex-
clusively belonged to him, and to have her share
of the laurels which he so proudly earned. As
she pretended to have contributed most effectually to the victory of Aboukir by her influence
in Sicily, so she had the hardihood to claim the
merit of having been the cause of that at Trafalgar. To substantiate this assumption, she
dictated to her amanuensis at Merton the following tale, which appeared first in the historical
romance published by Lady Hamilton's means;
and, what is still worse, it has been most
imprudently copied from thence into Southey's
Life of Nelson. The story is as follows: " When
Captain Blackwood arrived at Merton with the
news that the combined fleets had arrived at
Cadiz, Lord Nelson is stated to have treated it
lightly, having no intention to go to sea again,
and contenting himself with saying, ' Let the
man trudge it who has lost his budget :' but,"
observes the narrator, " amid all this *allegro* of
the tongue to his friends at Merton Place,

Lady Hamilton observed that his countenance, from that moment, wore occasional marks of the *penseroso* in his bosom. In this state of mind he was pacing one of the walks of Merton garden, which he always called the quarter-deck, when Lady Hamilton told him that she perceived he was low and uneasy. He smiled and said,—' No ! I am as happy as possible : ' adding, that he saw himself surrounded by his family ; that he found his health better since he had been at Merton ; and that he would not give a sixpence to call the king his uncle. Her Ladyship replied, that she did not believe what he said ; and that she would tell him what was the matter with him. That he was longing to get at these French and Spanish fleets ; that he considered them as his property, and would be miserable if any other man but himself did the business; that he must have them as the price and reward of his long watching, and two years uncomfortable situation in the Mediterranean ; and finished by saying,—' Nelson, however we may lament your absence, and your so speedily leaving us, offer your services immediately to go off Cadiz : they will be accepted, and you will gain a quiet heart by it. You will have a glorious victory ; and then you may come here, have your *otium cum dignitate*, and be happy.'

He looked at her Ladyship for some moments ; and, with tears in his eyes, exclaimed,—' Brave Emma ! good Emma ! if there were more Emmas, there would be more Nelsons. You have penetrated my thoughts. I wish all you say, but was afraid to trust even myself with reflecting on the subject. However, I will go to town.' He went accordingly, next morning, accompanied by her Ladyship, and his sisters. They left him at the Admiralty, on the way to Lady Hamilton's house in Clarges Street ; and soon after received a note, informing them that the *Victory* was telegraphed not to go into port, and begging they would prepare everything for his departure. This," says the biographer, "is the true history of that affecting affair. Her ladyship feels, most severely, that she was the cause of his going : but as she loved his glory, she could not resist giving him such advice."

Now in all this history, as the writer calls it, there is not one particle of truth ; for Captain Blackwood called at Merton by appointment, to apprize him of the news ; immediately on which, and before Lady Hamilton knew any-thing of the matter, his Lordship expressed his satisfaction at the intelligence, being convinced that he should be able to give Villeneuve a drubbing. He accordingly began to arrange matters for his departure ; having, indeed, already held consultations with the Admiralty on the subject. Bound, as Nelson was, in the fascinating arms of his Dalilah, he had not lost his sense of public duty, nor his love of glory. But though he cannot, in justice, be deprived of the merit of having acted with perfect freedom of mind, in following the call of honour to the last wreath which it procured him, yet melancholy evidence appeared under his own hand to prove how completely his affections remained spell-bound to the last day of his existence. In the morning, when he was preparing for action, with the enemy in view, he drew up the following statement, as a kind of testamentary bequest.[1]

" Whereas the eminent services of Emma Hamilton, widow of the Right Honourable Sir William Hamilton, have been of the very greatest service to our king and country, to my knowledge, without her receiving any reward from either our king or country :

" First, that she obtained the King of Spain's letter, in 1796, to his brother the King of Naples, acquainting him of his inclination to declare war against England ; from which letter the ministry sent out orders to the then

---

[1] October 21, 1805.

Sir John Jervis, to strike a stroke, if opportunity afforded, against either the arsenals of Spain, or her fleets : that neither of these was done, is not the fault of Lady Hamilton ; the opportunity might have been offered.

"Secondly, the British fleet under my command could never have returned the second time to Egypt, had not Lady Hamilton's influence with the Queen of Naples caused letters to be wrote to the governor of Syracuse, that he was to encourage the fleet being supplied with everything, should they put into any port in Sicily. We put into Syracuse, and received every supply ; went to Egypt, and destroyed the French fleet.

"Could I have rewarded these services, I would not now call upon my country. But as that has not been in my power, I leave Emma Hamilton, therefore, a legacy to my king and country ; that they will give her an ample provision to maintain her rank in life.

"I also leave to the beneficence of my country my adopted daughter, Horatia Nelson Thompson ; and I desire she will use, in future, the name of Nelson only.

"These are the only favours I ask of my king and country, at this moment, when I am going to fight their battle.

" May God bless my king and country, and
all those I hold dear ! My relations it is need-
less to mention ; they will, of course, be amply
provided for."

That his Lordship felt the truth of what is
stated in this paper cannot be questioned ; but
it has been already seen that her Ladyship's
merits, even as here represented, were greatly
overrated ; and that in reality she had no claims
at all for acts which her husband ought to have
performed ; while of the first it may be said,
that however adroitly it was managed, it had
more art in it than honesty.

When it was ascertained that the wound
which Nelson received was mortal, his thoughts
fluctuated wholly between his glory and his love.
" I am going fast," said he : " it will be all over
with me soon. Let my dear Lady Hamilton
have my hair, and all other things belonging to
me." Afterwards he observed, " What would
become of poor Lady Hamilton if she knew my
situation ! " On being informed of the number
of ships captured, he expressed his satisfaction,
and then reverting again to the subject most
interesting to his mind, he said, " Take care of
my dear Lady Hamilton, Hardy : take care of
poor Lady Hamilton." Among his last words
were these : " Doctor, remember me to Lady

Hamilton, remember me to Horatia ! [1] Tell her
I have made a will, and left her a legacy to my
country."

[1] If any further evidence is necessary as to the parentage
of Horatia, an extract or two from the letters of Lady
Hamilton is here given. While staying with Nelson's
brother, the Prebendary, at Canterbury, she wrote to
Nelson on Oct. 4, 1805, a letter which the admiral never
received, or it doubtless would have been destroyed, like
most of the others which came from the same person.
After a little gossip, she says : " I send you a letter of Miss
Conners, as their is much in it about our dear girl (Horatia). I allsoe had one from my mother who doats on her.
She says she could not live without her. What a blessing
for her parents to have such a child.—God spare her to
them." In another letter, sent from the same place a few
days after, and which Nelson never saw, as Trafalgar was
won, and he had gloriously fallen, before it could reach
him, Lady Hamilton writes : "I was obliged to send for
Mariana down, and my mother can ill spare her. She
gives me such an amiable account of our dear Horatia. I
have now had her so long at Merton, my heart will not
bear to be without her. You will be even fonder of her
when you return. Dearest angel, she is. Oh, Nelson !
how I love her, and how I idolize you, my dearest husband
of my heart." Years afterwards, when Horatia was about
twelve years of age, she was out of favour, temporarily,
with her mother, who smartly scolded her in a letter she
wrote to her on Easter Sunday, 1813 :—

"Listen to a kind good mother, who has ever been to you
affectionate and truly kind ; and who has neither spared
pains nor expense to make you the most amiable and most
accomplished of your sex. I grieve and lament to see the

Thus fell that illustrious commander, of whom, if we have been compelled to relate some circumstances that cast a shade over his private character, it has solely risen from the necessity of obeying the voice of truth, and of doing justice to the cause of injured virtue; not from a wish to wound the feelings of the living, or to disparage the real merits of the dead.

increasing strength of your turbulent passions. I shall go to join your father, and my blessed mother ; and may you on your death-bed have as little to reproach yourself, as your affectionate mother has. I shall to-morrow look out for a school for your sake, that you may bless the memory of an injured mother.—EMMA HAMILTON."

This letter was evidently written in a moment of irritation, and Horatia probably not so blameable as here represented. At all events, the threat of sending her to school was never carried out.

CHAPTER XV.

THE death of Nelson had a pro-
digious effect upon the public
mind, and the grief at his loss
was equal to the exultation produced by his victory : yet his
beloved Emma could not help
mixing much affectation with her real sorrow;
and while she lamented the breach which had
dried up the great stream of her pleasure and
ambition, she made such a parade of her concern
as tended to excite a suspicion that her affliction
arose more from a sense of disappointment than

from real affection to the hero. Of this, indeed, a striking instance appeared in her conduct at the theatre, when Braham brought forward the favourite song of the " Death of Nelson," in the opera of " Thirty Thousand." Her Ladyship was present at the very first representation, and at the conclusion of the song she fainted away. The house of course was thrown into confusion, and her Ladyship was conveyed to a private apartment till she recovered. She attended at the second performance, and again fainted. The same scene was exhibited on the third night, and likewise on the fourth, till at length the managers, expecting the regular return of this exhibition, prepared for it, adding to hartshorn and other restoratives a cordial of greater potency. The plain truth is, the whole was a mere trick, for she always contrived to secure one of the most conspicuous seats in the house, with the obvious design of playing her part to the greatest advantage.

The manner in which Lord Nelson remembered her Ladyship in his will[1] had a powerful

---

[1] By the will and codicils, Lady Hamilton was left—his diamond star, a sum of £2,000, an annuity of £500 per annum for life charged on the Bronte estate in Sicily, Merton Place, with its furniture, gardens, and grounds ; and the yearly interest of the £4,000 settled on his daughter Horatia, till she was eighteen years of age.

effect no doubt in consoling her mind under the
loss she had sustained by his death ; and the
neglect which it produced on the part of those
who out of complaisance to him had been
accustomed to treat her with superabundant
kindness, was somewhat alleviated by the conviction that her dominion over him was not
shaken even by the terrors of dissolution.

Her picture and that of Horatia adorned his
cabin, and these objects were contemplated by
him with as much delight as the representations
of saints are beheld by the devout Romanist.
Here let us close the catalogue of Nelson's infirmities, and the mournful display of his inex-
cusable failings ; but before the curtain is drawn
over the weak part of hisicharacter, it is necessary,
for the great end of moral instruction, that a
caveat should be entered against that unpardonable but too common error of making the
splendour of great actions and transcendent
talents an excuse for aberrations from the line of
private duty, and the still more shameful practice
of setting off occasional fits of devotion, and
instances of liberality, as an atonement for
habitual adultery. That this extraordinary man
had a general reverence for religion, and that he
possessed many excellent qualities of the heart
and understanding, cannot be denied ; yet,

amidst all this, it must be said of him that he was not so much a virtuous man as an admirer of virtue, and that religion in him was not an active operating principle, but a fluctuating sentiment of mental feeling.

It is greatly to be lamented that few if any exertions were made by those who enjoyed his confidence to draw him from that perilous situation into which he had been deluded ; while, on the contrary, it seemed to be the study of them all to encourage him in his folly, by redoubling their attentions to the enchantress who had bewitched him, in proportion as they saw that he was gratified by these courtesies. His nearest relations, instead of being scandalized by the connection which he had formed, were eager to gain his favour by courting the smiles of his mistress ; and while his unoffending wife was left to pick up the casual pity and consolations of strangers, the woman who had succeeded in exiling her from the house and heart of her lord revelled in luxury, surrounded by all the branches of the family, vying with each other for her friendship, and ambitious of the honour of receiving her into their habitations.

But no sooner did the moving power cease by which these persons were stimulated to cultivate the good opinion of a female, who had a sovereign contempt for the laws by which the social relations are preserved, than they all gradually dropped the mask, and abandoned the fascinating Emma, because she could no longer further their views, or promote their interest.

Some who had lived under her roof for months, and even years, who were entertained daily at her table, where they laughed at her witticisms, and were enraptured by her melodies, slunk away, as if they were anxious to discard her from their memories. Nay, there were not wanting others, who, after seeking her company with the most ardent professions of esteem, and feeling proud of her correspondence, now turned the heel upon her, and took a pleasure in magnifying her errors, forgetting that in so doing they condemned themselves for the want of delicacy, candour, and gratitude.

While her admirer lived, these birds of passage had no dislike to the hospitalities which she delighted to afford, but his death produced a wonderful alteration in their sense of propriety, and in the expression of their feelings. Their conduct plainly indicated by what principles they had been guided in seeking for the acquaintance of a woman on whom they now turned their backs, and whose character was thus admitted by themselves to have been undeserving of esteem at the very period when she was the object of their flattery.

All these proofs, however, of the capricious-ness of that friendship which results from mer-cenary motives, failed to operate on the mind of Emma, in producing a change of manners, and an attention to economy. Even the ex-tinction of her fondest hope, by the catastrophe of the hero to whom she was attached, had not the effect of correcting her love of pleasure, or of moderating her propensity to extravagance. She strove to counteract the mortification pro-duced by the contemptuous neglect which she experienced in one quarter, by enlarging the circle of her acquaintance. In the choice of these new friends she certainly was far from being over-scrupulous, and none who felt any concern about the moral qualities of their as-sociates would have been much at their ease in the companies that were usually assembled at Merton Place. The consequence of all this was soon felt in the embarrassments occasioned by the wanton profusion and indiscriminate waste which prevailed in her household, when the reservoir that had formerly supplied the means of indulgence was dried up. With ordinary prudence, indeed, the income which she derived from the settlement of her husband, and the donations of her noble admirer, would have been amply sufficient for her support in a style fully commensurate with her rank and pretensions. But the cast of characters which she delighted in consisted of creatures whose sole object was to devour all that came within their reach : and while they fastened like locusts upon the fertile spot which allured their presence, the moment that a change took place in its circumstances, they were the first to fly away. There were indeed two or three persons who offered their advice to this improvident woman, with the view of turning her from this course of dissipation and ruin ; but all their counsels were thrown away, till the clamours of creditors became too numerous to be slighted, and their measures too hostile to admit of compromise or delay. Within a few years after the death of Lord Nelson, an account was taken of her Ladyship's debts, by three gentlemen of reputation ; and it being found that she owed about eighteen thousand pounds, it was deemed necessary to dispose of the effects in Surrey, as well as the property in London, by which about a surplus of little more than two thousand pounds was saved from the wreck.[1] This was a lesson

[1] In November, 1808, a meeting of the friends of Lady Hamilton was held at the house of Alderman Sir John

which ought to have made a deep impression on
the most thoughtless mind : but though the
person who had been so severely taught still
possessed more than one thousand pounds a-year,
she soon contracted fresh debts, by continuing
to pursue the same career of folly. About this
time her mother died, at an advanced age, in
private lodgings in Bond Street ; and her remains were interred in the new burying-ground
at Paddington.

It is at least some relief from the general disgust excited by the consideration of a scene of
levity, that there was one feature of virtue
uniformly perceptible through the complicated
course of deception, voluptuousness, and depravity ; for through the whole of her life,
Emma behaved with the most dutiful regard
to her parent, of whom she was not ashamed,
even when her table was graced by persons of

Perring to see what could be done to relieve her from her
pecuniary embarrassments and difficulties. A statement
of her debts, &c., was submitted, and the result of the con-
ference was, that she gave up Merton Place, and other
property, in trust, to Sir J. Perring, Mr. Alexander
Davison, and three other gentlemen, with power to sell,
if they thought it necessary, for the benefit of her creditors
and the settlement of her affairs. Six of her sympathizers
present at the meeting subscribed over £3,000 for her
immediate benefit.

high distinction.   Let this then be remembered
to her praise, when the flagitiousness of her
conduct in wounding the peace of an excellent
woman, and tarnishing the laurels of a hero,
who but for those arts which she practised
would have shone with unspotted lustre, shall
be mentioned with regret and indignation.

After the death of Nelson, Lady Hamilton
was extremely piqued at the munificent grants
which were showered by Parliament upon the
several members of his family, while all her
claims, and the recommendations of the departed
chief, were disregarded.   The declaration, in
the form of a codicil, which his Lordship drew
up, and attested in her favour, the last day of
his life, having been delivered to his brother,
was kept by him till the earldom and the Parliamentary rewards were all settled; and then,
with an air of triumph, he threw her the paper,
because he knew that it could be of no other
use to her than as an additional proof of the
hold which she maintained to the last over the
heart of the illustrious writer.[1]   This, indeed,

[1] The Reverend William Nelson, D.D., *first Earl
Nelson*, was possibly a very commonplace kind of
person, who wanted, and took for himself, all he was
enabled to get in the shape of preferment or money ;
but the grave charge against him of concealing the
codicil of his brother's will, till all that Parliament would

was but a bad return for all the kindness which the new lord had experienced himself, and particularly for the liberal manner in which his daughter had been entertained at Merton, where grant was voted to him and his family, is quite contrary to fact, and has no foundation whatever. The purport of the note was well known to many persons—some of them staunch friends to Lady Hamilton, and in high positions—weeks before the funeral of Lord Nelson took place, on January 9, 1806. Some months before the Parliamentary grant was made to the Nelson family, the Hon. George Rose, M.P., and Paymaster to the Forces, in writing to Lady Hamilton on December 9, 1805, informed her, that she would learn from Captain Hardy, "that Lord Nelson, within the hour preceding the commencement of the action in which he immortalized his name, made an entry in his pocket-book, strongly recommending a remuneration to you for your services to the country when the fleet under his command was in Sicily, after his first return from Egypt, on which subject he had spoken to me with great earnestness more than once." He goes on to say that he would lay the memorandum before the Prime Minister, and support its request with all his influence. " My application must be to Mr. Pitt, but the reward (to which I have not the slightest hesitation in saying I think you are, both on principle and in policy, well entitled) must, I conceive, be from the Foreign Secretary of State." The pension Lady Hamilton sought for would most probably have been granted to her, but for the almost unexpected decease of Mr. Pitt. When Earl Nelson, on December 23, 1805, went to Doctor's Commons to prove the will of his brother, he took the pocket-book containing the note, or codicil, with him, and conferred with Sir W. Scott, the Judge of the

she was a settled resident several years. But
nothing better could well be expected of one,
who, after his advancement to the peerage,
with its lucrative consequences, continued to
hold tenaciously his ecclesiastical preferment, in
opposition to his brother's dying request, that it
might be relinquished in favour of the friend
who attended him in his last moments.[1]   This,

Consistory Court, as to the best manner of treating it, as
the memorandum had no relation to any portion of
the deceased Admiral's estate.   It was decided that there
was no reason for proving this note with the other codicils,
and the Earl left it in the care of Sir W. Scott (who was
a sympathizer with Lady Hamilton, and of opinion that
she had strong claims on the Government for a pension)
for more than seven weeks.   At the expiration of that
time the Earl took away the pocket-book, and, to quote
his own words, "gave it to Lord Grenville" (who had
succeeded Pitt as Prime Minister), "and at the same
time he read it to his Lordship, and strongly pointed out
to him the parts relative to Lady Hamilton and the
child; and in doing this Lord Nelson observed to Lord
Grenville, that he thought he was most effectually promoting the interest of Lady Hamilton, and doing his
duty, in which Lord Grenville acquiesced."   On receiving
the memorandum from the Earl, Lady Hamilton immediately registered it at Doctor's Commons, and charged him
with withholding it for the purpose of putting as much as
he could of the money voted by Parliament into his own
pocket, to her disadvantage.

[1] The Rev. A. J. Scott, chaplain of the *Victory*, in
whose arms Nelson died.   He was made D.D. by royal

therefore, is one instance among many which
might be adduced to show, that whatever be the
policy and justice of acting liberally towards
those who greatly distinguish themselves in the
cause of their country, there ought to be some
prudence and discrimination in apportioning
national honours and rewards. When a brave
commander falls in battle, let his widow and
children, if he has any, be properly remunerated ;
but there surely is little wisdom in conferring
high distinctions and immense grants upon
collateral branches of the family, without considering whether they have either virtue or
talents that may entitle them to such favours.
As Nelson died without legitimate issue, the
most proper course would have been to have
created his lady a peeress, in her own right,
with an ample estate to support the title. In
doing this, Government would have marked its
respect for virtue, at the same time that it
expressed a due regard for the extraordinary
services of the gallant admiral : but by passing
the widow entirely aside in the distribution of
honours, and pouring the whole, with immense
prodigality, upon persons whose own merits
would never have raised them to eminence,

mandate, but never obtained the prebendal stall at
Canterbury Nelson intended him to have.

something very like neglect bordering on injustice was committed.

Here then was a justifiable ground of complaint ; but Lady Hamilton most unquestionably
had no right to make any, since the very nature
of her demands prevented them from being
attended to by any ministers who retained a
reverence for private virtue.   But while the
suffering widow of Nelson [1] neither murmured
against the Government, nor resented the conduct of her relations, the woman who ought
to have preserved an absolute silence was loud
and vehement on the subject of her pretended
wrongs.   She also caused the life of the hero to
be printed, in which her merits were displayed
with great parade, and a bitter anathema was
denounced against the British nation, should it
still continue deaf to her claims.   She afterwards
printed a memorial, setting forth more in detail
these services, and the ill-treatment which she
had experienced, not only from Government, but
from individuals who owed her the greatest
obligations.   Though these representations were
properly disregarded, because they rested for
the most part on fallacious grounds ; still, it
cannot be denied, that the orphan, who was so

[1] Lady Nelson was granted by Parliament £2,000 per
annum for life.   She died May 4, 1831.

feelingly bequeathed to the nation by the dying
Nelson, has a just call upon the country for an
adequate provision suited to her origin. Let
not the faults of the parents be visited on the
head of the innocent : and while so much has
been showered upon persons, whose good-fortune
is owing solely to their alliance in blood to this
distinguished commander, it would be cruel to
withhold a portion of the public bounty from
the child of his dearest affections.

It is to be lamented that our great hero did
not himself take better care of this beloved
object, by his testamentary settlement, than
leaving her under the sole guardianship of Lady
Hamilton, with an encomium upon her Ladyship's moral and religious qualities, which, he
must have known, she did not deserve. As a
proof how well she merited this confidence and
praise, it may be mentioned, without any injury
to the survivor, that she made it her chief study
to instruct the young Horatia, when seven or
eight years old, in theatrical action, declamation,
and singing. So imprudent indeed was the
mother, as to cause the child to exhibit before
large companies in various characters, to show
her agility, the elegance of her attitudes, and
the powers of her memory in recitation.

Much as Lady Hamilton had to complain of

the inconstancy of her most intimate acquaintance, and of the want of gratitude in those
upon whom she placed the greatest dependence,
there were a few persons of rank and affluence,
who still admired her accomplishments, and
contributed to the supply of her wants. The
principal of these was the late Duke of Queensberry, who had followed her with delight in
former days, and who cheerfully renewed an
acquaintance with her on the return of Sir
William to England. When her Ladyship was
obliged to part with Merton,[1] and to lay down
her carriage, his Grace generously furnished a
house for her at Richmond, and allowed her a
sufficiency, by which she was enabled again to
set up an equipage. His presents also were
very large ; and when he died, at the close of
the year 1810, he bequeathed to her one thousand pounds, with an annuity, charged upon his
personal estate, of five hundred more. But as
the extent of the legacies appeared to go beyond
the means of defraying them, an application to
the Court of Chancery put a restraint upon the
payment, and her Ladyship derived no advantage
from the benevolent intentions of her noble

---

[1] In September, 1808, while at Richmond, she offered
Merton, with its furniture, to the Duke of Queensberry
for £15,000, but the offer was not accepted.

friend. This disappointment was rendered more severe by the folly of enlarging her establishment on the expected increase of her income. Fresh difficulties were the consequence, and many efforts were made to extricate her Ladyship from them by renewed application to Government; and even the patriotic fund at Lloyd's was moved to bestow a liberal grant upon one, who, it was alleged, had rendered essential service to her country. But none of these petitions proving successful, and most of her private friends falling off in the time of her utmost need, an execution was entered upon her property, the whole of which was sold by auction in Bond Street, not even excepting the presents which she had received from Lord Nelson, including among other valuable articles, the box with the freedom of the city of Oxford, given by that corporation to the hero of the Nile. But misfortune did not end here, for other creditors, being vexed at the loss which they had sustained, arrested her Ladyship, in the summer of 1813, and she was conveyed to the King's Bench, within the rules of which prison she resided,[1] with her daughter, enduring many privations, and feeling the instability of friendship, and the uncertainty of human enjoyments.

[1] At 12, Temple Place.

But, as if this extraordinary woman had been destined to endure the utmost mortification from the ingratitude of the worthless parasites who formerly basked in the sunshine of her prosperity, while she was thus in confinement, some of her confidants had the unparalleled impudence to publish the letters which passed between her and Nelson, adding to that scandalous collection several others, from various persons of eminence. It has been too generally supposed, that Lady Hamilton, in the season of her affliction, yielding to necessity and resentment, suffered these sad proofs of infidelity to be given to the world ; but in this she has been greatly wronged ; and amidst all her faults, the breach of faith in this instance, cannot with justice be added to the number. At the time when she was silly enough to cause a vindication of her conduct abroad, and her connection with Nelson to be written, she took a man and his family into her house, who lived there, entirely at her expense, for the space of two years. This wretch having constant access to all her papers and correspondence, thought proper to select from the mass what he conceived would be useful to his ends on a future day. When therefore the unhappy woman, who had so indiscreetly misplaced her confidence, could no longer be of service to those who had fattened upon her bounty, a foul advantage was taken of her helplessness, by publishing this correspondence, and artfully making the world believe that it was done with her consent. In vain did the sufferer protest against the iniquity of the deed, and assert her ignorance of the design; for the public declaration which she made to that effect only served as an advertisement to the work. In doing this, she acted by the counsel of a very worthy gentleman; but she would have been better advised, in applying to the Court of Chancery for an injuction to stop the publication of private letters, which were her exclusive property, and had been treacherously obtained from her for the worst of purposes. This was the only effectual course that could have been adopted in such a nefarious business; but unfortunately it was never thought . of by Lady Hamilton, or by the few friends who remained firm in their attachment, when the storm of adversity came upon her in the evening of life. After being in confinement above ten months, she obtained her discharge through the kindness of one of the city aldermen,[1] who pitied her case, and thought, that, with all her errors she had been cruelly treated.

[1] Alderman J. J. Smith.

Immediately on her liberation, she withdrew to
the Continent, and took up her abode near
Calais,[1] till she could have an opportunity of
seeking an asylum among her former acquaintance in Italy, to which country she looked,
with some degree of certainty, as affording a

[1] Lady Hamilton, in fear of being re-arrested at the
suit of a coach-builder, fled from London to Calais in the
early summer of 1814. She resided first at "Hotel
Dessin," then at a farmhouse a little way in the country
for some three months; and finally in apartments in the
Rue Francaise, where she died, January 15, 1815. The
stories of her destitution during the last few months of
her life are greatly exaggerated, and mostly fabulous. In
a letter written by her to her nephew, the Hon. R. F.
Greville, September 21, 1814, she says : " The best meat
here five pence a pound, 2 quarts of new milk 2 pence,
fowls 13 pence a couple, ducks the same. We bought
two fine turkeys for four shillins, an excellent turbot for
half a crown, fresh from the sea, partriges five pence the
couple, good Bordeux wine white and red for fivteen pence
the bottle, but there are some for ten sous halpeny. . . .
Horatia improves in person and education every day.
She speaks french like a french girl, italian, german,
english, &c." This is anything but starvation, and being
dependent on charity for subsistence ; and Lady Hamilton
had at least, to the last, the interest of the £4,000 settled
on her daughter, as well as the wreck of her property
she had brought with her from England, to keep her from
absolute poverty. Her daughter, writing years afterwards,
in 1874, says : "Although often certainly under very
distressing circumstances, she never experienced actual
want."

secure retreat from the chilling contempt and
severity that had so roughly assailed her vanity
in her native land. But, as if she had been
destined to find no resting-place in this world,
her means were so contracted, that she could
not follow her inclinations ; which disappointment, with the agitated state of her mind,
owing to the injury she had sustained by the
outrage committed upon her private papers,
preyed upon her spirits, and brought on a
disorder which soon assumed an alarming aspect.
She had for some years lost that elegance of
form which in former days rendered her an
object of general admiration. This corpulency
was increased by a gross voluptuary indulgence,
and an indolent course of life, which brought on
bilious complaints and flatulency. During the
whole of her illness she was attended with the
greatest affection by her child, and this alone
gave her comfort in her distressing situation ;
and when, at last, she found that there were no
hopes of a recovery, she employed the little
time that remained in preparing such documents
and memorials as might be of service to this
interesting object, who was now about to encounter the rude storms of the world, without a
relation or guardian to take a tender interest in
her welfare. This consideration pressed heavily

on the mind of the dying parent, who manifested the most affectionate concern for her child,
by endeavouring to soothe her mind, and to
allay her fears, giving her advice for her future
conduct, and settling her affairs in such a
manner as appeared best adapted to secure the
property which had been set apart for her use,
from any attempts that might be made to injure
the rights of the orphan and the destitute. A
sealed packet was also carefully entrusted to her
hands, but with strict injunctions that it should
not be opened till the attainment of her
eighteenth year ; which corresponded also with
the particular settlement in the codicil added to
the will of Nelson, providing for the maintenance of this very child under the denomina-
tion of his adopted daughter.

The author of these sheets had long suspected
that her Ladyship was secretly attached to the
Romish faith ; and her most intimate friends
who knew her in Italy will probably recollect
some particulars, which would serve to
strengthen the persuasion that she had been
reconciled many years ago to that Church.
One circumstance which may be mentioned was
that of her having a confidential monk to attend
her, who passed as her tutor in the languages,
but who, it is strongly suspected, acted as her

confessor. In England, indeed, she went sometimes to the parish church, but occasionally she
is known to have visited a Catholic place of
worship : and though persons of her character
have seldom any fixed principles of religion, yet,
towards the close of life, they have generally
some serious compunctions and reflections,
which incline them to embrace any persuasion
that holds out the strongest encouragements to
hope. That this extraordinary woman called in
the assistance of a priest of the Romish Church
in her last moments is certain,[1] nor is it less so,
that he administered to her the solemn viaticum,
which no ecclesiastic of his communion can
impart to any but baptized members and con-
verts. It has been said, that there was no
Protestant minister in the place, whose assistance
could be procured at this awful period ; but
though perhaps that may be true, it is equally
so that she must have been formally admitted
to the peace of the Church by a solemn recog-
nition, before absolution could be pronounced,

---

[1] Lady Hamilton was visited by a Roman Catholic
priest on her death-bed, and was buried according to the
Roman Catholic rite. The testimony of her daughter
Horatia on this matter is conclusive. Writing in 1874,
she says : " The service was read over the body by a
Roman Catholic priest, who had attended her at her
request during her illness."

or the eucharist, as the seal of her pardon, be administered.

Thus did one of the most extraordinary women of modern times terminate, on the 16th of January, 1815, her course of uncommon vicissitudes, in a foreign land, surrounded by strangers, and so oppressed by poverty, that her remains were nearly consigned to a spot of ground appropriated to the lowest description of the poor, for the want of means to defray the expenses of a decent funeral ; when an English merchant at Calais, shocked at the circumstance, undertook the charge ; and all the respectable gentlemen of this nation, amounting to about fifty, attended as mourners at the interment, which was duly performed in the principal cemetery of that place. The same generous person, who so humanely provided a decent sepulture for the dead, extended also his protecting hand to the child that she had left, and who was now in danger of suffering for her mother's folly and extravagance. But the liberal merchant rescued the orphan from the machinations of those creditors in France, who, according to the laws of that country, would have detained her for the debts of her parent.[1]

[1] Most of these statements are entirely incorrect. Lady Hamilton was interred in a piece of ground just

On her arrival in England she was entrusted to the guardianship of Mr. Matcham, the brother-in-law of Lord Nelson, and who, there can be no doubt, will watch over her interests with that concern, which he would have felt it his duty to discharge, had she been committed to him by the special request of his departed friend.

Thus did the last "scene of all" in the "strange eventful history" of the once enchanting Emma comport with the rest of her

outside the town of Calais, which was used as a public cemetery till 1816. The ground was shortly after this time used as a timber yard, and all vestiges of the graves it contained were swept gradually away. On the news of the decease of Lady Hamilton reaching England, a Mr. H. Cadogan and Earl Nelson went over to Calais, where the former paid the funeral expenses of the deceased, which amounted to £28 10s., and on his return brought her daughter Horatia back to her native land with him. Earl Nelson, as one of the trustees of Horatia, also probably thought it incumbent on him to see her safely back in England after the decease of her mother. On her arrival with Mr. Cadogan she was transferred to the care of Mrs. Matcham (Lord Nelson's sister) in accordance with the last wishes of Lady Hamilton. With Mrs. Matcham she remained for two years, and afterwards resided with Mr. Bolton (Lord Nelson's brother-in-law) until February, 1822, when she became the wife of the Rev. Philip Ward, sometime Vicar of Tenterden in Kent. By him she had a large family, and died in the 81st year of her age, March 6, 1881.

chequered existence; for her life was a series of
marvellous adventures, from the time when she
went barefooted in a Welsh village, to her
entrance upon a state of dissipation in London,
where her extraordinary beauty and accomplishments rendered her an object of universal
admiration, and occasioned her transplantation
to a soil perfectly suited to her taste for pleasure,
and to the versatile powers of her genius.   How
she figured in that land of voluptuous delight,
and the effects which her influence produced, it
will be for history to record, and posterity to
lament ; but after her return to England she
began very soon to experience the mutability of
fortune, which she wanted prudence to improve;
and, indeed, as her adversity came on, her folly
increased, till at length, solely from that cause
she was driven into exile, where she closed her
days in sorrow and poverty, unpitied by those
around her in the hour of sickness, while her
wretched remains were indebted for a grave to
the hand of charity.

SUPPLEMENTARY NOTE.

Since the note on page 235 was written, by the courtesy of J. C. Holding, Esq., of Kingsclere, Newbury, the possessor of the original, the editor is enabled to give *in extenso*, the text of the *first* letter Nelson wrote to his daughter :—

"*Victory*, off Toulon, Oct. 21, 1803.

"MY DEAR CHILD,—Receive this first letter from your most affectionate father. If I live it will be my pride to see you virtuously brought up, but if it pleases God to call me I trust to Himself, in that case I have left Lady Hamilton your guardian.

"I therefore charge you, my child, on the value of a father's blessing, to be obedient and attentive to all her kind admonitions and instructions. At this moment I have left you, codicil dated the Sixth of September, the sum of four thousand sterling, interest of which is to be paid to Lady Emma Hamilton, your guardian, for your maintenance and education. I shall only say, my dear child, may God Almighty bless you and make you an ornament to your sex, which I am sure you will be if you attend to all dear Lady Hamilton's kind instructions, and be assured that I am, my dear Horatia,

"Your most affectionate Father,

"NELSON AND BRONTE.

"To Miss Horatia Nelson Thompson."

INDEX.

UNWIN BROTHERS, THE GRESHAM PRESS, CHILWORTH AND LONDON.